The Man Called Messiah

The Man Called Messiah

A Novel

Corey Stumne

RESOURCE *Publications* • Eugene, Oregon

THE MAN CALLED MESSIAH
A Novel

Resource Publications
An Imprint of Wipf and Stock Publishers
199 W. 8th Ave., Suite 3
Eugene, OR 97401

www.wipfandstock.com

PAPERBACK ISBN: 978-1-6667-0685-7
HARDCOVER ISBN: 978-1-6667-0686-4
EBOOK ISBN: 978-1-6667-0687-1

07/26/21

For Ryan.

Look how much God loves you!

"How deep The Father's love for us,
How vast beyond all measure,
That He should give His only Son
To make a wretch his treasure.
How great the pain of searing loss,
The Father turns his face away,
As wounds which mar the Chosen One
Bring many sons to glory.

Behold the man upon a cross,
My sin upon his shoulders;
Ashamed, I hear my mocking voice
Call out among the scoffers.
It was my sin that held Him there
Until it was accomplished;
His dying breath has brought me life,
I know that it is finished."

—Stuart Townend, *How Deep the Father's Love for Us*

Contents

Preface

I love the St. Louis Cardinals.

St. Louis natives understand there's no other option. We're all baseball fans. Children are raised to root *against* the Chicago Cubs and root *for* the St. Louis Cardinals.

So, when the Cardinals had a 3-1 series lead over the Detroit Tigers in the 2006 World Series during my sophomore year of high school and someone offered me tickets to see the series-clinching game, I jumped at the opportunity. The bitter wind didn't deter me. I stood in one spot the entire game, afraid I'd miss something by being seated or waiting in a long line for hot chocolate. A bathroom break was out of the question. My legs grew sore, and my cheeks became wind burnt. After three hours, my persistence paid off. In the ninth inning, Cardinal rookie Adam Wainwright struck out the final Detroit batter to clinch the series. As you can imagine, I (along with the crowd) exploded with joy.

My bliss didn't end on October 27, 2006. In the weeks that followed, I consumed every bit of the victorious story I felt I was now a part of. I read every relevant newspaper article. I watched game highlights again and again on ESPN. I told anyone who'd listen about how I had felt as I watched the confetti fall from the pitch-black sky. I bought all the apparel. I breathed it all in.

As with any sports fan who watches their team win the championship, my love for the team remained, but my excitement gradually faded as winter set in. I still wore the championship shirts, but, over time, things returned to normal.

That year for Christmas, my parents gave me a gift I still have to this day—a Major League Baseball-produced DVD documentary that tells the story of how the 2006 St. Louis Cardinals won the World Series.

I'll never forget watching the documentary for the first time. Although I'd seen every minute of the action, the storytelling stirred me. Major League Baseball asked actor and longtime Cardinal fan Billy Bob Thornton to narrate the film. As the highlights rolled, Thornton's voice played over the video as he told, in his own words, the story of how the Cardinals became champions.

I remember being so . . . *moved.* I know that sounds dramatic, but it's an apt description. I understood, for the first time, the power of hearing a story I knew and loved so well from someone else's perspective.

Such is my goal for the story you're about to read.

The following pages contain my perspective of another victorious story. This novel is my viewpoint of the most famous story ever told about the most important event that ever happened in the life of the most significant person who ever lived.

Maybe you're somewhat familiar with the story. I hope so. If you're like me, this is a story you've consumed your entire life. Maybe you've even sometimes felt you're a part of this victorious story. If so—and if you're like me—the story may have lost some of the initial excitement and wonder. Sure, your love for the main character has never faded, but maybe those initial feelings of joy and bliss did (and do).

My hope is the perspective contained in the following pages reignite your feelings of affection and excitement for "The Man, fully Divine."

Acknowledgements

I'd like to show my appreciation to some of my close friends, mentors, and supporters who helped me bring this book to life.

First off, thank you to my wife, Meghin, for supporting me and being patient with me in the writing process.

Thank you to Hannah Curtis, Paul Runnestrand, and Ben Bradley for reading the very first draft of this book and encouraging me to press on.

Thank you to Ian Reynolds, Chase Stumne, Steve Stumne, Tori Richardson, Janet Johnson, Dr. Jim Miller, and Dr. Mike James for taking the time to read through my third draft and offer your critiques.

And, finally, a special thank you to the three men whose mentorship during this project meant more than they realized: Steve Johnson, for combing through every detail of this book and sharpening my prose and storytelling. Greg Petree, for walking with me through the intimidating world of publishing and showing me the ropes. And LaGard Smith, for believing in me and empowering me to take this writing journey.

Introduction

I'd like to take this opportunity to offer a few disclaimers. Before you begin, please understand:

1. You're not holding the Bible. This story, though based on biblical narrative, isn't the Bible. If it's been a while since you've read the actual crucifixion stories in the Bible, I encourage you to do so before you begin. You'll gain more from this story if you do. You can find them in chapters 26–28 of the Gospel of Matthew, chapters 14–16 of the Gospel of Mark, chapters 22–24 in the Gospel of Luke, and chapters 18–20 in the Gospel of John.
2. You're not holding Scripture. There are scriptures quoted in the pages of this book, but a large part of this book is conjecture, commentary, and paraphrasing—my perspective on how things could've transpired.
3. You're not holding perfect theology. If that's what you're looking for, you might be disappointed to learn I don't have perfect theology. Does anyone? This book's purpose isn't to present perfect theology but to reignite your affections for The Man on whom all theology is based.

For the three years I've spent working on this book, my prayer for you (the reader) remained unchanged morning after morning: "Father, please use this book to help people love Jesus more."

I believe your reaction to the story of Jesus is the most important thing about yourself. I believe your response to his heart will define your heart for the rest of your life. For I believe when Jesus' physical, earthly story ends, your story truly begins.

—Corey Stumne

Chapter 1

One More Meal

"SIX!" THE ROMAN CENTURION said as his voice thundered.

A soldier ran toward a naked, Jewish man shackled to a post soaked with blood.

The Man hemorrhaged as he recoiled and cowered like a dog. Bruises and gashes covered his body as he bled internally. Despite the relentless onslaught of the Roman soldiers' torture, he refused to plot his escape. Instead, he writhed on the ground and accepted his fate.

Clutching a whip equipped with pieces of bone, shards of metal, and fishhooks, the soldier swung and struck the right part of The Man's waistline, leaving it frayed.

The Man tried to scream, but no sound came out.

Several onlookers gasped and stepped backward as blood flung across the gray stone hall.

The wet post wobbled as The Man twisted in pain.

"Seven!"

The other soldier shredded The Man's ribcage, causing his eyes to roll back in his head. Blood poured from his wrists as his chains cut deep into his tissue.

One onlooker dry heaved.

With the next handful of strikes, the soldiers—breathing heavier and sweating—tore open his shoulders. The Man shook as he vomited onto his chains.

Some of the priests who chose to witness the flogging decided they'd seen enough. Unable to stand another brutal second, they left.

"Thirteen!"

The perspiring soldiers worked the back of his legs, starting with his hamstrings, before making their way to his calves.

"Fourteen!"

"Fifteen!"

"Sixteen!"

"Seventeen!"

"Father!" The Man said as he choked out the first distinguishable word he'd uttered since being chained to the post, catching the winded soldiers off-guard.

They paused and eyed The Man as he wailed tearless and dry cries.

His wails, however, weren't only from his physical pain. The Man mourned something much greater than himself, a condition more dismal than his own.

The soldiers glanced at each other and laughed.

"Ready for the front?" one asked the other.

They side-armed their swings to curl the tips of the whips around The Man's back to tear down his front side.

More bystanders headed home.

Oh, how he wished his anguish would end—even more how he wished his pain never had to be. Tethered to the post, The Man was completely alone. His heart longed to be surrounded by the people who loved him. But they were nowhere to be found. As he trudged through the hell standing before him, he yearned to draw strength from his loved ones but grew hopeless at the sight of their absence.

From The Man's perspective, the last supper he had shared with his twelve closest friends just fourteen hours earlier seemed like a clouded, distant memory . . .

* * *

Fourteen hours earlier

Betrayal.

The Man saw his disciples' faces twist from the sharp puncture of his words. Their bewildered expressions communicated that, after all they had been through the past few years, they believed none of their comrades could do something as heinous as this. But once they noticed The Man's somber demeanor, the all-too-possible reality sank deep into their being. The deeper the prediction sank, the more agitated they became.

Including The Man, all thirteen of them reclined at the cramped table, enjoying their special meal. The table sat in the middle of a small second-story room above a woodworking shop in the middle of the bustling city. The rough stone walls struggled to rise above the reach of the men sitting around the flimsy table. The aroma of strong herbs, bread, and wine rose from their table and permeated the small room. A steady breeze blew through an open window that carried smells signifying the arrival of the spring holy weekend: roasted lamb, budding flowers, and the influx of livestock.

All thirteen men were weary from their tumultuous week. Their leader, The Man from Galilee, seemed to be in a constant battle with the city priests and religious leaders. He opposed them with all his might. The Man taught publicly about who The Father really was. This was good news for some. For others, his teaching made their blood boil. The Man polarized the crowd with his instruction and his denouncement of the religious elite, making The Man seem like he might be a weight heavy enough to collapse the entire nation upon itself.

For a few years, his twelve disciples trailed him and saw things that didn't make sense even in their wildest dreams. The Man appeared to have control over everything. Demons, diseases, and the dead all submitted to him with complete obedience. His disciples believed he was the one their ancient scriptures spoke of who would free their people. He'd make everything right again.

And that's what confused them. All week long, the disciples asked questions among themselves under their breath. If he truly was the one sent from The Father, why did The Father's chosen nation hate him? Why wouldn't he be more unifying, especially toward his own people? Why upset the religious elite; shouldn't he want them on his side? They threatened him with death. How could The Man do what The Father set out for him to accomplish if he died? Why choose to create a gulf among the people?

One thing was clear; the people were either for or against him.

That evening at the table, The Man knew the disciples realized the same was true for them. They discovered they too would be cut to the core. They'd have to choose to be for or against The Man. Not everyone would choose the same.

"I'm telling you that one of you will betray me." The Man looked at the table, saddened by his words. He wished them to be false. The twelve men sitting around him were his friends and had travelled with him for the past three years. The Man loved the twelve as he loved his own brothers. It sickened him to believe what he knew to be true about one of them.

The disciples' eyes widened. Confusion spread across their faces as they stopped eating. They surveyed each other. Some whispered to their neighbor.

The Man sensed everybody wished to speak, but nobody dared open their mouth.

Scanning the table, one disciple—a fisherman by trade—got the attention of the disciple lounging next to The Man. *Ask him who he means,* his lips motioned.

The disciple reclined against The Man. "Who is it?"

The Man raised his head. His simple tunic, faded and dirty, gave the impression of a common man. Tight, short curls of hair clung to his head. Dark stubble wrapped around his neck and his cheeks. Slight emerald-green filled the irises in his eyes, giving him a bold and uniquely striking gaze. His hands remained calloused and rough because he built furniture for a living. He could meet any demand but specialized in elaborate tables for the rich—tables he could never afford himself. Although he was the head of this group, he never sat at the head of the table. He always sat among them, not in front of them.

"It's the one I'll give this piece of bread after dipping it in the dish." The Man broke off a piece of the bread and dipped it in the bowl of oil. He regarded the twelve sets of curious eyes staring at him. He gave it to another disciple sitting across from him, identifying him as the traitor.

The traitor took the bread and glanced at it. He blinked rapidly as his hands trembled. He swallowed hard. As he glanced up, his pupils dilated in an unnatural way, as if something in that moment filled a place in him he didn't know was empty. The traitor shivered and shook his head.

As soon as the traitor took the bread, The Accuser entered him. "You think it's me, teacher?"

The Man looked at him and loved him. "Yes. It's you."

The silence was deafening.

The Man looked at his meal and continued eating. Some later claimed they saw tears well in his eyes. "What you're going to do," The Man said under his breath to the traitor, "do it quickly."

The traitor looked around the table at his friends.

Confusion blanketed most of them. The disciples' furrowed brows and squinted eyes revealed the perplexity fogging their minds. Often, they found The Man's teachings and predictions muddy and puzzling, but this was on another level.

The traitor stood and fumbled for words, although he had none, exposed in a way he never knew possible. His mouth opened to speak, but nothing came out. He took his bread and ran out the door into the pitch-black night.

* * *

As the meal progressed, confusion still seemed to cloud the minds of the disciples around the table. The proclamation of betrayal from The Man still throbbed, and his lack of explanation did nothing to soothe. Conversation, sparse and choppy, continued awkwardly. The Man discussed how the time had come for The Father to glorify him and for him to glorify The Father. He explained how he'd be around them for just a while longer and then was going somewhere else but wouldn't tell them where. To their dismay, he withheld an invitation to join him.

Eventually, the conversation turned toward the traitor. The few who understood The Man's earlier prediction expressed their concern to act justly toward the traitor. The rest of the disciples came to understand the seriousness of the situation. They discussed an appropriate response to the traitor and what they'd do if he returned through the door.

But their leader refused to join the conversation. The Man sat in silence as he tried to eat his meal with his head down. His thoughts were elsewhere. His mind wasn't focused on the past or the present. Instead, he thought only of the future.

In his mind's eye, he saw the horror that would unfold in just a few hours. He saw the faces of hecklers cursing him. He felt their spit on his cheeks. He heard the hammering of iron spikes driving deeper into human flesh. His imagination allowed him to taste the familiar metallic liquid as his mouth filled with blood. The hair on his neck raised, as he could almost feel his bare back sliding up and down a wet beam. Dread lay mutely in his heart as he pictured what he supposed his tomorrow would look like. His palms were clammy, and his heart raced. What he visualized nauseated him, and he was unable to swallow. He couldn't listen to their conversation anymore.

"Friends," The Man said as he interrupted them. He did his best to push his imagination to the side and concentrate. "I want to give you a new command tonight."

His disciples stopped arguing about what to do with the traitor and glued their eyes on The Man.

"Love one another." He surveyed the room and fully loved them. He saw them the way The Father saw them and believed in their infinite potential to live the way The Father had desired. "Yes, love one another. Just like I have loved you, I want you to love each other. If you do this, everyone will know you're my disciples. You must love one another."

This command wasn't necessarily new. The Man had said it before. But this time was different. The situation was distinct. He meant more than just loving the people sitting at the table. His disciples were supposed to love *everyone*. They didn't need to ask the question they were all shamefully thinking, for they knew the answer The Man would give.

They were supposed to love the traitor too.

* * *

Reminiscence flowed like wine as the group continued with the traditions of their holy meal. As they consumed their fruits, grains, vegetables, and herbs, they reminded themselves of their Hebrew history, for they were Jews. Their prayers aided their ability to look forward and backward simultaneously with spiritual eyes. They celebrated the past and hoped for the future.

Perplexed by The Man's mysterious comments about traveling somewhere else soon, the fisherman pushed for clarity. "Teacher, where are you going?"

The Man knew the answer was too incomprehensible for the fisherman right now. "You can't follow me where I'm going now, but one day, you will."

"But why can't I follow you now?" the fisherman asked with a frown. "You know I'd lay down my life for you!"

The Man reached for the fisherman's hand and held it.

All other conversation waned as the group fixated on this interaction.

"You can't see things the way they really are. Darkness is coming. The Accuser plans to see what you're made of. But I've prayed for you—not for The Accuser to leave you alone but for your faith to remain strong and not fail."

The fisherman sighed and shrugged. He bit his lip. "Teacher, I'm ready to follow you to prison. I'm even ready to die with you!"

The Man smiled at his close friend, seeing beneath the fisherman's tattered, muddy tunic and underneath the splotches of dirt smattered across the fisherman's face. The Man admired the fisherman's fiery passion and excitability and the way he always desired to push forward. But The Man knew how soon the fisherman would fail. It wouldn't be but a few more hours until the fisherman was tearfully distraught and hating himself. The Man knew the fisherman was no match for the sifting of The Accuser. He knew this, because even though The Man was fully human, he was also fully Divine. "You'll deny you even know me three times before the rooster crows tonight." The Man closed his eyes and gripped the sides of his neck.

* * *

Teaching and instructing the group about things to come, The Man controlled the conversation for the next hour. He explained how he would leave them to prepare a place for them to stay—a room in The Father's own house. He told them they knew the way to the place where he was going.

A disciple tried to correct him, telling The Man they didn't know the way, because The Man refused to give them details on the precise location. Others chimed in with similar concerns.

"I *am* the way." The Man's tone communicated this truth to be a cornerstone in the foundation of what it meant to pursue the heart of The Father. "I *am* the way, the truth, and the life. No one comes to The Father except through me."

The way. *The only way.*

The Man saw understanding trickle into their minds. He was saying no other roads of religion, sacrifice, or penance reconciled humanity to The Father. Just one road existed—a narrow one. The path to the Divine couldn't be found on a map but at a table sharing food with them. Understanding this, The Man explained, was the ultimate truth that would lead them to life—*real life.*

The disciples expressed their longing to see The Father as they discussed what they thought it would be like to actually live with The Father in his house.

"Don't you understand?" The Man asked. "Anyone who has seen me has seen The Father. How can you say, 'Show us The Father?' Don't you believe I'm in The Father, and The Father is in me?"

Stunned, his disciples turned silent. They'd heard him say some wild things over the past few years, but this remark went against everything they'd ever been taught since their youth.

"Do you believe me?"

His disciples nodded in unison.

But The Man wasn't finished with his outrageous claims. He promised that once he went away, he'd send a part of The Father to his friends. The Father's own Spirit would live inside them and make a home in their heart.

The Man smiled as he watched the disciples ponder these things deep within their being. They'd been the handful of privileged men from their generation to witness what looked to be the rise of The Father once again. Centuries before, The Father had appeared to be distant and silent. But not anymore—not since The Man, fully Divine, stepped into the public eye and displayed signs and wonders attributable only to The Father's movement. The Man claimed to represent The Father without fault, and The Father's eyes beamed with satisfaction. They walked in total synchrony. As they moved, worshippers sensed the rhythm of their hearts.

Because of this Divine connection, they assumed The Man could make no mistakes and do no wrong. So why was this holy meal different? Why was it tense? Even though love filled The Man's words, sorrow filled them also.

And anxiety.

And stress.

Similar to the way an animal senses harsh weather coming even though the sky is clear, The Man felt a darkness encroaching upon their special time together. He knew a dreadful storm approached, and there wasn't shelter in sight. He decided to sing a psalm with his disciples, one about The Father protecting those who put their trust in Him.

After the song, they cleaned up their meal, left the warm, lit room and set out into the cool, dim night. The men filed out the door one by one. With no way of illuminating their path, their eyes took time to adjust to the dark. Some donned extra cloaks to shield the chill. Others braved it. They descended the steps leading to a narrow cobblestone road, empty and barren. Few people were out this late at night. It had been particularly crowded just hours before as flocks of Jews flooded the city to participate in the holy celebration. These travelers brought with them their families, belongings, and livestock.

Especially lambs. Evidence of lambs surrounded them; they heard the bleats in multiple directions and saw their wool scattered throughout the street and smelled their feces smashed into the stone beneath their feet. Hundreds of thousands of lambs were packed into the capital, all doomed to the same violent end.

The group weaved through empty carts and tables. The Man, fully Divine, led them, although each knew exactly where they were going.

They were on their way to a small mountain to pray.

* * *

Exiting the city walls through a small gate and proceeding down a steep, winding hill, The Man steered his group through a thick grove of trees. The mountain they marched to stood on the opposite side of the ravine they meandered toward. The moon shone bright. They hiked down the slope from the city, ducking under branches as their eyes strained to see ahead.

As they went, The Man gave them instructions. "Listen to me. I love you just like The Father loves me. Now remain in my love."

The path wove around a large boulder, forcing travelers into a brief yet steep climb.

The Man paused his teaching as he approached the boulder. He grabbed a tree limb with both arms and lifted himself. "When you do what I say, you remain in my love, just as I do what my Father says and remain in his love. I've told you these things so you'll be filled with joy. Yes, your joy will be complete and will overflow!"

Only three more men still needed to use the tree limb to scale the path's steep segment. The other disciples waited for them.

Once assembled, they attempted to push on, but The Man motioned with his hands for them to be still. The moon shone directly on The Man's face, illuminating him fully for the first time since they had left the city gates. His expression altered. Just a few minutes ago, joy and excitement had filled it as he had talked about his love for them. But now something was different. What he needed to tell them was complex. Joy still lingered on his face but now shared space with pain.

"My command is this. Love each other just like I've loved you." The Man grabbed one of his friend's shoulders and squeezed it. "Greater love—" The Man tried to speak again but couldn't. His head dropped. The all-too-familiar feeling in his throat climbed to the back of his mouth. Tears welled in his eyes and ran down his cheeks.

"Master," a disciple said. He was a tax collector and had been with the group from the beginning. "What's wrong? Why are you upset? Is it the traitor?"

The Man looked up at the tax collector and knew he simply didn't understand the gravity of the moment. He took two steps toward him and embraced him. The Man wept quietly into the tax collector's shoulder.

The tax collector did his best to console him, offering surface-level words of encouragement even though he had no idea what upset The Man.

The Man gathered himself and wiped his face on his cloak. He stepped backward. Love and sorrow crossed his face as he stared into their eyes. "You're my friends," The Man whispered. He spied his hands and imagined what they'd look like in just a few hours. "There's no . . . There's no greater love than to sacrifice one's life for one's friends."

The Man motioned for them to follow him. He wanted to show them through his actions he meant what he said.

* * *

As they approached the base of the slope, it gave way to a valley.

The Man gave them his final lecture. He predicted if they pursued him after the weekend's events, the world would hate them. Just like the world persecuted him, his disciples would also fall victim to persecution and hatred. He envisioned they'd be thrown out of towns and religious buildings simply because their allegiance lay with him. He assured his disciples a day was coming where people would reason if they murdered his disciples, they'd be offering a service to The Father, pleasing in his sight.

But there was good news. Stunning his disciples, he said it was a good thing he was going away and wouldn't be with them after a while. If he didn't go away, The Man explained, The Father's Spirit couldn't inhabit the disciples' hearts. The Man predicted their hearts would forever burn inside them, and the fuel would be the power of the Spirit.

Power, according to The Man, was the trait those infected by The Father's Spirit would be known for. The Spirit would guide them into all truth, interpreting between humanity and the Divine. The Spirit would be mankind's encourager, comforter, and translator. And if what The Man said was correct, then his disciples needed this in every way. If the world would loathe, harass, and even attempt to kill them, they'd need every benefit the Spirit would offer.

The Man saw the opportunity for them to pray together as a group.

It would be the last time they did.

The Man fell prostrate and looked heavenward.

Seeing he was about to pray, the others did the same.

"Father, the moment is here," The Man said as he addressed the Divine. "Glorify me so I can give glory back to you. You've given me authority over everyone. I give eternal life to each one you've given me. And I know this is the way to have eternal life—it's to know you, the only true Father, and me, the one you sent to earth. I glorified you here on Earth by completing your mission. Now, Father, bring me into the glory we shared before the world began."

Some disciples glanced around at the others, eyes squished and foreheads wrinkled in confusion.

"I showed what you're really like to the people you gave me. They were yours from day one. You entrusted them to me, and they've obeyed you. Now they know everything I have is actually from you, for I've told them the truth you gave me. They've accepted it and know I came from you, and they believe you sent me." The Man shifted his focus from himself to the ones in the circle with him. "My prayer isn't for the world but for those you've given me; they're rightfully yours. All who're mine belong to you, and you've given them to me, so they bring me glory. Now I'm leaving the world; they're staying, but I'm coming to you. Protect them so they'll be united just as we are. During my time here, I protected them. I guarded them and lost none, except the traitor. Now I'm coming to you. I told them all these things so they'd be filled with my joy. They know your words. And the world hates them because they don't belong to the world, just like I don't. I don't want you to remove them from the world but guard them from The Accuser. They don't belong to this world any more than I do. Please let your truth push them to become like you; teach them your word, which is truth. Just like you sent me into the world, I'm sending them into the world. I'm laying down everything I am so they can stand transformed, defined by your truth."

A chilly breeze rustled through the trees encouraging the men to pull their cloaks tighter around their bodies. As midnight approached, the night grew colder. Although it was shared just a few hours ago, their holy meal seemed like a distant memory.

The Man dipped his head, placed his hands on the ground and squeezed handfuls of dirt so tightly the soil protruded between his whitening knuckles. "I'm praying not only for these disciples but also for all who will ever believe in me through their message." He shifted his petition toward the immeasurable multitudes who would pledge their hearts to him over the course of history. "I pray they'll all be one, just like you and I are one, united in every way. Plant them in us so the world will believe you sent me. I've given them the glory you gave me so they can be united like us. I'm in them, and you're in me. I want them to experience perfect unity so the world will know you sent me and you love them as much as you love me. Father, I can't wait for my disciples to see where we're going. Then they'll see all the glory you gave me because you loved me!" The Man raised his hands and pressed them deeper into the ground as his prayer intensified. "O perfect Father, the world doesn't know you, *but I do*." The Man paused. A genuine smile crawled across his face as he recalled the immense delight he had in knowing The Father.

His disciples saw the joy sweep across his face; they understood he knew The Father in a way no one else did.

"These disciples know you sent me. I've showed them who you really are and will continue to do so. Then your love for me will swell inside them, and I'll be in them." The Man took a deep breath and stood.

The others followed. No one said a thing.

Awkwardness filled the air until The Man broke the silence. "Are you ready?"

"For what?" the tax collector asked.

"My time has finally arrived."

* * *

A couple hundred yards later, they arrived at the foot of the valley. Hearing a small stream bounce off the countless rocks as it wove through the dell, the men recognized the stretch of trail and hiked up the other side. It didn't take long for them to arrive at their destination. They waited in silence on the edge of a quaint olive grove. They had frequented this place many times, as The Man enjoyed spending time under the large canopy.

The Man's demeanor altered in a dramatic way. The peace and joy that had once covered his face during his prayer on the other side of the ravine was now gone. He tugged the neck of his tunic, as he suddenly felt hot. His fingers tingled as he shifted his weight, quickly feeling dizzy. Something significant troubled him. He stumbled over a stone and groaned. He clutched the part of his cloak that lay over his heart and twisted the garment as his face contorted. Air blew harshly out his mouth in short, raspy breaths. His hair became wet with sweat, making him shiver. He looked as if he were about to cry, but nothing came out.

The men were speechless. They had lost track of time. They didn't know if it was late at night or early in the morning or somewhere in-between. But this they knew; as they stood in front of the olive grove, hundreds of thousands of lambs in the city were waiting to be prepared for slaughter. The blood of countless sacrifices were about to run the streets of the holy city red. The suffocating aroma of metallic iron would soon fill the temple area. The bleating cry of dying lambs would echo through the capital nonstop once the sun rose. And, as they permitted this to be brought to the forefront of their minds, they were reminded of a timeless yet harsh truth; there's no forgiveness without the shedding of blood.

As they stood there, they understood hundreds of thousands of Jews in the city were sleeping next to their own sacrificial lamb destined to be slaughtered for the forgiveness of their sins.

The disciples failed to recognize they were standing next to theirs as well.

Chapter 2

The Trees and the Traitor

THE MAN TOOK A deep breath. He unclenched his fist and released his cloak. He glanced at the men and eyed the path behind them to see if anyone had followed. As he entered the olive grove, his misty breath dissipated into the night sky.

The small orchard was plenty spacious for what The Man had in mind. The moonlight looked like shattered pottery in the dirt as it sparsely lit the ground, struggling to find openings in the branches. The biggest trees stood only thirty feet tall, but their trunks were impressively wide. Normally, The Man would have daydreamed about the amount of wood just one of these trees would've supplied his carpentry shop, but his mind was focused on one thing; he was determined to meet with The Father.

For years, these trees had provided the perfect covering for The Man to find rest and solitude in times of prayer. He had developed fond memories of coming here and communing with The Father. He had spent much time with his disciples under these branches as they practiced how to pray to The Father in ways that seemed almost too intimate. These trees functioned as memory markers for him, helping him recall the special times in his life where he'd drawn near to The Father.

Although he had the same goal in mind tonight, something was different. He planned to approach The Father through prayer but not because his joy encouraged him to do so. This time, it was sorrow that propelled him to engage The Father.

And anguish.

And strain.

Feeling cold again, he pulled his cloak tight around his body as he shivered. He stopped next to a thick olive tree and turned to quietly address his disciples. "Sit here while I pray."

The men settled under a tree in a thicket of tall grass. Some took the opportunity to pray as they had done here so often in the past. Others whispered with each other, discussing when they would return home and what they would do tomorrow. A few lay in the grass and stared at the canopy. One told the others he sensed something dangerous was coming but didn't know what.

The Man motioned for his three best friends to accompany him. He left eight of the men in the grass while he and his inner circle went deeper into the garden.

They walked far enough where the others were barely visible.

The Man stopped. Stillness roamed ominously around the orchard. The breeze waned along with the sounds of the city. The Man's eyes shut. Then, in the hushed darkness, he moaned. He grabbed the middle of his cloak again with his right arm and twisted it tight. He fell against a nearby tree and slid down the trunk. His face grimaced and scrunched. He looked to be in physical pain, but his friends had no idea what was wrong. They'd never seen him quite like this. The Man labored for breath as his eyes stayed closed.

His inner circle eyed each other, none of them jumping to comfort their leader. Nobody moved.

Tears streaked The Man's face. "My soul is overwhelmed . . . with sadness."

His disciples saw this to be true but remained baffled as to why. This was supposed to be a happy and joyful weekend. What was gnawing at The Man?

"My soul . . . is overwhelmed with sadness." The Man's back tightened, and his fists clenched. "I feel like I might not make it through this."

His friends' eyes widened. Did The Man actually believe he might die of a broken heart? What was making him so dejected? Did someone say something they shouldn't have?

He stood and hugged each of them as he cried. Each embrace was longer than the previous. "Stay here and keep watch."

"Keep watch for what?" one asked.

The Man said nothing. He walked away from them into the dark silhouettes of the trees. The farther he walked, the more he filled with dread—a terrible dread.

Although his friends couldn't see him in the dark, they knew he was near. They could hear him crying quietly by himself.

* * *

The Man grew weary. He wished he could lie down and fall asleep in peace, but that possibility seemed to exist only in a different universe. The Man sensed he was destined to be exactly where he was: shivering alone and in the dark.

He dropped to his knees and looked up through an opening in the canopy. His shoulders sagged, as it felt like an invisible weight was devastating them. This unseen yoke was mental and emotional. It was soon to be physical.

But worst of all, it was spiritual.

This wasn't the first time in his life The Man felt burdened to the point of breaking. He knew what it felt like to consistently provide for somebody who had nothing. He'd visited countless funerals where hopelessness immobilized widows and weeping parents. He'd experienced living with lofty expectations that seemed impossible to uphold. But nothing like this. This weight seemed insurmountable and immovable, where one wrong move might just crush him.

He raised his hands. "Father, if you're willing, please take this cup of suffering from me." He strained to listen with his heart. He felt his blood run through his veins as his sweat intensified. His breathing quickened as silence met him. He waited a few moments. "Father, if you're willing, *please* take this cup of suffering from me."

Nothing.

Fresh tears streaked his face as he reminded himself of his reality. His nose ran as his soft cries turned into sobs. He clutched cold dirt in both fists as he tried to catch his breath. "*Please*," The Man said in a choppy whisper. "*Please*, Father. Please."

Another moment of nothingness passed.

"Please."

And another.

"Please!"

The Man understood his choice. Two paths lay before him. He could take the path humanity always took. He could do what he truly wanted, even though it lay outside The Father's will. This was the easy decision and, in a sense, the obvious one. It required nothing of him and, at the moment, was the best immediate option for himself. This path led to pleasure and comfort, but it also led to a selfish existence. The Accuser forever encouraged humanity to take this route. This path was saying yes to The Man's will and no to The Father's.

But he saw another path. He could choose to fully accept The Father's will for his life and embrace it perfectly and completely. No one had ever done that—at least not fully. Contrary to popular belief, this road wasn't lined with blessings, gratification, and security. A peculiar kind of death covered this path—death to one's own will. It would require everything of him. This path was saying no to his desires and yes to The Father's.

And although the allure to live life for himself and on his own terms was strong, he wanted to please The Father above all else. All along, The Man believed The Father had sent him to accomplish the one thing The Father had planned for him since the beginning of time. The Man would choose what humanity never could.

"Father, if you're willing, *please* take this cup of suffering from me." He paused before uttering the words that would echo for eternity and become the anthem for billions of people who would attempt daily to die the peculiar kind of death The Man chose that night. "Yet I want your will to be done, not mine."

Never again would the Earth witness a surrender so mighty.

* * *

The Man sat a while longer, meditating on The Father's will and asking for strength. Standing, he became surprised by his renewed energy. It felt like someone had shot him with a dose of Divine adrenaline. Sure, he was still mentally exhausted and emotionally drained. His pupils were dilated, and his skin was damp—it was actually just wet in some areas of his arm, although he couldn't quite see well enough to identify what it was, but it smelled like blood. The tips of his curly hair were now moist. He was still cold. But he felt well enough to stand.

He maneuvered to his friends through the brush and the trees. He found the three of them slumped against a tree, asleep. One snored off and on.

The Man grew disheartened. "Wake up."

Two of the disciples sat upright and strained to stand. The snoring one didn't move.

"Wake up!" The Man used his leg to nudge the one still sleeping.

Finally, the tired disciple opened his eyes, saw the three men standing over him and rose in a hurry. He flushed with embarrassment.

The Man took a moment and stared at his disciples.

They saw the disappointment in his gaze.

He wasn't standing in front of them as a teacher disenchanted by his students. He stood as a friend disappointed by his companions. He lifted his arms and shoulders slightly and opened his palms to the sky. "Could you not do it?"

The three glanced at him then each other. Their eyes finally adjusted from their sleep, and they realized he'd been praying longer than they had expected, which meant they'd been sleeping longer than they had thought.

The Man's appearance clearly changed. He continued to look worse.

"Do . . . what?" one asked.

The Man lowered his hands and sighed. "Couldn't you keep watch for me for even one hour?"

"We didn't mean—"

"Keep watch and pray."

"We will."

"Keep watch and pray so you won't fall to temptation."

The three disciples knew he meant it. For whatever reason, this was important. They had to be watching for . . . *something*. And they needed to be prayerful so they wouldn't fall into . . . *some kind of unknown temptation*. Although his command was perplexing, they fully intended to obey it, because they loved him and were loyal to following him.

"Yes, do this. For the spirit is willing, but the body is weak." He turned and walked back into the darkness.

* * *

Returning to the same spot as before, he found two marks in the damp ground where his knees had been earlier. He kneeled again. "Father, if you're willing, please take this cup of suffering from me, but, if it cannot be taken away unless I drink it, then have your way." He prayed this repeatedly, adamant and determined to ensure that before he proceeded with the night's events, his will was perfectly aligned with The Father's.

He prayed long enough for his knees to press deeper into the cold soil. Dismay rose from the pit of his being. The feeling suffocated him, tightening around his lungs. After fifteen minutes, he stood and returned to the three, hoping to receive encouragement from his friends.

But he found none, for his friends were sleeping again.

He glared at them. He understood how tired they were but wished they understood how badly he needed them during this time. Yes, The Man needed them. Although he was fully Divine, he was also fully human, which meant their comfort and support for him was crucial during this dark time.

The Man's breathing shortened more. For the first time that night, he felt something would worsen as the hours passed. This sensation was a feeling that crippled and debilitated the people it consumed, a feeling so insidious that it was found responsible for millions of people throughout history who fell victim to depression, suicide, hopelessness, and desperation.

Loneliness had engulfed The Man.

One of his disciples stirred. After opening his eyes, he sat upright and looked around, realizing he and his friends had failed The Man once again. The disciple opened his mouth to say something to enhance the situation, but nothing came out. He didn't know what to say.

Without word, The Man returned into the darkness to pray one more time.

* * *

His third prayer was nothing new. He repeatedly requested the same thing. He begged The Father for another way, but he understood none existed. Knowing this, he affirmed with The Father that he wanted The Father's will to be taken up and accomplished. He ensured his will was undeniably bound to The Father's and there wasn't a trace of hesitation in his heart as to the path he was choosing.

For The Man believed The Father was asking him to do something in the next fifteen hours that would alter the course of history. And although the thing The Father was leading The Man to do was wonderful, the task was also horrible. The Man's mission would be the best *and* the worst thing the Earth had ever and would ever lay its eyes upon. And to accomplish the task, The Man needed to relinquish any inkling of selfish inclination and chain himself to The Father's way.

The Man fully emptied himself and set out to wake his feeble disciples.

* * *

The Man blindly escorted his three yawning friends through the brush. After a few hundred feet, they found the other eight disciples sleeping in the tall grass.

"Go ahead and sleep," The Man said.

The disciples stirred.

"Go ahead and sleep. Have your rest; you'll need it." The Man sought for a place to lay down as well. He knew he needed every ounce of strength he could get.

As he crouched and prepared his spot in the grass, a flicker of light caught his attention. He rushed to his feet and peered through the trees. He saw a bouncing light in the valley. The Man couldn't tell what side of the stream the little yet distinct light was on. As his eyes adjusted, he realized the light wasn't just a meaningless point of light but a definite small flame, perhaps a torch. The Man studied the lively blaze until he saw a second one appear behind it.

Then a third.

Then a fourth.

Then a fifth.

Adrenaline coursed through his veins as he understood his time of woe had come. Without end, it seemed, the flames appeared from the trail on the opposite side of the valley. Before The Man said anything, the flames congregated at the bottom of the valley and dispersed up the trail toward his group.

"No." The volume of his voice was normal, but the silence filling the grove the past hour and a half made The Man's voice seem unnaturally loud. "No, you can't sleep anymore. Get up." He nudged them with his feet, and they stretched and labored to a stand.

"The time has come," The Man said with a quick voice and a gaze that didn't leave the flickering lights. "I'm about to be betrayed into the hands of sinners."

Some were painfully slow in rising to give him their full attention.

"Get up! Let's get going!" The Man pointed toward the path.

The men saw the torches approaching in the dark for the first time. With each torch they saw, their eyes grew wider.

"Look," The Man said in a hush.

As the group stared through the trees, they saw silhouettes and figures at the front of the line—three temple guards. They couldn't tell exactly what the temple guards were wearing, but they noticed two of them donned swords around their waist and one hefted what looked like a piece of wood. No, it was a club. Leading them was a man whose face gradually gave way to illumination by the flickering flames. They knew the face all too well.

"My betrayer is here."

The disciples stood shoulder to shoulder as the legion of men gathered around them. The two groups faced each other, neither choosing to speak first. The contrast between the factions was striking.

The Man's group was small. Including him, there were only twelve of them. They were unarmed other than a couple of small double-edged daggers. They were young, inexperienced, and poor. They shared nothing in common except their fellowship in following The Man. They wore simple clothes, tattered and worn. They hadn't bathed in over a week. Their eyes were bloodshot, and their muscles shivered in the cold.

Because they secretly feared The Man, the group the traitor led was large, almost thirty in total. Roman soldiers clothed in their full covering and armed with swords and shields stood beside Jewish temple guards and priests. Many of the men owned servants who accompanied them. Almost half of the traitor's group carried torches or lanterns. They held their heads high as they revealed their weapons to intimidate the other group. They were rested, equipped, and determined. They too shared not much in common except their hatred of The Man.

The two groups postured in awkward silence. Each waited on their leaders to do something.

For a moment, the traitor seemed unable to move, perhaps paralyzed by apprehension. He'd previously agreed with the soldiers and guards to confirm the identity of The Man by greeting him with a kiss. But now that the time had come, he looked unsure and hesitant, like a small boy who had devised the perfect scheme of trickery but, when the time came for execution, froze in fear. He couldn't see the other group's faces well and knew he wouldn't know where The Man was until he entered the circle of his previous friends and looked each of them in the face.

The traitor moved forward, face full of caution, and crossed the empty divide that separated the two groups. All eyes fixated on him. Going from the well-lit group to the dimly lit one, he squinted as he strained to see the details in their faces. He recognized the fisherman and the brothers and the tax collector and the zealot. Finally, he locked eyes with his former leader.

Stepping closer, the traitor touched The Man on the right shoulder and stared up at him. The traitor attempted to appear confident, but his quivering lip gave him away. A glint of sadness shone in his demeanor. The traitor seemed tired and worn out too, as if he'd been wrestling with someone all night long.

He leaned in to kiss The Man, but The Man placed his hand on the traitor's chest and stopped him. The Man bent his neck to look him in the eye. Then The Man said the one thing he knew to say in a last-ditch effort to liberate the traitor from his own destructive ways.

The Man called out to the traitor by whispering his name.

It was tender and subtle, and only the thirteen men clumped together heard it.

This was familiar. The Man had called out people's names before in similar ways. He possessed a knack for unearthing the original hearts of The Father's children who had become buried beneath The Accuser's devices used to smother them. When The Man would call their names, The Father's children seemed to become lighter and unrestricted, like they were free to return to who The Father had created them to be. He would call out the names of people once tormented by demons but now weren't. His disciples had watched in awe as he would call out the names of blind beggars and lepers and would encourage them to use their faith and proceed toward healing. He had even done the unthinkable by calling out the names of people in graves, leaving onlookers in holy wonder as they had watched previously dead people stride from their tombs and into life again.

And, as The Man touched the traitor on the chest and looked into his eyes and whispered his name, he hoped his original friend might return to life from the deathtrap The Accuser had placed him in. The Man yearned for this because he loved his friend dearly and believed in his potential. But the spark of life and love The Man remembered in his disciple's eyes had disappeared. It was clear The Accuser had consumed the traitor from the inside out.

"Are you really going to betray me with a kiss?" The Man whispered.

The traitor flashed a fake smile and placed both hands on The Man's shoulders. "Greetings, teacher!" the traitor said loud enough for the soldiers behind him to hear. He leaned in and kissed him on the cheek.

For The Man, his demise had begun.

The Man stepped forward to fully reveal himself to the armed group. He separated himself from his friends, but his face remained in the shadows, because no flame was close enough to illuminate him. He knew exactly what was to take place and how the rest of the evening would shake out, for he was fully Divine. "Who do you want?"

Three men—a temple guard and two Roman soldiers—came forward to confront The Man. Two of them grabbed torches from onlooking servants. They marched in confidence through tall grass, stepping over an abnormally large root exposed just a few inches off the ground. One of them lifted his torch forward to see his silhouette better, but his cloak covered his head to whisk away the cool breeze, making his facial features difficult to recognize.

"Who do you want?" The Man asked again.

They said The Man's name, identifying him as the one they desired.

The Man approached them. Once he stood in front of them, he removed his cloak and revealed his face to the torch lights.

From what they could tell, he resembled a common Jewish man—dark skin, black and short, distinctively curly hair. But it was his eyes that made them nervous. Even in the dim orchard, his green eyes were exceptionally *intense*. The Man could read their thoughts; his gaze made them nervous. They felt exposed, as if he could see everything about them even though this was the first time these four men had interacted. His stare made them more uncomfortable with each passing second.

The Man stepped forward again, putting himself fewer than three feet from them. "I'm him."

His unnatural boldness forced all three of them to step backward to create space. His gaze was strong, but his fearless demeanor from which he had revealed himself was too much and too stark for them. During it all, they had forgotten the exposed root behind them, and they tripped backward over it.

The Man could see right through their armor and shields. He could see their hearts. He could see they were frightened of The Man, for they'd heard about his power and authority to do anything he wanted, even supernatural things. "Who are you looking for?" The Man asked again with a sigh.

The three men scurried to their feet, brushed off their garb and raised their torches again for lighting. They said The Man's name once again, identifying him as the one they desired.

"I already told you that's me. If you're looking for me, let these men go." He turned and pointed to the group of twelve standing in the shadows. The traitor remained among the group.

As he looked at the group behind him, a stocky temple guard with a club ran behind him and struck him on his lower back. The sound reverberated through the otherwise still night.

The Man yelped as he fell.

Four others jumped on top of him and pinned him down. Two held his hands, one held his legs, and one held him by his hair. The Man's head pressed into the cold dirt as the guards and soldiers attacked him.

No voice was heard, and no words were uttered. The disciples didn't wait for instruction; the eleven men charged forward while the traitor stood taken aback at the sight of violence. They tackled the guards who were assaulting The Man.

Chaos ensued. Torches fell, and the area darkened. The grunting and moaning of the two clashing groups drowned out the sounds of the punches. Some disciples flung rocks at the soldiers. People screamed. Some grasped for the necks of their foes. Noses broke, and bruises formed.

The soldiers drew their swords. And with those swords, a few disciples drew the double-edged daggers they hid beneath their clothing. The fisherman swung wildly at anyone he thought was trying to arrest The Man. He swung to kill, but fortunately for the group of soldiers and guards, he had no idea how to fight.

As the violence erupted, few noticed the goodwill that happened.

The armed soldiers abandoned The Man as they struggled to fend off the disciples who attacked them.

The Man laid on his stomach for a few seconds as he tried to catch his breath from the club knocking it out of him. He put his hands underneath his chest and groaned as he struggled to his knees. Straightening up, what he saw upset his heart.

A young boy, about sixteen years old, sat on his knees nearby. The Man could tell the boy was a servant of one of the men in the group, as he looked like he just didn't belong. Shabby clothes hid his underdeveloped muscle tone. He breathed in spurts as his face pinched together in pain. He held both hands to the right side of his head as he cried. His face articulated fresh and raw throbbing. Blood escaped through the cracks in his fingers, soaking the right side of his body.

The Man barely saw it, but in front of his own knees was what looked to be a bloodstained ear.

As the conflict raged on above him, The Man crawled to the servant and faced the boy. The Man sensed The Father's Spirit move inside his own heart. Sympathy swelled from within The Man as compassion overwhelmed him. The Man leaned in and bent his neck to look the servant in the eye. Taking his own cloak, The Man wiped the fresh tears that flowed down the young man's face. Although violent commotion surrounded them, the servant's sobs echoed in the orchard as he tried to catch his breath.

"It'll be okay." The Man retrieved the mangled ear from the dirt and smiled. "Watch. I make all things new." He removed the servant's hands from his head, revealing a small, open wound where his ear used to be. The Man wiped the wound clean and fastened the ear to the boy's head.

Miraculously, the skin on his head latched onto the skin from his ear, and the bleeding and the pain stopped in an instant.

After having been thrown to the ground, kicked, and beaten with a club, The Man never once attended to his own needs but chose to serve a servant.

The servant touched his ear. As he felt the rigid line of new skin that sealed his ear to his head, his jaw dropped as his eyes opened as wide as they could. He watched the Jew crouched before him, unsure how to respond. Still attempting to control his emotions, he shuffled to his feet and ran into the woods.

The Man glanced at two Roman soldiers standing to the side, gawking at him, astonished at what they'd just witnessed. Their jaws hung low, just like the boy's. The Man saw they were no longer interested in arresting somebody who had what appeared to be magical powers. They too left the fight and fled into the night.

"Put away your sword!" The Man whipped around and glared at his disciples.

Due to the madness, nobody noticed The Man they'd come to arrest had stood on his own, unbound, right in the middle of it all. Everyone remained still.

With the crook of his arm, a disciple squeezed the skull of a temple guard. Two disciples lay on the ground, bleeding from their faces. The fisherman held up his dagger but stood motionless and frustrated that The Man had stopped him.

The Man frowned at the fisherman. "Put it *down*!"

The fisherman dropped his dagger. The rest of his disciples released their opponents and straightened up. One emerged from the bottom of a pile with his tunic torn and ripped from his body.

"Those who use the sword will die by the sword." The Man was no longer addressing just his disciples but the whole crowd standing in the grove. "Don't you realize I could ask my Father for thousands of angels to protect us, and he would send them instantly? But, if I did, how would the scriptures be fulfilled that describe what must happen now?" He turned his attention to the opposing group but specifically to the temple guards, for the chief priests had ordered them to unlawfully arrest The Man by any means necessary. "Am I some dangerous revolutionary that you felt the need to come at me with swords and clubs to arrest me? I know that's what your chief priests told you. I was among you all week. I was in the public eye. Why didn't you arrest me in the temple? I was there, teaching every day."

No response.

The Man waited a moment and faced his disciples. "This is all happening to fulfill the words of the prophets from Scripture." The Man's face changed. What his face had communicated before no one could tell, because his expression was riddled with emotions. But now his face transformed as one specific emotion overtook him and changed his demeanor. The Man's countenance could've been mistaken for disappointment. But it was much more than that. His expression communicated monumental sorrow, as if he was about to experience the full scope of an inexpressible evil he'd only heard of from afar but now would take on face to face.

He turned toward the mob and accepted his fate. "Go ahead and do it. This is your hour, when darkness reigns."

The crowd moved in and bound The Man. They forced chains tightly around his hands and another around his neck. They put a sackcloth bag over his head and tied it around his neck. A few hit The Man in the face, the last one causing The Man to fall over. They all laughed.

A disciple made a move toward his leader, but a Roman soldier stepped between them and drew his sword. "This man is under arrest," the soldier said with a sneer. "Don't even think about coming after him or following us. If any of you do, I'll make sure every one of you sorry fools regret you even knew this Jew."

The disciples stood wide-eyed in disbelief.

"Get out of here," the soldier whispered. "*Now*."

A handful of them escaped up the path deeper into the grove. Some scurried down the mountain but through the brush to not take the trail the mob would be traveling. The disciple whose tunic was ruined ran toward the city, plain naked. The traitor stood still, unsure of what to do or who to follow.

This was the first time The Man's true disciples had ever deserted him. But it wouldn't be the last.

The Man would grow accustomed to this. To his dismay, this desertion would start a trend that would continue throughout history. Followers would abandon him in times of trial and trouble. Even though his followers would forever change the world, they would always grapple to remain faithful when they sensed the Divine was fighting a losing battle. Although they claimed to follow the One whose name alone made the demons flee, they would always struggle to pursue him fearlessly at any cost.

This wasn't the only time disciples would abandon him when they realized that following him meant that they too must march to their own death.

* * *

After brushing off the dirt and gathering their belongs, the soldiers grabbed The Man's shoulders and hoisted him onto his feet. "Let's get going, you dog."

"We've got someone who wants to see you."

"Where are your friends now?"

"You won't like what we've planned for you."

"Let's hope this Father of yours can protect you."

"You scum! Let's go!"

"You remember how to walk, don't you?"

A servant gave one of the soldiers a switch, and they whipped him like a horse to push him along a path he couldn't see. The strikes stung, especially when they hit the lower part of his back where the club had landed just a few minutes before.

The Man attempted to walk at an appropriate pace to elude more whippings but struggled to maintain his footing.

They proceeded down the trail, across the stream and into the city. They were going to the residence of the most powerful Jewish man in the city—the high priest. The high priest had ordered the arrest hours earlier. The Man knew the high priest hated him because The Man disrupted everything about the high priest's way of life. The high priest found The

Man to be an offense toward The Father and his law. Therefore, he had to be dealt with.

Across the city, the high priest stood upstairs, staring out his bedroom window with his cloak wrapped tightly around himself. As he waited for the mob to return, he prayed to The Father. He always made it a habit and tradition during the holy weekend to persistently pray and ask for The Father to send the promised messiah to save the Jews and restore the nation of Israel.

What he didn't grasp was the person he'd been earnestly praying for was the same person he earnestly hated, and, at that moment, he was stumbling toward his palace.

Underneath the bag, The Man closed his eyes as he strained not to cry. It wasn't the pain that hurt but the abandonment. As he marched, he knew no one was coming to rescue him.

Chapter 3

Showing True Colors

For over thirty minutes, The Man marched with the bag covering his head. He knew he was traveling to the home of the high priest. He'd seen the home before but had never been invited in.

He knew they had returned to the city by the stone pressing his feet. The fresh smell of livestock overwhelmed his nose and ears. The Man couldn't see anything; the thick bag on his head forbid light to penetrate. The soldiers' tireless whipping numbed his back. The switch put The Man in a relentless discomfort and unease. As the group moved through the city, their hecklings and profane taunts grew silent. The Man understood they didn't want to wake anybody. This wasn't due to the holy weekend; their dealings with The Man were suspect and would eventually, as the night progressed, become highly illegal.

The irony was everywhere, yet they all missed it. This specific and unique detachment, composed of Roman soldiers who upheld governmental law and temple guards who upheld spiritual law, was oddly unified in acting unjustly and unlawfully toward The Man on whom all morality and justice would forever be based.

The chain around his neck tightened and jerked him backward to a halt. The group stopped. The Man's heart raced as his limbs tingled in anticipation. He heard a loud knock on a door followed by somebody answering and encouraging the group to enter. They pushed him up a handful of steps and through a doorway.

Although he recognized that with each new setting he moved one step closer to his demise, The Man found a small degree of relief inside. The pleasant warmth radiating inside the building gave him momentary comfort. He still couldn't see, but he could tell by glancing down through the bottom slits of the bag that the room was well lit. It smelled of incense and herbs, something The Man only ever smelled at the Jewish temple. The smooth marble floor beneath his feet boasted of strength and status.

Whoever lived there was incredibly wealthy.

* * *

Thirty minutes before The Man stepped foot onto the marble floor, the fisherman found another disciple.

They both fled the scene at the warning of the Roman soldier and sprinted down the mountain through the brush, avoiding the trail, fearful of what might happen if they were to encounter the mob again. The fisherman bent over, attempting to catch his breath, when the other disciple spoke up.

"We can't just desert him," the disciple said as he slapped his hand against his own leg.

The fisherman tried to speak but couldn't, because he was winded. He straightened up and put his hands over the top of his head and peered back up the path. Then he saw them.

The flames bounced in the black night as the detachment wound down the path heading for the city. The fisherman and the other disciple stood fifty feet from the trail behind trees as the mob passed. They saw their leader in the middle of the group bound by chains around his hands and his neck. They couldn't quite make out the strange covering over his head. The soldiers struck him repeatedly with something, perhaps a switch.

"Let's follow them," the fisherman said.

"We have to," the other disciple agreed.

"He won't suffer alone. We can't let that happen."

Stumbling through the dark, they found the footpath and hiked down. They kept at least a couple hundred feet between them and the last member of the group to not expose themselves. They glided across the stream, up the other side of the ravine and back through the city entrance. Following the mob, they trekked to the upper part of the city. The fisherman and the other disciple had never ventured into this division of the capital. Due to its reputation of affluence and luxury, they understood they simply didn't belong.

The detachment stopped in front of a palace and waited for the property gate to open.

The two disciples gawked at what they saw. The palace was magnificent. The front gate had two bulky wooden doors with scripture carved elegantly into the frames. Walls extended from both sides of the gate and led to multiple towers that squared the property. They couldn't see everything hiding behind the walls, but it didn't matter. They couldn't take their eyes off the two main housing structures that soared above the walls and sat boastfully in the middle of the estate. Picturesque marble columns appeared to stand guarding the architectural treasure that rose behind them. Prominent red tiles covered the roof. Second and third stories overlooked the holy city as their many windows provided openings that the homeowner seemingly could reach through and grab elaborate blessings from the hand of The Father Himself.

The gate opened, and the crowd entered, but not all of them. About half left and departed for home, as their duty was done.

The fisherman and the other disciple saw their chance.

The disciple slipped through the gate, but the gatekeeper, a middle-aged woman, shut the gate on the fisherman.

"He's with me," the disciple said.

She opened the gate again and eyed the fisherman. He looked unlike the other disciple who appeared clean shaven and wore fresher clothes. He had a strong jaw and was handsome.

The fisherman was not. His beard was unkempt, and his clothes were frayed. His left eye was blue and swollen from the fight in the orchard. He stunk miserably.

She regarded the fisherman then faced the disciple. "They just brought in a man accused of stirring up division among our people. They say he's a magic man, you know, does incredible things, but they all lead to trouble. He'll be the downfall of our people."

The two disciples struggled for words.

She bent down and peered up at the fisherman, convinced he looked familiar. "You're not one of his disciples, are you?"

"I'm not." He eyed the other disciple who shot his glance to the ground.

She motioned forward and welcomed them inside the gate.

As they walked through, they almost missed The Man blinded by a bag over his head and a handful of guards climbing the steps into the building on the left. A sizeable bonfire blazed in the courtyard between the two housing structures and, after checking to ensure no one might recognize them, they went to warm themselves.

* * *

Light. For the first time in over thirty minutes, The Man could see. They removed the sack from his head, and he beheld his surroundings.

Eight men stood glaring at him, but The Man didn't meet their gaze. He couldn't keep his eyes from wandering in amazement at what he saw. The home was stunning. He stood in what looked to be the focal room of the house, large and open. Scenic tapestries covered the walls depicting mountains and valleys and animals of every kind. To his left extended a hallway with six singular doors that led to different rooms; slave quarters, he presumed. The house radiated with heat. Multiple fireplaces crackled in the dim light. Greeting him like a warm hug from an old friend, the comforting smell of herbal bread rising in the oven drifted into his nostrils. Beneath his feet lay an intricately detailed mosaic that covered almost the entire floor. A meticulous pattern of small square marble snaked across the room and down the hallway. The Man had never stepped foot in a house like this before. After realizing everyone was still watching him, he lifted his head and at last observed who was in the room.

Three men were the temple guards who had arrested and bound him earlier. Four men were members of the Jewish Council, a body of seventy-one men who oversaw all matters of the law in the city. They wore bright robes with long blue tassels hanging off at the bottom. Small wooden boxes attached by headbands hung off the sides of their faces, reminding the Jewish people to be holy. The Man recognized them instantly, because they had harassed and threatened him earlier that week as he had taught at the temple.

But the last person was different from the rest. Much older than the others, he wore even more extravagant clothing than the councilmembers. He was the father-in-law to the residing high priest who lived in the other house on the property, but it was understood by everyone in the city this fellow still pulled the strings behind the scenes, for he used to hold the office of high priest. He was a wise elder to everyone on the council, and they all revered him.

The elder stood in the middle of the group with his back hunched and taking deep, meticulous breaths, eyeing The Man. He motioned for a nearby slave to fetch him something to drink. The Man realized the home belonged to the elder.

"So," the elder said in a quiet, low voice, "I hear your disciples were violent toward my men tonight. Is that what you teach them to do—extract violence on The Father's temple workers?"

The Man remained motionless.

The elder gave him a moment to respond, but The Man declined. "Son, it's my understanding you're a miracle worker, a magic man as some have said. Where do you get your powers?"

No reaction.

"You won't respond to me? Surely, you know who I am. If you realized who you were speaking to, you would indeed consider changing the way you're dealing with me."

The Man didn't answer, but he thought the exact same thing.

The elder regarded the councilmembers and laughed. The Man didn't appear to be a powerful magic man but a mute fool. "It's a shame you won't talk to me. I'm a teacher of the people just like you. But my concern is that you teach them to sin. You undoubtedly have communicated to your followers that the Sabbath means nothing, haven't you?"

The Man dropped his head. He wasn't interested in responding to this illegal cross-examination.

"Son, I'm speaking truth, correct? You teach your followers to ignore the Sabbath. You disrupt the temple marketplace. People are even saying you claim to be Divine. Do you seriously claim such an arrogant blasphemy? Lift your head and answer me!"

The Man sighed. "Everyone knows what I teach." His brow furrowed as he lifted his head, revealing the cuts on his face. "I've preached regularly in the synagogues and the temple, where the people gather. I haven't spoken in secret. Why are you asking me this question?"

"Because the rumor we've heard—"

"Ask those who heard me. They know what I said."

One of the councilmen's jaw dropped.

The Man knew he'd offended the elder; everyone in the room understood this wasn't the way to respond to the elder and former high priest. The Man had spoken as if he truly wasn't under the elder's religious authority.

Spittle bubbled in the corners of the elder's mouth as his nostrils flared. His lips pulled back, revealing his yellowed teeth.

A councilman stomped three steps forward and backhanded The Man across the face. "Is that the way to answer the former high priest?"

The Man rubbed his face as it came out of its grimace. "If I said anything wrong, you must prove it. But, if I'm speaking the truth, why are you hitting me?"

The Man was correct, and everyone in the room knew it. They must prove his errors, not just accuse him of them.

"All we need are a few witnesses," the elder said through gnashed teeth. "And I know just where to find them."

The temple guards grabbed the chain around The Man's neck and yanked it, sending him to the floor. The councilmen snickered at the sight of The Man attempting to rise despite his substantial shackles.

But the elder didn't. The Man sensed the elder found nothing comical about the situation. The Man, as helpless as he appeared, was too threatening. He had to be taken care of promptly and quietly to ensure a peaceful holy weekend. The elder would personally see to it that he was.

All eight men left the house, forcing The Man to totter behind them. They were going to the home of the high priest.

Bitter cold wind blew across the courtyard as The Man walked from one house to another. He realized many more people were gathered on the property than he first thought. A robust bonfire roared in the middle of the courtyard where over twenty men and women congregated.

He looked up and surveyed the palace in front of him. The one he'd just come from looked essentially the same as the one he was headed for. The structures left common men like himself astonished. It was difficult to believe someone actually *lived* there. And yet, that wasn't what really caught The Man's eye.

As he stared up, he looked skyward and, for a split second, felt overcome with wonder. The stars filled the sky in a way that seemed new. Nobody could count them—not even close. It seemed to The Man there were more areas of light in the sky than darkness. Light wisped back and forth across the heavens, parading the best Creation had to offer. Bright twinkling stars flaunted the imagination of The Father. No matter which way he craned his neck, he viewed constellations and star clusters that all seemed to be watching what was happening. It was as if everything in the entire universe paused their endeavors and strained their necks down to the Earth to peer into the holy city, even though the city and its splendor wasn't what caught their eye.

It was The Man. In great anticipation, the entirety of the universe fixed its eye solely on The Man.

And it too was filled with wonder.

* * *

The two disciples pulled their cloaks over their heads to block the cold and keep their identity hidden as much as possible. They'd been standing inside the gated property for only twenty minutes or so when they couldn't take the chilly temperature anymore and decided to warm themselves. They slunk to the bonfire in the middle of the courtyard. The fire felt good. It warmed their faces and their hands and especially their backsides as they occasionally turned. They said nothing and kept their head down.

The bonfire seemed to attract a unique crowd. Servants, temple guards, and family members all gathered around, discussing what was happening inside the house regarding The Man.

"But how?"

"It's obvious. He just is."

"But you have to have proof. Where's their proof?"

"He's been uttering blasphemies ever since he came out of Galilee. This is nothing new."

"But have they . . . you know, recorded them somewhere? Has a judge heard these?"

"No, but everybody knows—"

"But that isn't good enough for our court of—"

"It has to be! For the sake of our nation and our religion, it must be! The outcome is far more important than the process in this case."

The fisherman accidentally looked up and made eye contact with what looked to be a servant girl. He shot his gaze downward, but the damage had been done.

"Hey, this fellow is one of his followers," a girl said, pointing at the fisherman.

All conversation ceased as the fisherman lifted his head and looked around. An empty feeling planted in the pit of his stomach. His gaze darted toward the gate, wondering if he could make it. He wet his lips and cleared his throat. "I don't even know him."

"Are you sure?" the girl asked. "I thought I saw you—"

"Did you not hear me? I said *I don't know him*. Let it go."

As the conversation continued with the rest of the group and the attention taken away from the fisherman, he considered what he said. He hated his lie but trusted that to be the last occasion he'd have to.

* * *

The detail in the table was remarkable. Pressed planks zigzagged across the surface in a unique pattern he'd never seen. The Man loved the way slim pieces of trim hung underneath the edges of the table. Lovely vines and roses were carved into the six legs that supported the table's bulky mass. Imagining how much the table weighed confounded The Man's mind.

Even more shocking, this table clearly wasn't made from pine or even cypress. No, the rings The Man could discern in the wood seemed too dense. This was Lebanese cedar. It would've been harvested hundreds of miles away and floated down miles of rivers just to get to the carpentry shop.

The Man could appreciate the table because his father was a carpenter by trade. Over the years, The Man had adopted the skills of his father, and he too mastered the art of carpentry.

Father would've loved this, The Man thought.

Twelve chairs with high, arching backs sat around the table—five on each side and one at each head. They each had pillows for luxury and support. Roses and vines were etched into the legs of each chair. A table like this would've cost at least a year's wage. Possibly even—

The Man was slapped in the face, and he fell backward against a wall.

"Are you not going to answer?" a councilman asked as spit flew from his lips.

The Man straightened upright and held the left side of his face as it throbbed. He realized he hadn't been paying attention to the cross-examination, because the table in the other room had distracted him. Over forty councilmen surrounded him, donning the same bright robes with long tassels. Others stood outside talking. Slaves came and went as they served the men.

In the back of the room stood the house owner and the leader of the Jews. He was the high priest and had been for almost fifteen years. He was the most influential Jew who lived in the city. He wore a bright blue tunic with tassels, but his extravagance didn't stop there. He sported a coat with bells fastened at his waist. The coat flaunted gold embroidering across its front that spelled the names of the twelve tribes of Israel next to the precious stones that clung to the fabric. He normally wore a three-tiered golden crown when in public, but not tonight. His bloodshot eyes communicated he normally wasn't awake at this hour. For him, this was a special occasion. As wolves had stalked their prey for days, the high priest was weary yet resolute. He had his target lined up and was ready to strike.

"I heard him claim The Father now favors Samaritans over Jews!" one councilman said.

"He's taught the young men of Israel the Sabbath should be ignored," an older gentleman said as he walked through the door.

"You've been sleeping with the whores you spend time with, haven't you?" another councilman asked as he pointed at The Man. "How do you expect to be a teacher of Israel when you abuse our women?"

The Man merely looked at him but didn't reply. He knew their accusations were false and couldn't be proven, but it didn't matter. The Man fully understood it didn't matter.

* * *

As the night progressed, the allegations grew more absurd. Many of their testimonies against The Man throughout the night were senseless and contradictory. They bullied him by using intimidation tactics, but he remained silent.

After much discussion outside, two male slaves strode into the room.

"We've heard this man claim to do something impossible yet destructive to our nation," one slave said.

"Yes, I heard it too," the other chimed in.

"We heard him say, 'I'll destroy this temple made with human hands, and in three days, I'll build another made without human hands.' He said it!"

"Yes, he did! Well, he said he'd do it in five days, but yes, he said it."

"No, he said three. Trust me."

"I thought he said it would take him three days to tear it down and five to build another."

"No, that's not what—"

"*Silence!*" The high priest rose, cheeks flush with anger and frustration, and sauntered toward the front of the room. He dismissed the babbling slaves, knowing their story was useless if it wasn't congruent.

A hush plastered the walls as the council watched The Man and the high priest meet eye to eye.

"Well," the high priest said. "Aren't you going to answer these charges?"

The Man said nothing. His gaze lingered on the high priest.

"These are serious charges and could have serious consequences. You're aware of that, right?"

No response.

"What do you have to say for yourself?"

No response.

The high priest pursed his lips as his muscles tensed. He stared at The Man as his breathing shortened. Shaking his head in disbelief, he quickly stepped toward The Man, looking like he might strike him. But suddenly, he stopped. His body went slack as his face relaxed, as if he had just figured out a clue to a puzzle. "Tell us . . ." The high priest turned his back to The Man and played to the Jewish Council. "Are you the messiah, the son of the Blessed One?"

An uncomfortable pregnant tension filled the room.

"I am," The Man said with a puffed-out chest.

With the proclamation, the high priest's eyes widened.

The councilmen gasped.

"And you'll see me seated in the place of power at The Father's right hand and coming on the clouds of Heaven."

Then, in a room filled with spiritual leaders, religious lawmakers, Jewish priests, and even the Divine Himself, all hell broke loose.

* * *

The Man's words weren't just an offense, they were an accusation. His words denounced the Divine-given authority the council assumed they possessed. The Man, in essence, had claimed he was fully Divine and The Father was entirely on his side, not theirs. He foresaw a day coming soon when the current situation would be reversed, a day when he'd be sitting next to The Father in judgement of *them* and they'd have no answers to give.

The high priest screamed as he raised his hands high. He turned in aversion and shot a disgusted expression at The Man. He clutched the top of his tunic above the precious stones and ripped the seam in half as he shouted, showing his horror in response to the wickedness he believed The Man had just spoken. "We don't need any other witnesses!" The high priest tore at his clothes. "Why do we need other witnesses? You've all heard this blasphemy. What's your verdict?"

The councilmembers stood in pandemonium. Some yelled he was guilty, others that he deserved to die. Some tore their clothes. Others left the room in utter repulsion.

But they all hated him.

* * *

The high priest gathered in a separate room with a few of his closer allies in the council. They knew they wanted to put The Man to death but were nervous to do so during the holy weekend, because the crowds adored The Man. The Roman Governor warned them earlier if they couldn't control their own people, Rome would. They needed to devise a cunning plan.

Meanwhile, in the main hall, the priests unveiled the vileness of their hearts as they attempted to strip The Man's dignity and mock his connection to The Father.

The councilmen took the chain around The Man's neck and tied him tight to a supporting post. They took turns spitting on him and slapping him across the face. They held his head high to allow themselves the pleasure of looking into his eyes as they laughed at him. Eventually, when they grew bored, they made a game of his scorn. They grabbed some cloth and blindfolded The Man and punched him in the face and ribs, imploring him to prophesy as to who had struck him.

Blood from The Man's face flowed down his neck and wet the front of his cloak.

A few priests held dramatic mock prayers, begging The Father to interrupt their fun and rescue his false messiah. Full of hateful joy, they giggled like children as they prayed.

This proceeded for over an hour.

* * *

The high priest saw his plans coming together. He had been concocting a way to finally trap the elusive man in his words and trick him into speaking blasphemous words in front of the council. There now was no chance their testimonies against The Man wouldn't agree, for they'd all heard the blasphemy themselves. Even better, all this had happened in the privacy of his own home while all the city slept. Neither Jew nor Roman could say they had watched the illegal proceedings that followed. Nobody could confirm how The Man had become covered with abrasions and bruises. Nobody could do this, because nobody had seen the shocking evil hidden behind the walls of the high priest's home in the middle of the night.

At least nobody *they* noticed.

Unfortunately for the high priest and his council, uninvited guests had arrived undetected.

The Father witnessed everything; nothing escaped his sight. He saw a part of Himself covered in the disguise of human flesh, mistreated and insulted by the creatures he had fashioned. As The Man's face grimaced and winced, so did The Father's. Even though he was the Creator of the Universe and the Master of Time, The Father had never experienced anything like this before. The scene was as if he was watching his own heart being pulled from his body and stomped on. He intensely desired to hold The Man close to his heart, heal his wounds and wipe the tears from his eyes. But he prevented himself from doing so, for he had planned from the beginning of time to rescue the world from their sin by withholding rescue from The Man that night. Because of that, his heart filled with an unspeakable sorrow as he watched.

But The Father wasn't the only overlooked guest in the home.

The Accuser watched from a distance as well. He had abandoned the traitor earlier that night, refusing to deny his own heart the indulgence of watching the exciting events unfold in the palace. He longed to see this night for some time now and found pleasure in watching. Hiding in the shadows of the house, he made no sound. With each strike, kick, insult, and charge, his grin widened.

* * *

An hour had passed since the two disciples decided to warm themselves by the fire. They didn't know what else to do. Rushing in and trying to save The Man would do no good, as they would've been captured with ease and placed in custody. But they couldn't go home and abandon The Man. That's not what a loyal disciple would do, so they waited by the fire, trying to map out their next move.

Many crowded around the bonfire. Nobody stayed longer than the two disciples. Almost everyone chatted casually about what they believed was transpiring inside the palace. Occasionally, their conversation turned to their plans and traditions for the holy weekend. Nothing about their conversations threatened the disciples.

Two temple guards approached the fire and joined the circle.

At once, the fisherman recognized the guards as being a part of the mob who had arrested The Man. His heart raced as he nudged the other disciple to confirm their identity.

But the other disciple looked up impulsively and completely revealed his face to the two temple guards.

In an instant, the guards noticed the two disciples.

"Hey, I recognize you two." The temple guard eyed his companion. "Weren't they in the olive grove earlier?"

"Yes. In fact, I'm sure of it."

"He's the one who had one of the daggers."

"Yes, they both were there."

They ceased talking to each other and glared at the two disciples.

All conversation around the fire halted.

The fisherman rose and scurried away.

Following closely, the temple guards wouldn't let it go. "Didn't I see you with The Man in the olive grove?"

"I don't know what you're talking about!"

The crowd surrounded him.

The other disciple stayed behind at the firepit.

The fisherman panned from the guards to the property gate to the disciple at the fire. He tugged at the neck of his tunic as he attempted to think quickly. "Leave me alone!"

But, as he tried to walk away, the crowd trailed him, convinced he was one of The Man's disciples.

"These temple guards wouldn't lie!"

"We know you've spent time with him in the temple while he taught."

"You dress just like him."

"Are you trying to rescue him from the council?"

"You must be one of the disciples. We can tell by your northern accent."

The fisherman swung around, eyes wide and pointed skyward. "A curse on me if I'm lying! I don't know The Man!" Immediately, he looked left and up at the palace. For the first time since the olive grove, he saw The Man's face through an open window as one of the councilmen slapped it.

The Man fell backward, stood up again and peered out the window. For a moment, he made eye contact with the fisherman. Their gaze lasted a mere two seconds before someone grabbed The Man's chain and pulled him out of sight.

Not far away on the property, a rooster's crow echoed in the night, signifying the approaching daybreak.

The fisherman remembered The Man's prediction of his own unfaithfulness and how vehemently the fisherman had denied it. The rooster's crow brought an ugly irony to the front of the fisherman's lips, forcing him to drink. Its bitterness seemed to be too much. Dropping to his knees, the fisherman buried his head in his hands in disbelief. For the first time in his life, he realized just how weak he actually was. He stared at his own disloyalty that night face to face and became overwhelmed with the ugliness he saw. He had failed his messiah in every way, and he knew it. The feeling of extreme disappointment swelled in his heart as he slowly believed his discipleship amounted to absolutely nothing.

He stood and pushed down a woman attempting to identify him. He ran from the crowd, out through the gate and into the darkness of the city. He wept bitterly the rest of the night until he fell asleep under a tree.

* * *

"We've officially decided," the high priest said, "that The Man has blasphemed against the Divine and deserves to die for his crimes."

The councilmen erupted in applause. The high priest's words seemed to bring a fresh sense of relief to them, signifying their work that night wouldn't be in vain.

"But it's the holy weekend. It would serve us well to not stir up any crowds who might still view this man as someone exceptional. Therefore, we'll not be stoning him. Once the sun fully rises, we'll take him to the governor's home and explain to him the crimes we've witnessed tonight. Surely, he'll see the threat this man brings to both Rome and the Jews. If any of you'd like to follow us and see to it the governor understands the seriousness of the situation, it would be much appreciated."

The councilmen whispered to each other and discussed whether they'd be joining.

"Sunrise is still not for another hour or two. It'd be in our best interest to not rouse the governor before he wakes. Once daybreak comes, we'll take The Man to him so he can try to convict him. Until then, get something to eat and drink. What we'll do tomorrow will please our Heavenly Father.

Make sure you eat something so you have the strength to do his will." He pointed to The Man chained to a post in the corner.

Blue and purple contusions covered his distended face. One eye had swelled shut. Blood stained his cheeks and neck red.

"And put him in the cellar. Make sure at least two of you guard the door until it's time for us to go." The high priest retired to his bedroom to sleep.

Four temple guards loosened the chains from the post, led The Man outside and threw him into an underground food cellar. The rest of the councilmen inside ordered the servants to fetch them water, wine, and warm bread. The rest of the evening, they reclined at tables and couches as they refreshed themselves. Some fell asleep, for they'd grown exhausted from the long night.

Nobody spotted the skinny, young man peering through the window.

* * *

A shiver crept down the traitor's back as he stared through the high priest's first-story window. He had followed the mob from the mountain and had entered the property. He didn't feel it to be appropriate to enter the high priest's home, because he didn't really know any of them. He didn't belong to the temple guard, the Roman military, or the Jewish Council. And he understood he had lost his place that night among The Man's disciples. The traitor belonged to no group or community, so he had carefully watched the proceedings unfold through the shadows of an open window.

He had assumed they might contemplate the idea of stoning The Man, but he didn't actually believe they'd try to go through with it. Maybe, he thought, they'd hold him in prison over the weekend. They might even physically punish The Man. But *kill* him? That's not what the traitor had in mind, and it wasn't what he had signed up for. The Jewish Council had paid him thirty pieces of silver to deliver The Man into their hands; he hadn't considered the money would soon be blood money.

"*You're an accomplice to murder*," someone whispered.

The traitor turned but saw no one. Other than the crowd at the firepit, no one stood within a hundred feet of him.

"*You're a murderer*."

The traitor's eyes sagged as he grew frightened. The voice he heard wasn't audible. It came from deep within himself. Something—or *someone*—was speaking not to his ears but to his heart.

It was The Accuser.

Everything had gone according to plan inside the palace. The Accuser had been wanting to destroy The Man ever since he was born. He believed it was necessary if he wanted to defeat everything The Father stood for. So, when the high priest announced his decision and the plot was fully in motion, The Accuser left after he noticed the traitor outside alone in the dark. He saw guilt overcoming the traitor's heart. The Accuser's opportunity to steal whatever hope he might have left presented itself. "*You're the worst kind of person.*"

The traitor felt tears running down his cheek. He detested himself as something worse than guilt gradually overwhelmed him—shame. Shame swarmed his heart.

The Accuser spoke deliberately to ensure the traitor believed who he'd become was even worse than what he'd done. "*You sold Heaven's Treasure for a small bag of silver. The Father hates you.*"

The traitor cried harder as he put his hands over his head, trying to catch his breath.

"*What future do you possibly have? You have no one to go to, nowhere to belong. The disciples hate you, and the councilmen used you. You have no worth to anyone anymore.*"

The traitor sobbed. He walked farther from anyone on property to not draw more unwanted attention to himself.

"*You are The Father's worst mistake.*"

"*No, you are not,*" another voice said. This voice too wasn't audible, but it clearly spoke to the traitor's heart—The Father's voice. The traitor didn't recognize The Father's voice, for he hadn't heard it with this kind of clarity before. The voice was peaceful, warm, and clear. *And soothing.* But because the traitor didn't recognize the voice, he found it, in a way, *unbelievable.*

As The Accuser continued to shame the traitor, The Father counteracted the charges.

"*You're The Father's worst mistake.*"

"*I make no mistakes.*"

"*You can't do anything worthy of The Father's love.*"

"*You can't do anything to make me stop loving you.*"

"*You're the trash of the Earth.*"

"*You're the treasure of my heart.*"

"*Everyone hates you because of who you've become.*"

"*I love you simply because of who you are.*"

The traitor couldn't take the back-and-forth banter anymore, so he ran. He scampered out the gate and through the upper part of the city toward the temple. As he sprinted, he could hear the clash of voices wage war against each other on the battleground of his heart. He stopped by the temple and tossed his money through the doors as a final act of desperation to relieve himself of his guilt and shame.

But his remorse endured. Although The Father did everything he could to reveal how he truly felt in a clear and obvious way, the traitor simply didn't recognize his voice. But the traitor *did* recognize The Accuser's voice and believed it was true.

Throughout history, men and women alike always believed the horrible things about themselves The Accuser whispered in their hearts but continuously struggled to believe the profound truths The Father proclaimed about who they were. The traitor was no exception, as he felt The Accuser's overwhelming lies descend deep into his heart.

"*Your life has no point anymore.*"

Devastation. The traitor yearned for the voice to grow silent, but it only grew louder.

"*There's no point anymore.*"

The traitor sobbed as he fixed the ears of his heart on The Accuser's words.

"*You might as well kill yourself.*"

The traitor scampered through the dark and quiet city and found some frayed rope in a trash heap. He tugged at the twine, testing for durability. He went outside the city walls and found a field with a large, sturdy tree in the middle. He climbed the tree and tied the rope to the branch. On the other end of the rope, he created a noose and placed the rope over his head. He sat on the branch for no more than five minutes as he cried in the dark by himself. He struggled to think of reasons to live, but The Accuser had extinguished all hope and reminded him this was the only logical thing to do.

The tree shook as the traitor fell through the air and hung himself.

* * *

The Man sat shivering alone in the dark. He imagined what lay before him in the next few hours, his stomach churning with nauseating discomfort. He couldn't tell if his body was shaking because of the cold or his own nerves. He tried to think of anything but his future, so he sang some hymns his mother had taught him as a child. The songs were meant to be sung joyfully, but only sorrowful notes echoed off the walls.

At daybreak, the guards would march him through the city to meet with the governor at his headquarters. The governor fully represented the Roman Empire and everything the kingdom stood for. His job was to ensure he fully executed the emperor's rule and will.

But what the governor didn't understand yet was The Man also represented a kingdom and everything it stood for. The Man's mission on Earth was to ensure he fully implemented The Father's rule and will.

Two kingdoms were about to clash. Only one could prevail.

The door burst open, startling The Man. Four temple guards stood at the top of the stairs. One held more chains. Another held a whip.

"Let's get going," one said.

The Man climbed the stairs and peered out the door to see the sun was about halfway risen and flooding the land with beautiful shades of pink and orange.

They shackled him with more chains and pushed him forward to the property gates.

All the councilmen stood waiting for him.

"It's time to meet your ruler," the high priest said.

The procession set off toward the Roman headquarters.

Chapter 4

A Governor, a Magician, and a Tetrarch

THE COUNCIL FORCED HIM along a winding road through the upper city. They passed many homes but none as extravagant as the one they had just came from. As the sun rose, some people in the capital were stirring. Other than the bleating of sheep and bellowing of livestock from multiple directions along the street, the city rested in silence.

The Man's posture toward his oppressors was fully submissive. He willed himself to obey their orders along the road. But his compliance didn't halt their cruelty.

As the procession marched, they hurled insults on him and whipped him.

He remained silent through it all.

With only a quarter mile left on their journey, The Man spotted one of the most beautiful trees he'd ever seen. Striking, plump blooms covered the branches. The tree towered twenty-five feet over the few empty market stands nestled next to its trunk. Two of the branches swept low to the road, inviting travelers to take a closer look. The Man paused and surveyed the tree on his right. He beheld the stout pink and red blooms that covered the tree all the way to its top, each one complementing the next. How he wished to break his chains, dismiss his captors and sleep peacefully under the scenic canopy of colors and listen to the birds sing their annual spring songs.

Spring had always been his favorite time of year. Everything appeared to have new life, as if the Earth was in a deep sleep but now rose from its slumber to welcome a new season. The creeks seemed to sing as they fed the mighty trees whose roots held them in place. Beautiful budding flowers of pink and violet and scarlet and yellow adorned each tree. Birds sang their heavenly songs as they cared for their chicks. Bees of every kind awoke from their wintry nap to push forth new life as they pollinated countless plants and blossoms. The Man thought the sun even appeared to shine brighter.

Yes, springtime was always his favorite season of year simply because he loved The Father's handiwork. He adored every part of creation and viewed The Father's work as a priceless treasure, understanding The Father had created nature for his glory as it redirected humanity's heart toward him. How sad, The Man thought, that so many people refused to give creation even a passing glance as they go about their day.

For as much as The Man loved The Father's creation, he also was empathetic. Just like creation, he believed The Father had sent him to Earth to redirect the people's hearts toward their Creator. Just like the springtime, The Man had come to Earth to awaken the people from a deep sleep so they could rise to a new season of life.

"No time for gawking!" A temple guard shoved The Man in the upper back, causing him to stumble forward.

The sun now shone fully above the horizon as the morning warmed. The road snaked throughout the capital. As they approached their destination, he could see more and more evidence of Roman oppression. Latin scratch covered signs and tablets everywhere. Roman soldiers in their full garb came and went. No matter their race or religion, everyone in the city fell under the emperor's rule.

And then they saw it.

Just like the high priest's, the governor's palace was a marvel to behold. Beautiful gardens covered the gated property. A main archway led visitors to the center of a large courtyard where countless Roman statues appeared to guard it. Marble columns supported the walls that hemmed in the courtyard. Although smaller than the high priest's home, the governor's palace still demanded guests to regard its grandeur. Two bulky wooden doors sat on top of a spacious marble porch that extended about twenty feet into the courtyard with stairs that travelled down both sides. Beneath every window of the home sat rose gardens in full bloom.

The procession walked through the gate. They marched through the archways and past the statues and fountains and stood in front of the porch. They refused to enter the governor's house, because they believed doing so would make them unclean and unfit to eat the Passover meal during the holy weekend.

The high priest demanded the two Roman soldiers guarding the door to tell the governor they had a need of utmost importance.

* * *

"What do you want?" the governor asked, leaning against the porch railing. Blinking slowly, he crossed his arms as his lips pressed together. Glossy eyes with bags underneath stared without emotion at the group of Jews. He wore a white tunic with a burgundy cape that clung to his back. His brown hair was short and his face cleanly shaven. He wore Roman sandals with leather straps wrapping around his calves. Multiple rings on his hand boasted his wealth. He was thick and muscular. His yawns didn't negate the fact he exuded confidence.

The governor had dealt with the high priest and his associates many times and had formed a respectful working relationship with him. But, according to some of the high priest's closer associates, this Roman Governor couldn't stand the Jews. They were, in his eyes, religious fools who struggled to behave properly. The emperor had sent the governor to rule over this region known for being wild and disorderly. He didn't like his job but viewed his post as an ugly steppingstone toward his ultimate goal: ruling side by side with the emperor in Rome.

"We have brought you a criminal who is a thorn in the heel of both Israel and Rome," the high priest said as he looked up at the porch.

The priests elbowed The Man toward the front of the porch.

After looking at The Man, the governor tilted his head and pursed his lips. "What charges are you bringing against this Jew?" the governor asked with a yawn.

"If he were not a criminal, we would not have handed him over to you."

"Did you really pull me from bed to play word games with me? You, of all people, should know how busy this weekend is for us all. I have things to do. Get on with it. What crimes has this man committed?"

The council shouted all kinds of accusations at The Man.

"He disrupts the Temple proceedings and stirs up the worshippers!"

"He violates our traditions and our timeless values."

"Everywhere he goes, he causes trouble."

"Throngs of crowds follow him everywhere. They adore him!"

"He practices dark magic!"

"He disrespects our leaders and believes he's superior to you!"

"He doesn't pay his taxes and encourages others to do the same."

The last accusation caught the governor's attention. Sure, plenty of people evaded paying their taxes to Rome. It wasn't uncommon. But the governor ensured they were jailed if found guilty. He couldn't care less about the other accusations. Collecting taxes was one of his important, though monotonous, jobs. And he, along with everyone else, knew the emperor wouldn't stand to be cheated out of his money.

"What did you say?" The governor's brow furrowed as he pointed at the councilman who had just spoken.

"He does not pay his taxes."

The governor stopped and considered this. If true, The Man would be dealt punishment. But why did this large group of the Jewish religious elite care about this? Was imprisoning this man more important to them than tending to the hundreds of thousands of worshippers who had flocked to the city?

Stepping forward, the high priest puffed out his chest and lifted his finger, as if to lecture anyone who would listen. "We have found this man undermining our nation. He opposes payment of taxes to the emperor and claims to be a messiah." When he saw he had the governor's full attention, he delivered the final blow. "He claims to be a king!"

The governor's eyes widened. Avoiding taxes was one thing but claiming to be a king was an entirely new level of offense. This was a bold threat to the emperor himself and would be dealt with the most serious of consequences. But the governor had to act with cunning wisdom. On one hand, if multitudes really pledged their allegiance to The Man and revered him as someone special, punishing him in a public way could backfire on the governor. What if his followers rioted? What if things got out of control? And on the holy weekend! An uprising surely wouldn't bode well with the emperor. Unrest might be a major setback in the governor's political career.

But, on the other hand, if word reached Rome about a king strutting around the governor's jurisdiction with hordes of admirers following his every move, that *also* could cripple his career. He had worked tirelessly to come this far, yet he acted like there was more to be had for him. One wrong decision could ruin everything for the governor. "So, this Jew claims to be your messiah, correct?"

"An incorrect claim, yes," the high priest said.

After taking a moment to scrutinize The Man, the governor's face pinched together as his eyes squinted. The governor shook his head and huffed. He'd heard of people with similar claims; he'd even met a few. Dirt and abrasions—even some dried blood—covered this Jew standing below his porch. His clothes were disgusting and tattered. And he just stood like a fool, staring at the ground. He was the most pitiful messiah the governor had ever dealt with. "It sounds like the Jewish people should punish this Jewish man who incorrectly claims to be the messiah for the Jews." The governor raised his eyebrows toward the high priest.

Silence filled the courtyard.

"Take him yourself and judge him by your own law."

"But this man poses a serious—"

"Take him yourself and judge him by your own law!"

The high priest bit his lip. "But we have no right to execute anyone."

The Man glanced up at the high priest. *There it is*, The Man thought, *their true intentions.* After waking up the governor early and beating around the bush, the high priest had finally stated their true intentions. The Man knew the council wanted to kill him, but they wanted the governor to do it.

The governor's calculating prudence and political wisdom was about to go toe to toe with a formidable opponent—the high priest himself. The governor needed to be careful. If he underestimated just how dangerous and volatile the situation really was, things could get out of control. He leaned over and whispered to a soldier standing nearby.

The soldier didn't say anything but simply nodded.

The governor left the group and returned to his chambers. The doors closed softly.

"You!" The soldier pointed at The Man. "Come with me now."

"But that's our prisoner! You aren't going to release him, are—"

"Stop talking!" the soldier said. "You've made enough noise this morning."

The temple guards unbound the chains from The Man's neck and hands.

The Man meandered up the left porch stairs past a few rose bushes as the soldier grabbed his arm. The door opened, and he walked through.

This time, the door slammed shut.

* * *

The governor turned his back toward The Man.

A servant gave the governor a chalice to drink from.

Once refreshed, he took a towel, wiped his hands and gave it back to the servant. He let his head fall backward as he sighed. He turned around and approached The Man until he stood face to face with him. He opened his mouth to begin his questioning but caught himself staring.

Being fully Divine, The Man saw through the governor's disguise of confidence and poise.

The governor was put off by The Man but couldn't explain why. He knew this feeling had something to do with the way The Man carried himself. The Man's demeanor was different than everyone else who'd ever been in his situation. Many prisoners and criminals responded dramatically toward the governor. Some sobbed and explained their innocence. Others refuted their charges using logic and reason. A few even admitted their wrongdoings and begged for mercy, telling the governor how their life would be different if he just gave them a second chance.

But not this Jew. Something was unique about him, something different. He stood unshaken before the most powerful ruler in the region. Even though he knew the seriousness of the consequences that lay before him, he appeared unmoved and unfazed. He possessed silent sureness, unafraid of anything, as if he wholly believed the ending of his story would be a positive one even if his current situation was not—total confidence but completely silent.

The Man didn't let his gaze fall from the governor's eyes, causing the governor to shift his weight on his feet. The green shades in The Man's irises were striking. They wouldn't look down in submission or away in deceit. They locked onto the governor with silent confidence.

"Are . . . you the king of the Jews?" A slight grin crept across the governor's face, as if his question was almost funny.

"Is that your own idea, or did others talk to you about me?"

"Am I a Jew?" the governor asked arrogantly. He showed The Man a ring on his finger adorned with Roman symbols. "It was your people and your chief priests who handed you over to me. What is it you've done?"

The Man smiled and broke his gaze with the governor. He glanced at a small statue in the corner commemorating a Roman god.

"Answer me," the governor said.

"My kingdom is not of this world," The Man said as he stared at the statue. "If it were, my followers would fight to prevent my arrest. You see, my kingdom is from another place."

The governor chuckled. A kingdom not from this world? Perhaps this man actually believed he ruled a kingdom that formed the stars and instructed them how to shine. Or maybe he thought his kingdom had dominion over the depths of the ocean and that the sea creatures obeyed his every whim. Instead of making fun of The Man, he prodded the declaration. "So, you're a king?"

"That's correct." The Man looked the governor in the eyes again. "I'm a king. In fact, ever since I was born, I've been destined to be a king and to testify to the truth." The Man took two fingers and tapped them on his chest then pointed to himself. "Everyone on the side of truth *listens to me*."

The Man knew he was agitating the governor. As the governor stepped backward, The Man saw the governor's anxious thoughts.

The governor wanted to believe The Man was just a poor fellow who couldn't think straight. Some things he said could be used as evidence to support the claim, but some things The Man said frightened the governor. The more The Man talked, the more the governor's heart twisted and turned. It felt as if it were burning, but in a good way—like he possibly wanted to hear more even though he found The Man delirious. The governor wanted to quickly end *and* continue his conversation with The Man simultaneously. The northerner standing in his chamber was more than intriguing; he was, in a bizarre way, gently authoritative. He spoke to the governor with the confidence of a king but in an intimate way, as if he'd always known him.

Then, without understanding the weight of his words, the governor asked the most important question he ever could. "What is truth?"

* * *

Truth. Since the beginning of time, humanity had struggled with truth more than anything else. Mankind found nothing more elusive and daunting than to know the truth. At its core, truth had always been the pursuit of philosophers and academics and thinkers and theorists everywhere. Mankind had always sought to know and understand their reality with complete accuracy. What was the Earth? Why was it here? What was humanity's purpose? Were men and women good or bad? Or both? Did some supreme morality everyone must attend to exist? Would people ever truly be held accountable for their actions? And the most daunting one of all: where was this all going?

Truth had always baffled the minds and hearts of men everywhere who searched for certainty, and the governor was not exempt from the never-ending chase. The questions that had plagued the hearts of all mankind had also been quietly haunting him from childhood. *What is truth?*

The question had escaped his mouth like uncontrolled vomit. He hadn't been able to resist the opportunity to turn the words back on the apparently renowned teacher of the Jews. But he also couldn't see the irony in his question. He had inquired about truth even though it stood right there before him.

Yes, The Man *was* the Truth. He was the Truth at the beginning of time. He was the Truth that all wisdom flowed from. He was the Truth that gave people—every race, every age, every gender, every nation—the answers to the ageless questions they'd always wrestled with. He was the Truth that perfectly revealed the disposition of The Father's face.

And he was the Truth that would set mankind free.

The governor asked the personified Truth, "What is truth?" without even realizing it.

* * *

The Man chuckled. He regarded the governor and gave him a warm smile. Even though the governor was arrogant and full of false wisdom, The Man couldn't help but love him.

"Yes, what is truth?" the governor whispered to himself as he walked away from The Man. He stood at a window and glanced at the councilmen. The gathering of Jews grew. They wanted the governor to execute this peculiar man who stood in his room. And he knew he could; The Man clearly understood he was a king of some mysterious, invisible domain. That was grounds for execution. But the governor had to be wise, for if The Man possessed a following like the council said, then allowing the weekend to pass and punishing him in a few days would be ideal.

Above all else, he couldn't afford to have a riot on his hands.

"Come with me," the governor said. He called for soldiers to escort The Man behind him as he walked through the double wooden doors.

They moved to the front of the porch to address the crowd.

* * *

"He's not guilty of any crime," the governor said. "I find no basis for a charge against him."

"Did you not hear what we said?" the high priest asked as spit flew from his mouth. "He stands in defiance of the emperor. We demand he be treated like the traitor he is!"

The crowd cheered and screamed. Some cursed The Man. Others jeered at him. Many continued to heap charges against him.

"He cares nothing about honoring his heritage, even less about honoring Rome!"

"The Man is good for nothing and needs to go!"

"He poisons the minds of our children!"

"He's a liar and a deceiver!"

"He doesn't pay his taxes!"

As the accusations continued, the governor faced The Man and saw something about his demeanor changed.

As The Man watched his own people heave insults at him, the warm smile he gave the governor inside left. Sorrow and dejection plastered his face.

"Don't you hear the testimony they're bringing against you?" the governor asked The Man as he stepped toward him.

But The Man didn't reply. He didn't even look at him. As the allegations thundered, The Man stared at the ground in complete and utter silence. The Man's strange enigma grew, leaving the governor baffled.

"He turns your tax collectors against you!"

"His disciples go from town to town causing trouble!"

"We heard he encourages cannibalism!"

"How can you let a man like this walk the streets you rule?"

"If he disrespects our laws, he is sure to disrespect yours!"

"Nothing good ever comes out of Nazareth!"

The governor's hand shot up to quiet the crowd. He pointed to a councilman in the back and asked him to repeat what he had said.

"Nothing good ever comes out of Nazareth."

The governor turned toward the man again. "Is that where you're from?"

But The Man didn't move nor did he speak.

"Yes," the high priest said. "He is from Nazareth—that small, good-for-nothing town on the edge of the water."

The governor understood little about Nazareth. According to his informants, it was a tiny, poverty-stricken village of a few hundred people. The governor knew nothing of the town besides that most people used the lake the town sat on to fish for a living. To him, Nazareth was just another nasty settlement about seventy miles north of the capital that he hoped he'd never step foot in.

"He stirs up people all over Judea by his teaching," the high priest said. "He started in the province of Galilee and has come all the way here."

And there was his solution. The governor finally found the missing puzzle piece to help him escape this political dilemma. The Man was from Galilee, a northern province separate from the governor's jurisdiction of Judea. Legally, The Man ought to report to the ruler of his region. And luckily for the governor, the Tetrarch of Galilee happened to be staying just down the road for the holy weekend.

"This man is a Galilean," the governor said. "Therefore, he ought to be judged like one." He turned to his soldiers. "Take him just down the road to where the Tetrarch of Galilee is staying. Let him judge The Man, for it's his right and duty. He'll know what needs to be done."

The crowd complained, but the governor ignored them.

He turned, sauntered inside and ate breakfast with his wife.

The soldiers tied chains around The Man's neck. They yelled at the Jews to back away as they pressed through the courtyard. A select few councilmen followed closely behind. Exiting right out of the property gates, the soldiers traveled a few blocks down the road to another palace, one hosting the Tetrarch of Galilee.

They knocked on the door and waited.

Finally, it opened and the soldiers, The Man, and the handful of councilmen entered.

* * *

The Man stood in the middle of a large chamber filled with natural light. Beneath his feet lay the biggest carpet he'd ever seen. Lavish purple and red fibers weaved an intricate crisscrossing pattern all along the edges that eventually led to the middle of the carpet surrounding a stitching of two lions. Tapestries covered almost every square inch of the walls. A fire burned to The Man's right as servants boiled water in it. The Roman soldiers, along with a few councilmen who'd followed, stepped behind The Man, leaving him on the middle of the carpet by himself. Multiple underdressed teenage girls reclined on an elegant couch to The Man's left. They composed a part of the tetrarch's harem brought from his fortress in Galilee for his sexual entertainment.

And in front of The Man sitting on a tall, cushioned chair sat the Tetrarch of Galilee.

His jurisdiction included numerous towns, villages, and provinces in the northern region of the country. The tetrarch had developed a suitable reputation for making his life easier by making others' lives harder. He taxed the Galileans like no ruler before to ensure all his palaces and vacation homes were appropriate to his standards. Even though he was a Jew himself, the Jews hated him.

A long black beard covered the tetrarch's chin and neck. He wore a golden tunic with a green sash. A silver crown sat on his head. A servant girl occasionally wiped fruit juice from his mouth and neck as he devoured plums and nectarines. He was exceptionally obese. The tetrarch was never denied and enjoyed every pleasure his heart desired.

But as the tetrarch observed The Man, a puzzled look crawled across his face. Although they both came from the same region, they had never crossed paths. The tetrarch had heard many stories about how The Man was a powerful magician who could bend the rules of nature. The tetrarch had always hoped to have The Man to his palace sometime to perform and entertain him. But The Man standing before the tetrarch now looked nothing like a magician but rather a homeless beggar who'd just been robbed. The tetrarch was hopeful this wouldn't deter The Man from showing him a trick.

"So," the tetrarch said as he let out a smile, "you're the carpenter from Nazareth, right? The . . . famous one? I've heard many great things about your abilities."

The Man said nothing. He hadn't even raised his face to the tetrarch since entering the room.

"I want to see your talent. Would you show us all a magic trick? I heard you can turn water into wine. Shall our servants fetch you some?"

The Man remained mute.

The tetrarch chuckled as he peered down from his elaborate chair. "Excuse me," the tetrarch said sarcastically as he tilted his head. "Did you hear what I said? Are you going to show me a magic trick?"

No response.

"Raise your head and look at me, you fool!"

The Man lifted his head and, for the first time, looked at the tetrarch. He did his best to control himself, for he remembered vividly what the tetrarch had done not long ago to cause him and his family gut-wrenching pain.

A few years earlier, the tetrarch had murdered The Man's own cousin.

* * *

It had all started with a birthday party. Two years earlier, the tetrarch threw The Man's cousin, who was a prophet, in prison. He ministered to the Jewish people by preparing their hearts to receive The Man. He did this by baptizing them. Thus, The Man's cousin was nicknamed the Baptist.

The Baptist and the Tetrarch of Galilee had developed a tense relationship. Because the tetrarch was a Jew by birth, the Baptist felt it was The Father's will for him to call the tetrarch out of his sin and prepare his heart to receive The Man. In those days, the tetrarch had become overwhelmed with lust toward his sister-in-law and had forced her to marry him, stealing her from his own brother. This prompted the Baptist to publicly ridicule him. The tetrarch would have none of that, for he loved the pleasurable wickedness of his ways. To stifle the Baptist, the tetrarch had cast him into prison.

That year, the tetrarch had thrown himself a birthday party that rivaled no other. Hundreds of guests had attended and joined the fun. Barrels of wine emptied as the tetrarch had encouraged the guests to reach new levels of intoxication. People had gorged themselves full on delectable vegetables, fruit, bread, fish, and lamb. But the revelry didn't stop there. For the evening entertainment, the tetrarch had decided to give himself something he had secretly always wanted.

He had instructed his own niece, the daughter of his new, controversial bride, to entertain him. He had told her to braid her hair, don fine jewelry, makeup, and perfume, strip and dance for him and his guests. As the music played, the tetrarch had become so satisfied by his arousal that he, in his drunken state, immediately told her any wish she desired would be granted.

The girl had asked her mother what she should request. Her mother had instructed her to demand the head of the Baptist on a platter. Her mother had also been embarrassed from the Baptist's public denouncement of her new relationship and had wanted him killed for it.

Regretfully, the tetrarch had given into her demand. He had executed the Baptist and brought his head to her on a platter in front of all his guests. The tetrarch had murdered an innocent prophet from Galilee and caused an unspeakable amount of pain to The Man and his family.

Two years later, the hurt still felt fresh in The Man's heart.

* * *

"Is he dumb?" the tetrarch asked the councilmen standing in the back of the room. "Can he not talk?"

"He talks all the time! He never stops talking; he's a false teacher to our people!"

"Well, it sure doesn't look like it."

The tetrarch stood and approached The Man. He took The Man's chin in his hand and lifted it to have a better look. After examining the bruises, he gave The Man's chin a slight shake. "Why won't you talk to me?"

The Man didn't move nor speak. He regarded the tetrarch in silence.

Finally, the tetrarch laughed.

His harem and servants followed suit and laughed as well.

He returned to his chair as his stomach rippled underneath his clothing. Taking a glass of wine, his eyes narrowed at the councilmen as his laughter dissipated. "Alright, what is it you really want?"

"This man deserves to die!"

"But why? What has he done?"

"What hasn't he done? He stirs up trouble in Galilee and in Jerusalem. He's a headache to the Jewish people and to Rome."

"He doesn't look like a revolutionary. What kind of trouble does he stir up?"

Then the accusations started again.

"He is! He denounces you just like his cousin did."

"He tells people to not follow the law."

"He's trying to ruin our religion!"

"He claims to be a king and is apparently after your throne!"

"Is this true?" the tetrarch asked The Man. "Are you really a king? Do you think you will one day sit on a throne like mine and judge other fools like yourself?"

The Man remained silent.

"Do you not like me? What poor things have you said about me?"

Silence.

"What are you teaching our people?"

More silence.

The tetrarch belly laughed as he said, "This man is no king! This man isn't even a revolutionary! He can't even talk. He's just a poor, mute dog!"

The Roman soldiers along with the harem and servants laughed.

"There's nothing I can do with this man, nor is there anything I need to do! Is this man really upsetting you that much? Why? He doesn't do anything! How am I supposed to judge someone whose actions are untraceable because he just . . . stands there?" The tetrarch laughed so hard he spilled his wine all over the floor.

The Roman soldiers also laughed, but the councilmen did not.

"Go on," the tetrarch said to the councilmen. "Return to the governor. Tell him I'm sending The Man back to him because he hasn't done anything wrong. But give me a minute with him. I still need him to entertain me."

The councilmen left flustered and upset. Reporting this to the high priest would certainly earn them no reward. They closed the door behind them, leaving The Man inside with the soldiers and the tetrarch.

The tetrarch grinned. "Bring The Man to me."

* * *

For the next fifteen minutes, the tetrarch had his fun. He mocked The Man and his claims to be king. He ordered the servants to bring him an elegant purple robe from his own closet and dress The Man in it. The tetrarch also put his own crown on The Man's head. "Your Majesty!" the tetrarch said as he laughed. "Your rule knows no end! Everyone is subject to you and your throne!" The tetrarch struggled down to his knees, bowing before The Man with his arms outstretched.

Everyone in the room howled with laughter.

The tetrarch tried his best to continue his mockery without snickering. "You have no rival to your power!" the tetrarch said as he giggled. "There is none like you, Mighty King!"

And even though the tetrarch spewed what he thought to be humorous lies, The Man understood the truth of the matter. For there was a day coming soon when everyone—man and woman, king and slave, Jew and Gentile, young and old—would see The Man for who he really was. He truly was a king, a glorious king who would set in motion a new way of living through The Father's Kingdom. He was the seamless mediator who came to bridge the divide between The Father and his children. He was the spotless lamb who was preparing to lay his life down so others may live. He was the perfect redeemer who spoke with a thunderous voice declaring freedom for all who would hear him.

The tetrarch was right; there really was none like the Jew he was bowing before.

* * *

The tetrarch labored to his feet and slapped The Man in the face and laughed. He retrieved his crown, sat in his seat and ordered more food. "Take him away. He's boring."

The soldiers led The Man from the palace and through the city to return to the governor's mansion. As they passed through the property gates and headed toward the courtyard archways, they heard the buzz of a large crowd.

"Wow," one soldier said as he first peered into the courtyard.

The crowd had tripled in size with well over a couple hundred people. While The Man had been at the tetrarch's residence, the council had recruited many other Jews to help convince the governor of The Man's fate.

The Man recognized some of the people from his time teaching in the temple courts a few days earlier. However, he failed to recognize the new people joining the crowd in the back who were all accepting small bags of silver from the councilmembers.

As the soldiers led him up the porch steps, the crowd bellowed their displeasure and threw things at him. As he stepped through the governor's doors, The Man understood he was on the threshold of his personal doom.

Chapter 5

Bending

"WHAT DO YOU MEAN he didn't do anything?"

Irate upon hearing the Tetrarch of Galilee had returned The Man to him without a resolution to please the Jewish Council, the governor paced back and forth as he cursed under his breath. Thinking his cunning politics had gotten him out of this administrative conundrum, the governor clenched his teeth as he snarled. His situation wasn't better. It was deteriorating right before his eyes as the crowd outside his door grew.

"The tetrarch lounged on his seat and requested The Man to show him a magic trick," one of the soldiers explained. "The Man stood unresponsive the entire time. The tetrarch even struck The Man in the face, and he didn't react."

"So, the tetrarch did *absolutely nothing* to appease these Jews?"

"Nothing. How could he? The Man didn't and hasn't, in the tetrarch's eyes, done anything that deserves some extreme punishment."

The governor approached a basin of water and washed his face. He looked into the bowl as if he might find a solution in the water. "There must be a way out of this," he said out loud to himself. Giving up or giving in wasn't an option. His political career depended on it. "I can't mess this up."

He instructed the soldiers to bring The Man onto the porch with him to address the gathering. As he stepped through the door and breathed in the sharp, cool air, a bead of nervous sweat rolled down his upper jawline. The morning sun rose higher while the tension among the Jewish people spread.

"Jews!" the governor said with raised hands.

The crowd hushed.

"I must let you know, just like me, the Tetrarch of Galilee has found nothing of importance to charge The Man with. He has found him innocent."

The crowd groaned in collective disappointment. Cursing dispersed throughout the courtyard as the people raised their fists and shouted at the governor.

A dozen Roman soldiers scurried through the courtyard arches and surrounded the porch, forcing the crowd to keep their distance from The Man and the governor.

As The Man scanned the crowd, he saw countless faces regarding him as if he were the scum of the earth.

"Councilmen, you better get your people under control before we have to!" a soldier said, exciting the crowd even more.

The governor attempted to address the assembly multiple times only to have their volume and disdain overpower him. He whipped around to instruct his commanding officer to teach the Jews a lesson, but he was interrupted.

"Sir," a servant girl behind him said, "your wife has a message for you."

"Doesn't she know I'm busy?" The governor's back stiffened as his fists clenched.

"She said it is of utmost importance."

His brow loosened as his muscles relaxed. The governor followed the girl inside and shut the doors behind him, still hearing the hum of the crowd. After taking a deep breath, relief swept over him in the privacy of his home. "What does she want?" the governor asked with a calmer tone.

"She sends you this message: *Don't get involved with that innocent man. I've lost sleep because of a disturbing dream about him.*"

"A dream?" The governor's eyes narrowed. "Am I supposed to change the way I govern Judea because my wife had a bad dream?"

"She is just concerned that—"

"I know she's concerned! Does she not think I'm concerned as well? Does she not think I'm stressed beyond my limit from this unpleasant surprise I walked into this morning? What's she expecting me to do?"

"She said her dream was more than just a dream; it was an alarming vision of what will happen to you and your legacy if you do not remove yourself from this situation."

The governor paused. *Legacy*, he thought. Legacy was something he held dear. He desired to see his name last forever. He hoped and prayed that, for millennia to come, his name would be a household name among the peoples of the world. He longed for his name to be used in the future to inspire others to greatness simply because they mentioned him. He yearned, just like the other emperors in his nation's history, to live forever through the bedtime stories fathers passed along to their sons.

A dreadfulness overwhelmed the governor as he understood his wife *actually* believed this current situation might be the thing to ruin his chance to leave an everlasting legacy.

"Did she . . . tell you what the dream was about?" the governor asked quietly as he sat at a table with his head in his hands.

"She said in the dream you were holding a desirable piece of undiscovered fruit. No one had ever tasted this fruit before, but a group of Jews came and slapped it out of your hand, because they claimed it was rotten inside. You wanted to keep the fruit, because you saw nothing wrong with it, but they insisted you get rid of it. You showed the fruit to a few friends who also saw nothing wrong with it, but the Jews were persistent in making sure it was thrown in the trash. After much pressure, you gave in and threw the fruit outside and—"

"How does this have anything to do with—"

"And forgot about it. You threw the fruit outside and forgot about it. But three days later, according to your wife, the fruit's seeds sprouted. A substantial tree grew where you had discarded the fruit. The tree produced countless fruit that also fell to the ground and degraded into the soil. But the seeds of those pieces of fruit also sprouted, and quickly, a forest of these massive trees grew. This forest started in Jerusalem then spread all over Israel. The forest crept into the surrounding lands bordering the sea and even made its way to Rome. Eventually, this great forest covered the entire earth." The girl paused to let the governor take in what he had heard.

Two soldiers in the room listened intently.

The governor lifted his head to reveal a puzzled look as he pondered what the dream might mean.

"Your wife said the dream ended with her in Rome. She was a lonely, elderly widow because you had already gone to the dust. In the dream, she decided to visit a great library where the annals of Roman antiquity were held. To her delight, she found many scrolls that spoke of you, but once she read them, she grew greatly distressed."

The governor licked his lips. "What did they say?"

"She found nothing about your wisdom or your honor or your might. Each scroll simply repeated over and over you were the Governor of Judea who threw away the perfect piece of fruit."

As the governor put his elbows on the table and buried his head in his arms, his lungs tightened and refused to take in full breaths.

"Sir," the servant girl said with caution, "she is terrified that this man is innocent. She fears if you treat him unjustly . . . your reputation will never escape it."

The governor silently took in what he was hearing. He had no response. Fear bubbled inside him as it crawled up his throat.

* * *

The governor stood emotionless on his porch in front of the Jews. "I've spent much time this morning judging and considering The Man you're heaping these charges against, and I've found him not guilty."

Again, the Jews erupted in their displeasure.

"We won't leave this courtyard until justice is carried out and this criminal gets what he deserves!" the high priest said with a raised fist.

"You brought me this Jew because you claim he provokes the people to rebellion," the governor said with a sharp tone and quick pace. "I've examined him in plain sight and found no basis for your charges against him. Neither has the Tetrarch of Galilee, because he sent him back to us. As you can see, he has done nothing to deserve death."

At this, the Jews screamed even more.

"That's not true!"

"There's no other option!"

"What more do you need to condemn him?"

"Don't make this mistake!"

"Bring in a third opinion!"

"No!" the governor said. He thought his teeth might break from his clenched jaw. A blue vein running up the side of his temple now bulged visibly for all to see. "My rule's impartial and final! I won't stand to be coerced into acting unjustly by a bunch of self-righteous, disrespectful Jews!"

The Roman soldiers drew their swords and positioned themselves to attack the unruly mass.

When the Jews saw this, they remembered their place and settled down. They desired bloodshed but not their own.

Once the crowd quieted, the governor decided to remind them who he was. "I am *the* ruling power over all of Judea!" His voice bellowed through the courtyard. "There's no other. There's no one else who rules over you!

There's no other judge, no other governor, no other authority! It'd be in your best interest to act in a civil manner. That is unless you wish to be standing on my judgement porch as well."

The governor's threat silenced the Jews.

Eventually, the high priest chuckled. "Authority?" the high priest said, laughing and pointing a crooked finger up toward the porch. "You're just the emperor's puppet sent here to do the job nobody else wants to do."

The blatant disrespect was shocking. The high priest had never spoke to the governor like that, even when they vehemently disagreed, which they did often. Some sort of new, malevolent spirit seemed to be driving the heart of the high priest to do away with a man who seemed so, in the eyes of the governor, *unimportant*.

"Don't speak to—"

"If I need to send a group of my men to Rome to sort all this out, I can," the high priest snarled. "I'm sure the powers that be will be swift to act when they hear a self-proclaimed king walks freely under the mighty rule of the Governor of Judea."

The governor wanted to kill the high priest right then and there but knew that would be the worst thing he could do. He couldn't afford to make an enemy out of the high priest. The high priest understood this and used it as back-breaking leverage. The invisible weight resting on the governor's shoulders felt unbearable. He would have paid a reckless amount of money for somebody to give him the answer to solve this problem so everyone could leave content. Unfortunately for him, there simply wasn't an easy solution.

The governor realized the best outcome for him was to ensure the high priest could walk away happy with the least amount of people knowing. The governor hated what he was about to do but felt he had no choice. "Fine," the governor retorted. "I'll punish this man. He will learn the error of his ways and be sure to not repeat them. He will learn submission to your law and to ours."

The governor acknowledged The Man standing beside him and pitied him. He wanted to have compassion on what he believed to be an innocent Jew. But he couldn't—not at the cost of his own future.

"But he claimed to be a king!"

"He will *never* claim that again!" The governor scanned the crowd with a stern glance they hadn't seen yet. "I'll punish him and release him."

Once again, the Jews verbalized their disapproval and argued the sentence was too weak.

The governor turned and headed for the door.

* * *

Inspiration struck a few minutes after lounging by a hissing fire. He couldn't believe he'd forgotten about this.

A few years prior, the governor had started a tradition where he'd occasionally pardon a Jewish prisoner of the people's choice as an act of goodwill toward the Jewish nation. The Jews had come to look forward to this and expect it. This tradition had strengthened the governor's credibility and favor in a region where he desperately needed approval.

And now, the governor understood, this tradition could be used as his way out. The more he contemplated it, the more it seemed almost too easy. Another Jewish man currently sat in a nearby prison. He was known throughout the region to be a notorious thug. He was a thief, a rebel, and a liar. He'd even led uprisings against a few local governments. But worst of all, he was a cold-blooded murderer.

The thug was the last creature any civilized person, especially any priest, would want to stalk their streets. All the governor had to do was place The Man next to the thug and ask the people who they wanted to be released this year.

The governor sent soldiers to immediately bring the thug to his judgement porch.

* * *

He couldn't tell what kind of bird it was. The Man had been standing silently on the porch with soldiers at his left and right for at least twenty minutes. He struggled to keep his mind from picturing what he would look like in just a few hours. Although he appeared to be a dumb, mute fool who didn't understand what was happening, internally he fought a battle no one could ever understand.

He lifted his gaze to focus on something else and saw an eagle perched on top of one of the courtyard archways. He strained to discern any markings on the bird to determine the species, but his swollen eye hindered him. All he saw was a large bird of prey.

Like The Man, the bird perched silently, peering across the horizon. Its intimidating claws gripped the marble beneath its body. The eyes dilated as it scanned the ground, searching for food to rip apart with its sharp beak. In an instant, the bird leapt into the air and flew away.

Two words came to mind as The Man watched the eagle disappear beyond his vision—*powerful* and *free*. The creature, in all its majesty, exhibited an unmatched strength as it soared freely to wherever it pleased. The contrast was stark when compared to The Man who, currently, was so weak in his captivity. The Man, fully Divine, had chosen to relinquish his unmatched strength and freely walk into the hands of cruel oppressors who would hold him captive.

The Man was choosing to set aside his power and freedom to take up weakness and captivity so his oppressors might set aside their weakness and captivity to take up a powerful freedom. "Strengthen me, Father, so I can walk the path you've set before me."

* * *

"Friends," the governor said, "give me your attention." Something about the governor's mood had changed. He stood on the porch, smiling next to The Man. The governor appeared upbeat and cheerful, as if he were about to give the crowd a gift.

The Jews hushed and waited in anticipation.

"As you know, it's my honored tradition to release to you a prisoner of your choice. It's my pleasure to extend great mercy to the Jewish people today by looking at one of your own with compassion."

The double wooden doors flung open behind him. Two Roman soldiers stepped forward, holding chains tied around the notorious thug's neck.

Because of his lengthy stay in prison, the thug's long beard seemed wild and unkept. Long, matted hair dangled in front of his dirt-covered face. Only half his teeth remained in his mouth. His left ear hung mangled and deformed. He stunk terribly.

The crowd collectively stepped backward as they recognized this Jewish man as somebody who they were both afraid of and repulsed by.

The thug intimidated them in a cold way. Not one facial muscle moved as his eyeballs scanned the crowd.

The Man stood on the governor's left, the thug on the governor's right.

"Both these men standing beside me are Jewish criminals. The one on my left claims to be a king to your people even though you say he's certainly not. The one on my right is a proven rebel who breaks both Roman and Jewish laws. He's a thief and a murderer, killing both Roman and Jew alike."

The crowd listened intently as they considered both men.

"Do you want me to release to you the King of the Jews?" the governor asked even though he believed he already knew the answer.

The Man looked down and surmised the high priest's blood was boiling as he read his thoughts.

The King of the Jews, the high priest repeated internally. The way the governor had worded his question rubbed the high priest wrong in every way. The high priest envied The Man, and The Man knew it. Of course, the high priest would never admit it. He'd never even come to grips with it inside his heart, but that didn't make it any less true. Many of the Jewish people adored The Man and held him in high regard. Those same people honored the high priest, but they didn't admire him, much less adore him. This fueled the hidden envy the high priest felt toward The Man.

"No," the high priest said quietly.

The governor frowned. "What did you say?"

"No."

Silence filled the courtyard.

"No, not him," the high priest repeated. "Give us the thug!"

The governor's eyes widened in dread as the high priest turned to the Jews, confirming they too wanted the thug to be liberated to them.

"We don't want The Man, do we?" the high priest asked with a shout.

"No!" the people said in unison. "Away with this man! Release the thug to us!"

The governor tried to start over. "Which of the two do you want me to release to you?"

"Give us the thug!"

Everything was backfiring on the governor in an appalling and spectacular way. He had deeply underestimated the malicious, envious hatred the council had been concealing deep within their hearts.

* * *

The governor briefly considered the possibility that perhaps the councilmen didn't loathe the thug like the Romans did. But he was wrong. The councilmen *despised* the thug. He epitomized everything they stood against. He was corrupt, violent, impure, abusive, irreverent, and profane. He truly was, in their view, a waste of The Father's creation. They supposed The Father makes no mistakes, but if he did, it would've been the thug.

At the end of the day, the thug was sinful. And the way the councilmen understood things, they weren't.

They were completely repulsed by the thug, because they thought The Father was completely repulsed by the thug. If someone wasn't good enough for The Father, then they weren't fit for fellowship with the council. The thug had clearly turned his back on the Jewish people and their religion through his careless actions. He was a threat to eradicate everything they stood to accomplish. Because of this, the councilmen *hated* the thug.

But they hated The Man even more.

* * *

"Then what should I do with The Man called Messiah?" The governor grew exasperated with each passing minute as he saw more of their disdain toward true justice.

A hushed silence fell on the crowd until the high priest raised his fist in determination.

"Crucify him!" he said with fiery eyes and a snarl.

The entire crowd thundered in agreement.

The governor struggled for words but found none. He felt the situation slipping through his fingers. The people weren't just demanding The Man be executed but *crucified*.

The governor knew crucifixion was the most heinous and diabolical form of torture ever devised. Executioners would force their victims to carry a crossbeam to their own execution site where they'd be made to lay across the beam on the ground. Sometimes they were tied to the beam with thin rope, and the beam was attached to a sturdy wooden stake in the ground where they would hang for days, eventually succumbing to the exposure. Often the executioners would take tapered iron spikes about six inches long and a half-inch thick and drive them through their victims' limbs, pinning them permanently to the wood. It was wickedly cruel yet effective. The governor had only witnessed a few crucifixions from start to finish; after the last one, he decided he didn't have the stomach for it.

"W-Why?" the governor asked. "What crime has he committed?"

"Crucify him!"
"But . . . why?"
"Crucify him!"
"But The Man is innocent."
"Crucify him!"

* * *

The governor was correct; The Man was innocent. He didn't abuse women or lie to his followers or miss his tax payments. He never taught people to disrespect authorities or forget the law. It was the opposite. He encouraged men to treat women with the utmost respect. He commanded his followers to be full of truth in all circumstances. He wanted the Jews to respect the authorities so much they even prayed for them.

The Man wasn't just innocent—he was *pure*. He was the definition of purity. Contrary to the views of the councilmen, a multitude of wrongs weren't lodged deep within The Man's heart. Only one thing comprised the foundation of his heart, driving everything he ever did: *goodness*.

At his core, The Man was *good*. His goodness reflected The Father's goodness. The Man had every opportunity to show something other than goodness to the world, every opportunity to show hate or prejudice or indifference or selfishness. But The Man simply couldn't, because The Man was simply good.

So, while the governor was correct in his assessment that The Man was innocent, he missed the fact that The Man was *good* in every way.

* * *

The crowd's chants overwhelmed the governor.

"Crucify! Crucify! Crucify!"

"Why?" The governor's face sagged, and his head hung lower and lower. "Why? What crime has this man committed?"

But the Jews persisted. Their demands slowly wore the governor down as they pinned him into a corner. "Crucify! Crucify! Crucify!"

The governor made a last-ditch effort to stand in the middle of the demands of the councilmen and the demands of justice. Rather than hold firm in his authority, he shrank to the council and offered them a cowardly resolution. He chose to bend so he didn't break. "Silence!"

The crowd quieted after the soldiers stepped forward with drawn weapons.

"I've found in him no grounds for execution." The governor licked his lips and inhaled sharply. "Therefore, I'll have him punished and release him."

The crowd erupted in rage as the governor had soldiers bring The Man inside his home.

Once inside, the governor locked eyes with his two soldiers holding The Man. "Listen to me . . ." Sweat slid down the governor's flushed cheeks. He looked flustered and upset, something the soldiers had never seen in him. The governor bit his lip. Disappointment filled his eyes. "Take this Jew and have him flogged."

The Man's head fell to his chest. He pinched his face together to control his emotions.

"The punishment must be severe, but he can't die. His blood will be your blood if he dies."

"Yes, sir."

"Ensure this doesn't cause a ruckus."

"Yes, sir."

"There'll be no riots in my streets. Understood?"

"Yes, sir."

"Take him quickly to the centurion and clearly explain to him my instructions. Have him and his men bring The Man back to me."

"Yes, sir."

"Get going."

"Yes, sir."

The Roman soldiers led the chained Jew out the house's back door toward the scourging hall.

* * *

Emotions flooded The Man as he walked the cobblestone path. His limbs shivered in the brisk morning wind. He knew what his body would look like within the hour. Even though the walk was less than five minutes, the time still afforded him the opportunity to be overcome with every kind feeling.

But two emotions rose above the rest.

Sorrow engulfed his heart. A deep sadness attacked his soul as he felt the burden of humanity's sin weigh on him. *Mankind has wandered so very far from The Father's heart,* The Man thought. As he walked, the distance between The Father and his children seemed greater than ever.

And because of that—because he felt the immense divide between humanity and The Father's heart—The Man's heart was also overcome with love. As he walked, he remembered the people he loved effortlessly and how his actions would set them free. But he also called to mind the people who'd abused him and now were about to torture him. Moved by the thought of mercy, sparks of excitement flickered inside his heart as he pictured their transformation once he showed them just how much The Father truly loved them.

Yes, as he walked toward an unspeakable agony, he was completely filled with sorrow *and* completely filled with love.

Chapter 6

An Appropriate Crown

THE SCOURGING HALL WAS much larger than The Man expected. The spacious rectangular room seemed almost empty. Its grey stone walls rose about ten feet from the ground. Because no ceiling covered the hall, the sun fell on most of the uneven cobblestone floor. A sturdy table with scrolls stacked on the tabletop leaned against the southern wall. Three baskets of towels and a basin of water sat to the left of the table. A single wooden stake three feet tall loomed in the middle of the floor. Iron shackles fastened to the top of the stake. The post looked like something normally used to restrain livestock. Dried blood stained every square inch of it.

For decades, this post collected the blood of countless criminals. Some were thieves, some murderers, and some rebels. Some came with dignity, but all left with none. The post symbolized a stark reality; Rome gets the last word.

Always.

The Man's stomach churned. His throat tightened, causing him to strain the muscles in his neck as he fought off a strange choking sensation. A sudden and overwhelming sense of dread filled his spirit. The chains around his wrists clattered softly as his hands shook. He knew, in just a few moments, the stake in the ground would be soaked wet once again. He stood, staring at the post.

A Roman soldier on his left held a chain bound to The Man's neck while the soldier on his right proceeded forward across the hall. He opened a small door on the far side and ducked in.

As the minutes crawled by, people trickled in behind The Man and lined up against the walls. Many had come from the governor's palace—even a few priests arrived. As people filled the hall, a quiet buzz echoed endlessly off the walls from their conversations.

Finally, the far door opened again. The soldier returned to The Man's side. Five other Roman soldiers, all dressed in matching scarlet tunics, metal breastplates, leather aprons equipped with their sword and dagger, and brown sandals appeared through the door. The first one was clearly the centurion in charge of overseeing the scourging. He held authority over the others. Tight, curly black hair clung to his scalp; smooth skin wrapped around his tight jawline. The next two soldiers stooped through the door; one held a few scrolls while the other carried some smaller chains. Eventually, the last two entered the hall with baskets. They approached the table where the centurion sat and placed their baskets on the tabletop.

The Man's heart raced as he watched them pull the items from their baskets and set them along the ground—whips. Each had a wooden handle about a foot long. Three to five skinny, leather whips were fastened to each handle. A variety of items fashioned to cause a wide range of suffering to their victim were joined on the end of each whips. Some whips had sharp metal fragments and shards of bone attached to them. Others had lead-weighted balls used for bruising. Some even had fishhooks.

The Man's gaze darted around the crowded room. He saw no one he recognized other than a few priests. None of his disciples had come to save him. His family members were nowhere in sight. With a brittle voice, he whispered as he prayed, "Father . . . *please be with me.* I need your strength."

The soldier holding him overheard his prayer and chuckled.

* * *

"People of Judea, give me your attention." The centurion stood with his hands raised to quiet the onlookers. As the crowd hushed, the centurion motioned to the soldier holding The Man.

The soldier retrieved a small piece of parchment stamped by the governor from his belt. He gave the document to the centurion who unrolled the text and skimmed it.

He blinked rapidly as his brows squished together. After a few moments of running his hand through his hair, he spoke with a deep voice that demanded respect. "Our governor has found this Jew standing before you now guilty of stirring a rebellion and claiming kingship. He's been placed in my custody for punishment. This morning, his crimes will be dealt with . . . accordingly." He stamped the parchment with a hot wax seal and returned the document to the soldier.

The four soldiers operating under the centurion began their duties. Two of them loosened the chain from The Man's neck and stripped off his tunic. They led him forward to the post and shackled his hands to it, forcing his whole upper body to hunch over. He stood shivering in just his undergarment. The other two soldiers snatched the lead-weighted whips and sauntered to the crowd for a bit of show and tell. As they went, they laughed and boasted of what they were about to do.

The two soldiers who bound The Man to the post stepped aside while the other two found their way behind The Man. They loosened their arms and their shoulders.

"Are you ready?" one of them asked The Man.

The crowd fell silent as they held their breath. Some slowly covered their eyes as the soldiers waited for the centurion's approval to begin.

The Man, fully Divine, had chosen his entire life to set aside the privileges of being equal with The Father to take up the status of a slave. He was now about to eat the fruit of his choices.

* * *

"*One*!" the centurion yelled.

With his arm cocked, one of the soldiers ran behind The Man and struck him in the lower left part of the back as hard as he could.

The lead balls landed with a terrible thud just above The Man's kidneys, sending shockwaves throughout his entire body. Pain vibrated beneath his skin as he bellowed. The Man's back recoiled and arched. His gnashing teeth felt like they might shatter into tiny pieces.

A handful of onlookers gasped.

"*Two*!"

The first soldier rolled to his left to make way for the other.

The second soldier ran forward and, with two hands, whipped the lead balls down vertically like he was chopping wood. They landed on top of The Man's right collarbone. His right arm jolted as he screamed. The soldier rolled to his right.

"*Three*!"

They struck him again and again. The torture continued for what seemed like an eternity. This was much to the soldiers' delight, for they found pleasure in their job.

Many in the crowd pitied The Man but believed he deserved the abuse.

But none was more pleased than The Accuser. Just before the whip's first strike, The Accuser had slipped into the corner of the hall unnoticed and unseen. With wide, ecstatic eyes, he watched with unrivaled joy as Heaven's Treasure was beaten and bruised. The Accuser's plan was being carried out to perfection. A nasty smile edged across his face as the centurion counted.

With each blow, The Father looked on altogether heartbroken. With each strike, he grimaced as he watched a part of his own self suffer a sinner's fate. The Father's suffering was not the same as The Man's, but it was no less devastating. Ever since the beginning, he had witnessed countless acts of hateful violence that men inflicted upon each other, but now he watched as it was exacted upon his own flesh and blood.

* * *

"Halt!" the centurion said.

After the twentieth strike, The Man lay trembling on the ground. Blood poured from his wrists as the shackles cut deep into his flesh. Large bruises ranging from blue to purple to black covered his entire body. Air left his body in quiet whimpers.

One of the soldiers stood bent over, trying to catch his breath. Both breathed hard and were sweating.

"Let him catch his breath while you catch yours and exchange tools," the centurion said.

The soldiers wandered to the table. They both grabbed a towel and wiped the sweat from their faces. They took turns drinking from the basin as they rested.

The centurion approached one of the soldiers who had brought The Man from the governor's house and casually conversed with him.

The Man didn't move. The Man *couldn't* move.

Many in the crowd had quiet conversations. A few left, and a few came. Some mocked The Man and reenacted his beating. Others laughed.

But the priests did not. They had no reaction. They stood in silence with an intense gaze. Just like The Accuser, a simple beating would not satisfy what they were truly after.

Five minutes passed, giving the soldiers plenty of time to rejuvenate.

Ready to finish his obligation, the centurion clapped and told his unit to proceed with their duties.

The whips the two soldiers grabbed this time no longer had lead-weighted balls attached to them but a variety of hooks, pieces of bone, and shards of metal. The first beating was intended to bruise The Man. This next one intended to slice those bruises open.

"Get up, Your Majesty," one of them said as they walked behind The Man.

He didn't move. His lungs were just now catching up and attempting to take full breaths for the first time in minutes.

"Help him," the centurion said.

The two soldiers set down their tools and lifted The Man to his feet.

Standing upright, he groaned as a new wave of pain set in. He struggled to not give into despair as he realized what he had just experienced was only round one. He looked for family and friends but saw none. However, something did catch his eye—the glare from one of the priests.

The priest stood rigid in his religious garb and regarded The Man with loathing.

The Man saw the priest's heart filled to the brim with hatred toward him.

In the priest's view, the Jewish people had encountered countless enemies over the centuries. Nation after nation had risen to destroy the Jewish way of life. It wasn't just Rome; they'd faced every kind of oppression, poverty, strife, war, famine, captivity, and godlessness. But it was this Jew—a simple carpenter from a small northern town—who felt like the greatest threat of all. Because of this, the priest recognized The Man to be his biggest enemy. Therefore, he hated him.

And, as The Man regarded the priest, he too understood this priest to be his enemy as well. After all, the priest belonged to the council; their lies, unjust court proceedings, bribery, and jealousy had put The Man in his shackles. The council was responsible for all his aching wounds. Yes, The Man stared at the priest and considered him to be his enemy just like the priest considered The Man to be his enemy.

But The Man didn't hate the priest.

He didn't hate him at all.

* * *

About three years earlier, The Man had stood on the edge of a great lake in the northern region. Hordes of people sat on a mountainside to listen to him teach.

"The Father blesses those who are poor and realize their need for him, for the Kingdom of Heaven belongs to them," he said with a wide, welcoming smile. The Man began his monologue with encouraging statements about the condition of the underprivileged Jewish peasants who listened to him. But, as he spoke, his teaching increased in difficulty.

He articulated to them that following The Father's law wasn't just about their actions; it was about their heart. It was more than just not murdering people. They weren't permitted to stay angry with anyone. It was more than just not making unfulfilled vows. They must be a people whose every word was truthful and trusted. It was more than just not committing adultery. They were to regard all people the way The Father did.

But the most difficult instruction of all pertained to how they treated their enemies.

"You've heard the law that says, 'Love your neighbor, and hate your enemy.' But I say . . . *love your enemies*! Pray for those who persecute you! In that way, you'll be acting like true children of your Father in Heaven."

The crowd had never heard a more difficult teaching. After all, this wasn't the way humanity worked. The instruction seemed unreasonable. And, in a way, the teaching was. It was indeed impossible for them to truly love their enemies and pray for The Father to bless the people who preyed upon them.

The Man understood this. No one could love their enemies outright without Divine help. The Man would one day teach them that following The Father's *true heart* would certainly be impossible unless something much greater than themselves enabled them.

They had to be empowered by The Father's Spirit living inside them.

This was the only way it could be done.

* * *

Trembling, The Man stood shackled to the post and stared at the priest. On the outside, The Man was battered and bruised. His eyes swelled, and his back throbbed. His wrists continued to bleed. He could barely stand. Hateful people surrounded him. He felt helpless and weak.

But, on the inside, rooted deep within his being, was The Father's very own Spirit. This Spirit stood in stark contrast with The Man's body. The Spirit living inside him was mighty and powerful. And although no one could hear it, the Spirit was roaring loudly.

The Man shackled to the post looked at the priest and fully loved him.

It was a mighty, roaring love.

* * *

"Ready?" the centurion asked.

The soldiers nodded.

"The count will start again," the centurion said to the crowd. He glanced around and gave them one last chance to leave if they didn't want to witness what was about to happen.

A handful of people scurried out.

Then the centurion yelled, "*One*!"

The first soldier ran forward and, with all his strength, slashed The Man across the upper part of his back.

Sorrow rushed through The Father's heart.

The Accuser stepped forward as delight flooded his being; he had longed to see this day and became overwhelmed with emotion.

The Man shrieked in agony as his weight fell against the stake. The hooks, metal, and bone gashed into his flesh a half-inch deep. Multiple bruises burst open. Blood splattered on the ground as many of the onlookers looked away.

The soldier peeled off to his left to make way for his partner.

"*Two*!"

The second soldier side-armed his whip into the side of The Man's right thigh.

The Man's arms jerked against his shackles as he fell to one knee. He strained to stand when the centurion shouted again.

"*Three*!"

"*Four*!"

"*Five*!"

"*Six*!"

On and on the flogging went as the soldiers struck The Man again and again. They cut his legs, slashed his flanks and wounded his stomach. They even mangled his ear as one blow missed his shoulder and struck the side of his face. But his back received the worst of the beating. The soldiers shredded his back in a gruesome manner.

Plenty of people in the crowd left. They couldn't stomach the sound of splattering blood.

The higher the centurion counted, the more The Man lost his focus. He felt his body numbing in an eerie way. His arms tingled slightly, and his eyes couldn't focus on anything. Eventually, he blacked out.

"Halt!" the centurion said as he noticed The Man's unconsciousness.

Unable to stop his momentum, the soldier slashed The Man in the lower part of the back.

"*I said stop*!" the centurion said with roar as he stood.

The few in the crowd who remained were struck mute. For some, this was the first flogging they'd ever witnessed, and the sight was much more difficult to observe than they had expected. For most of them, what they experienced that morning would keep them awake at night for years to come.

An unnerving silence fell upon the hall.

"You better make sure this man wakes up," the centurion said to the soldiers after a moment. "Take him to a holding cell and give him water."

"Give him water?" one of the soldiers asked.

"*Yes, give him water*," the centurion said flatly. "This man desperately needs water. According to the governor, his blood is our blood. Remember?"

"Yes, sir."

The sparse crowd trickled out quietly as the soldiers cleaned up the blood.

The Man, fully Divine, lay there a mangled ball of flesh, unconscious, and shackled to the post.

With anguish in his heart, The Father looked upon The Man. He deeply desired to restore The Man not just to full health but to the glory that had been his from the beginning. But he didn't, for The Father knew the suffering of The Man wouldn't be in vain.

The Father fully trusted The Man's suffering would bring deep healing to the wounds of humanity. Through the horror unfolding before him, The Father planned on ushering in a new age into the world where everything was finally made new, only possible because The Man chose to become despised and rejected and familiar with pain.

* * *

As The Man lay unconscious, he dreamed fondly of the memories of when he and The Father had chosen to step down into time and partner together to fashion the universe. In his mind's eye, he remembered the wonder he had felt watching light flow from The Father's mouth as he spoke effortlessly. At first, darkness smothered everything. But then The Father spoke, and light pierced through the darkness at the sound of his voice.

In The Man's subconscious, he recalled the sense of splendor and glory he had felt when he worked with The Father to separate the waters, the land, and the sky. The Father spoke billions of galaxies and planets into existence, and The Man named them all, deeming each one priceless. Together, they commanded the trees to take root and the flowers to bloom and the fish to swim and the creatures to roam. And they called for mankind to care for it all.

Their creation was formed to ultimately reflect their own true, primary character.

The creation was *good.*

As he lay there, The Man dreamed peacefully about his good and perfect masterpiece.

* * *

The Man woke to water dousing his face.

"Wake up!"

Confusion swept over The Man as he had forgotten where he was.

Four Roman soldiers stood in front of him, occupying a small room with grey stone walls and a low ceiling. Other than a small table in the corner and a candle fixture on the wall, the room was mostly empty.

In an instant, The Man remembered his circumstances as he tried to sit upright. Pain radiated throughout his entire frame. He attempted to move his neck, but the muscles in the upper part of his back refused. It almost felt like they weren't there. He glanced down and found his stomach unrecognizable. Realizing his right eye was swollen shut, he did everything he could to raise his arm to touch the right side of his face. He couldn't tell if his ear was attached or not. Causing him extreme discomfort, his muscles contracted involuntarily as he vomited on himself.

The soldiers laughed. They threw more water on him to wash the bile from his wounds.

"Get the king to sit up," one of the soldiers said as he chuckled.

They grabbed The Man underneath his arms and propped him against a wall. The stone dug into the wounds on his back.

Another soldier dipped a cup into the basin and put it to his lips. "Your Majesty," he said with a grin, "you *must* drink some water."

The Man tried to drink as much as he could, but plenty of the water spilled out the corners of his mouth.

The soldier dipped the cup again and put it to The Man's lips.

He attempted to drink but ended up choking.

The soldier tossed the rest of the cup into The Man's face.

"The fool forgot how to drink," one of them said in disgust.

The soldiers stood and stopped paying The Man attention. Two of them grabbed the cup and the water and left the room while the other two discussed why the centurion hadn't sent The Man back to the governor yet.

"What's taking him so long?"

"He's a high-ranking official and has more things to take care of than just this."

"How much longer did he say he'd be?"

"He didn't mention, but I figure it wouldn't be more than twenty minutes. He understands the predicament the governor's in and will want to return The Man as soon as possible."

"Why'd he even send him to us? Normally, the crime he's been accused of calls for immediate execution."

"I was wondering the same thing. Maybe he's a special case? Maybe he actually . . . is a king?"

"If he truly is a king, where are all his subjects?"

"Maybe none of his followers—"

"Does he look like a real king to you?" The soldier pointed to The Man sitting in a pool of his own blood, unable to move. "Be logical." The soldier made eye contact with his comrade. "What kind of king doesn't fight back? What kind of king just accepts this fate?"

They both eyed The Man and eventually cackled at the thought that this Jew might be someone special. One bent down to get face to face with The Man and—

"Come quick!"

The two soldiers turned around to find the two other soldiers standing in the doorway.

"You'll enjoy this. Look what we found!" One held up a tattered scarlet robe. "Don't you think the king deserves to greet the people in his royal outfit?"

The other two soldiers standing next to The Man snickered. They took the robe and held it high to admire. Then they looked back at The Man.

"Don't you think you'll look good in this?" one of them said.

The Man didn't respond.

"Oh, my apologies. *Your Majesty*, don't you think you'll look good in this?"

They all laughed.

Once the laughter dissipated, the two soldiers who had found the robe whispered something under their breath to the other two. Both pairs of soldiers exchanged a quick and quiet conversation. A smirk slithered across their faces like it would for children who had just been invited to join a fun game.

One soldier eventually approached The Man and squatted. "We figured while we wait we would present to you, *our king*, a few small gifts," the soldier said with a dark, low tone. "You don't mind if we fetch them, do you?"

The Man didn't react. He didn't even look the soldier in the eye.

"I thought that's what you'd say," the soldier said with a snort. "We're going to step outside for a moment. You aren't going to run away, are you?"

Silence.

"Good. Stay here."

The four soldiers slipped out of the room and shut the door.

* * *

Stillness.

The Man breathed slowly and painfully. He didn't know how long the soldiers had been gone, as time seemed to elude him. This was the first interval he found himself truly alone since he was thrown in the cellar at the high priest's home. A peaceful hush reverberated in the room as The Man closed his eyes.

Oh, how a part of him wanted to just strut out of the room and demonstrate his true identity. He could have done it, too. He understood walking out of the room would've been effortless for him. But he didn't just want to show everyone who he actually was. He wanted to reveal who The Father was as well.

The path he'd been walking his entire life was leading to this day. Yes, the mission was to restore the relationship between The Father and his children. And The Man knew he would do that by redeeming humanity from their self-inflicted shackles and standing victorious over The Accuser.

But The Man was trying to accomplish something else through his suffering, and although this aspect of his mission was different from bringing salvation to the world, it was equally powerful. The Man would uncover and reveal who The Father actually was.

And he knew if he chose to stroll out of the room and escape the pain set before him, his mission would be compromised. The Man's flesh desired to walk out of the room, but his spirit was determined and set. His entire being joyfully submitted to The Father's will, because he knew it to be perfect and complete.

As The Man sat alone, an unfulfillable desire to be surrounded by his loved ones overwhelmed him. He recalled the large family he had grown up in. His father was a carpenter and had slowly passed the trade to The Man as he grew. The Man was the oldest child; his brothers and sisters all looked up to him. He treasured each of them and always enjoyed their company.

But he was closest with his mother. Like many sons, he believed The Father gifted him with the best mother in the world. Although he was fully Divine, The Man looked up to her in every way. Her natural, selfless love inspired him. Before he could walk, she had been the one who had cared for him. She had cleaned him, had fed him, had played with him and had held him.

As The Man sat alone, he craved to be at home with his family. And although he was a grown man in his thirties, he sought to somehow go back in time so his mother could embrace him once again.

* * *

The door burst open, and the four soldiers strolled in.

"We come bringing gifts, oh mighty king!" one of them said.

Two of them grabbed The Man's arms and lifted him to his feet. As the soldiers held him upright, the two others forced The Man's arms through the sleeves of the scarlet robe. The robe, in a way, acted as a grimy bandage as its fibers clung to the wounds and clot the blood. After ensuring The Man could stand on his own, the soldiers stood back to mock him.

"Beautiful!" one said. "Simply stunning!"

"Every king has a scarlet robe, and now our king does too!"

"Your royalty will never be in question again!"

One soldier lunged forward to ask a loaded question. His eyebrows bounced as his cheeks flushed red from excitement. "But where's a king's honor without a crown?"

From behind his back, the soldier revealed to The Man a makeshift crown fashioned just for him. The crown was made from what looked to be thorny vines twisted together multiple times in a circular shape. The thorns were bulky and sharp, many of them well over an inch long.

"Hold still now." The soldier gently positioned the crown on the brim of The Man's skull.

One soldier slipped behind The Man and held down his arms while the other two revealed sticks they hid behind their backs and softly placed them on top of both sides of the thorny crown. With the help of the sticks, they pulled down the crown so it wrapped tightly against The Man's forehead and wound around his skull just above the ears.

The Man moaned as the thorns dug deep under his flesh.

The soldier who had placed the crown upon The Man eyed him with a sadistic stare. "Perfect," he said in a low whisper.

Another soldier ran outside, retrieved a much larger stick and placed it in The Man's hands. "Don't forget your scepter, mighty king."

They stepped backward to admire their work.

The Man stood shaking in his disgusting robe as he leaned against his mock scepter. The crown of thorns was tightly buried into his skull, making blood trickle into his left eye. He was the most deplorable excuse of royalty they'd ever seen.

"They say you're the King of the Jews," one of them said, "but we know that can't be true. If it were, they wouldn't have handed you over to us!"

The others laughed as the soldier continued.

"So, tell us, who're you king over?"

The Man kept his mouth shut as he focused on maintaining his balance.

"He just looks pitiful to me," one soldier said. "He's a sad king for sure!"

"Sad because he suffers."

Then it clicked with the soldier who had originally inquired to know what kind of king he was. The soldier clapped his hands together and spun to face his comrades. "He is the king of sorrow and the king of suffering!"

The others shrieked with laughter, for they all believed a fake scepter, a dirty royal robe, and a crown of thorns to be completely out of place for this stupid Jewish peasant.

In reality, his look suited him perfectly.

* * *

Yes, beneath the soiled robe truly was the king of sorrow and suffering. He was the one true king to those in the world whose lives were defined by sorrow. For ages to come, the people of the world who knew sorrow in an intimate way would forever look upon the lonely man and imagine the tears in his eyes and say, *That's my king.*

And he was, undeniably, the king to those in the world who suffered in every way. Never again would people contemplate the suffering in their lives and wonder if their anguish was unique. Those who bore innumerable hardships could always gaze upon The Man who wore the thorny crown and boldly proclaim, *That's my king.*

The Man, fully Divine, chose to set aside his heavenly privileges and accept a life well-acquainted with sorrow and suffering. The Father had commissioned him to walk alongside the downtrodden and the hurting and take up their afflictions to demonstrate the Divine bleeds as well. Because of The Man, the children of The Father would forever know they would never walk alone in their sorrow or suffering because *they served the king of sorrow and suffering.*

* * *

"All hail the King of the Jews!" the soldiers said in unison.

Three soldiers dropped to their knees and bowed before The Man. The other soldier tried to join but struggled because he was bent over, laughing. The other three hurled sarcastic praises toward The Man.

"The King of the Jews is strong and mighty!"

"His subjects praise him!"

"His splendor reaches throughout eternity!"

The soldiers cackled for several minutes as they couldn't contain themselves.

The door opened, and a servant boy poked his head inside. "Excuse me, but . . . he's to be taken back to the governor's palace now," he said then exited.

The laughter waned. The soldiers looked back and forth at each other. They didn't have to say anything in order to communicate their desire to have one last moment of fun.

One soldier approached The Man and looked him eye to eye. "No, you're no king," he said through gritted teeth. "You're not even a man. You're just a misbehaving *Jew* who deserves to be beaten." He spit in The Man's face, took his scepter and belted The Man in the head, driving the thorns deeper into his skull.

The Man fell backward against the wall and to the ground.

The soldier continued to swing the scepter at The Man who recoiled into the fetal position as he blocked his head with his arms.

After a moment, one of the onlooking soldiers intervened. "Stop!"

The soldier paused.

"You can't kill this man. If you do, our blood is his blood. Remember?"

The soldier holding the scepter looked down and considered the strength of The Man, seeing his health teetered toward disaster.

"Let's get him back to the governor so our task can be complete." The soldier dropped the scepter and spit on The Man.

The other three did the same as they showed their utter contempt toward him. They put chains around his neck and his hands.

The centurion walked in the door. "What's this?" he asked in a deep tone as his eyes bulged, and his nostrils flared as his lips pressed together. He shook his head in a jerky motion as he held his chin high. The soldiers had clearly gone above and beyond their duties to physically punish The Man by taking on the task of mocking and humiliating him.

The centurion approached The Man to have a closer look, bent down and investigated the thorny crown. It was obviously causing The Man severe pain as the blood refused to clot. "*You idiots*!" The centurion got nose to nose with a soldier. "Why can't you do as you're commanded? I asked you to watch this Jew . . . not continue his punishment unsupervised!"

The soldiers stood silent.

"What were you thinking? Did you think at all? This Jew . . . he could've died! Do I need to remind you what happens to us if he dies?"

Silence.

"You fools put me at risk simply because you wanted to have your fun!" The centurion approached another soldier, grabbed the soldier's hair and pulled it down, bringing the soldier to his knees. "*Do you think you can follow my orders this time*?" he asked quietly.

"Y-Y-Yes . . . sir."

"*You really think so*?"

"Yes, sir."

"Good. Then lift him *gently* to his feet. Get him more water. Make sure he drinks. Then hand him over to the two soldiers who serve the governor's palace. They're waiting outside for him and will walk him back." The centurion paused and surveyed the other three soldiers to determine if they understood the gravity of his command. "Have I made myself clear?"

"Yes, sir."

"Do it." The centurion thrust the soldier's head out of his grip, turned and slammed the door shut as he left.

Two soldiers lifted The Man to his feet while the other two fetched water. When they returned, they gave it to The Man.

He drank it all except the small amount that escaped his lips. The water did much to help The Man ward off dehydration as he continued to lose fluids.

The four soldiers took The Man outside and found the two soldiers who served the governor and relinquished The Man to them.

The governor's soldiers chuckled at the sight of seeing The Man in his scarlet robe and thorny crown.

"Come now," one of them said to The Man. "It's time to decide your fate."

Led by the two soldiers, The Man limped back to the governor's mansion.

Chapter 7

The Trade that Changed the World

THE SUN ROSE INTO the late morning sky as a light breeze swept through the city. Although there wasn't a cloud on the horizon, a storm was brewing. More and more people heard about the commotion at the governor's palace. Tension gripped parts of the capital as people waited anxiously to see what would unfold. If the councilmen got their way, hordes of The Man's followers would be distraught. If the governor released The Man, the Jewish Council might riot. No matter what happened, numerous people were sure to be disappointed.

The governor paced in his mansion as he watched the gathering in his courtyard multiply. His palms grew clammy and wet. He ordered nothing to eat because his stomach swirled. He hoped with everything in him The Man's punishment would be enough to satisfy the agitated mob.

Only time would tell.

* * *

The governor's door thumped. A young male slave scurried to open it.

The governor couldn't see who was there and couldn't quite decipher what was said.

After a moment, the slave hurried toward the governor for a briefing. "It's The Man. He has returned from the scourging hall."

"Good," the governor said in relief. He paused to wait for the slave to say something. When he didn't, the governor continued. "Well, bring him inside already."

"I'm . . . I'm not sure that's a good idea, sir." The slave squinted and bit his lip. "Bringing him inside—"

"What do you mean it's not a good idea?"

The slave searched for the best way to say what he needed to say without distressing the governor. "Bringing him inside is not . . . well, it might be too . . . *messy*."

Confusion crossed the governor's face as his brow tightened and his lips pursed. He stood and went to the door himself. What he saw left his jaw hanging open.

Two soldiers standing behind The Man had their forearms underneath his armpits.

The Man teetered in a filthy scarlet robe, panting quick, short breaths. One eye was swollen shut while the other blinked slowly. A vinelike, weedy plant wrapped around his head, its thorns digging into The Man's skull. The governor couldn't examine The Man's back but could see the front of his torso, as the robe was slightly open. Deep gashes covered The Man's entire body from his knees to the right side of his face. As he swayed, blood dripped gently off the ends of his robe, creating a puddle on the floor.

"Those *imbeciles*," the governor whispered through gritted teeth. "Quickly!" the governor said to the soldiers and the slave. "Bring him inside and sit him on the floor. Fetch water and force him to drink. Find some towels and clean him up."

The slave froze. He attempted to speak but stuttered through his words. His eyes darted back and forth, unsure what to do.

"And you," the governor said as he looked at the slave, "get a few of the others and tell them to bring us more towels. We won't have enough inside. Make sure this gets cleaned up completely."

"Yes . . . sir," the young slave said hesitantly as he left.

The soldiers brought The Man inside and did just as the governor had directed. The Man sat on the governor's floor as he drank water. Multiple slaves attempted to clean his wounds but couldn't get to most of them because his robe clotted to his back. The water helped, but the bleeding continued. Ten minutes later, he sat on the ground in a pool of his own blood.

As the time passed, the governor gradually grasped he couldn't assist The Man anymore. "It's time," he said to the soldiers. "Bring him outside at my command." The governor opened the double wooden doors leading to the restless crowd and took his place at the front of the porch. A sharp breeze sent a chill up his back as he rubbed his hands together. Although the crowd couldn't see them, the governor's knees shook. "Jews! Listen to me!"

The hushed crowd gave the governor their full and undivided attention.

"Earlier this morning, I sentenced the Jew you brought before me to a thorough scourging so he might understand the seriousness of his crime. The mighty hand of Rome has taught him a lesson he'll never forget."

People in the courtyard stirred and murmured as they could see the governor beginning to construct his excuse as to why the time was now appropriate to release The Man.

The governor sensed their frustration building, so he decided to let them see for themselves. "Look, I'm bringing him out to you." The governor motioned to a solider through a window. "I'm bringing him out to you to let you know I find no basis for a charge against him."

The mass growled their disapproval. Some shouted insults toward the governor while others cursed.

"I've punished him severely!" The governor raised his voice louder as he pointed at the high priest. "You accused him with a multitude of charges, and his flesh has paid the price! There's no use for further reprimands!"

Growing louder, the outcry from the Jews rang throughout the courtyard as they communicated their disgust.

Then the double wooden doors swung open to reveal two soldiers with The Man between them, and they strode to the front of the porch. As The Man approached the gathering, the Jews grew quiet as their gaze feasted upon his distorted figure. Most wanted to look away but found their eyes disobeying their mind's command.

He looked almost unrecognizable from the Jew who had stood before them just an hour ago. His clothes had been taken from him. Now a foreign, scarlet material clung to his back like a cape and wrapped over his shoulders, partially concealing his chest and stomach. His skin appeared soaked in a dark red dye. The Jews at the head of the crowd noticed the trail of blood on the porch that followed The Man from the double wooden doors. His face was mutilated, and his eyes remained shut.

The contrast couldn't have been more striking as The Man took his place next to the governor. Both men claimed to rule throngs of people with ultimate authority, yet one looked the part while the other didn't.

The governor was clean and strong. He slept in a palace and had no request denied. Hundreds of thousands of people obeyed his every command. Power radiated from his presence.

But the Jew standing next to him was disgusting and weak. He didn't crave to be served, but to serve. He had no true place to lay his head. His handful of followers constantly waivered in their obedience. Humility radiated from his presence.

The governor grabbed the front hem of The Man's scarlet robe, opened it and placed it over The Man's shoulders and behind his back, revealing to the crowd for the first time his grisly torso. "Here is The Man!"

The crowd groaned. Even though they hated The Man, the Jews couldn't prevent themselves from being taken aback at the lacerations across his stomach. Some of the parents took their children's hand and escorted them through the back of the courtyard.

The Man squirmed as the robe rubbed against his flesh. His head fell backward slightly as his teeth clenched. For the first time, he opened his eye and looked skyward. A deep moan came from his throat in spurts as he tried to keep his frame still.

The Jews grew grimly silent.

The Man gazed across the crowd for the first time since his flogging, and something caught his eye. Tears ran down his face as it winced.

Standing toward the back of the courtyard was his mother.

* * *

His mother stood next to the disciple who was with the fisherman in the high priest's courtyard the night before. Three other women accompanied them. All five believed The Man spoke the words of life. They tethered their hearts to The Man's. Because of this, each of their spirits broke as they observed The Man abused and stripped of his humanity, presented as the governor's peace offering to the priests.

But none of their hearts broke like his mother's.

Her covered head bobbed as she wept painful tears in silence. As her lips trembled, her heart felt physically heavy. Her whole body seemed weak, making her think she might collapse. There was absolutely nothing she could do to help her precious child, and she knew it. She would have given anything, even her own life, to march through the crowd and onto the porch and rid her son's enemies for him. All she wanted to do was nurse him back to health, bandage his wounds and lay him in a comfortable bed. His mother would soon be able to fully and completely fathom the most appalling nightmare one could experience on this side of eternity; she was about to watch her own child die a slow and painful death.

She noticed her son, and her son noticed her. In the short hush that presented itself, they merely stared at each other from across the courtyard. They needed no words, for their gaze communicated what a conversation couldn't.

As his mother observed her wretched son, three emotions flooded her soul: unquenchable love, unthinkable pain, and utter helplessness. She gasped a sizable breath of air that made others around her stare, then she sobbed. Although she didn't recognize it, The Father came close to her that instant and held her heart gently.

* * *

"Crucify him!" The high priest's shout seemed unusually loud in the midst of the quieted crowd.

"Now wh—" the governor began to speak.

"Crucify him!" the Jews cheered, as they refused to let their bloodlust be satisfied. "Crucify! Crucify! Crucify!"

The governor's body contorted as a snarl distorted his face, and his cheeks reddened. "*You take him and crucify him*! As for me, I find no basis for a charge against him."

The high priest motioned to a handful of other priests to quiet the Jews so he could have a conversation with the governor in front of everyone. "We abide by The Father's law given to our fathers long ago. We are committed in our hearts to following that law at all costs. I understand you, being a Gentile, have not read our law book before, is this so?"

"I haven't." The governor's gaze shot the opposite direction of the high priest. He wasn't sure where the high priest was going with this.

"We have a law, and according to that law, he must die, because he claims to be fully Divine."

The governor's eyes widened as his heart raced. His mouth became dry. His limbs tingled as another chill ran up his back. *Fully Divine*, the governor thought.

Some of the Jews hurled insults and accusations toward the porch again.

The governor needed more time to process this. Suddenly, he felt extreme anxiety from the surrounding mob. He ordered his soldiers to bring The Man inside for more questioning.

As they meandered toward the door, dread shoved its way into the governor's heart.

* * *

Fear wasn't something the governor was used to. He was the most powerful man in the entire region. He had nothing to fear. And yet, as he walked into his mansion, he stood face to face with an emotion he hadn't wrestled with in years.

Fear.

Something about the way The Man carried himself was just . . . *different*. It bothered the governor even though he couldn't explain why. He just knew this man was unusual in every sense of the word. Therefore, in a way, he feared him.

But, if The Man's demeanor cracked a leak for fear to drip into the governor's heart, the high priest's statement opened the floodgates.

The Man truly believed he was fully Divine. And apparently, as the governor continued to learn about The Man throughout the morning, so did hundreds of other people throughout the region. Some people were abandoning everything they owned to follow this northerner simply because they believed he was equal with the gods.

Only one other person with a large following on planet Earth claimed to be fully Divine—the emperor. Yes, the governor fully believed with all his heart the Roman Emperor was a son of the gods and, therefore, fully Divine himself.

And that's why The Man's claim to Divinity troubled the governor so much. The Man's claim to kingship threatened the emperor's throne, but his claim to Divinity was a direct attack to the emperor himself.

The Man must've been completely insane and hellbent on his own destruction. Or he was who he said he was.

Both options disturbed the governor.

* * *

"Alright," the governor said as he whipped around and gazed sternly at The Man, "*who are you really*?"

The Man ignored the governor. His head hung low while his gaze remained glued to the floor.

The governor fidgeted with a handful of trinkets he had grabbed from a bowl as he paced the dining room. He huffed and snapped his head toward The Man. "I asked you a question. Answer me!"

No answer.

"Why are you not bothered by the accusations?"

No response.

The governor's head fell back as he pressed his palms against his temples. "When did the priests first accuse you of . . . these things?"

Silence.

The governor's voice shook as he lost his composure due to a mixture of frustration and fear. "W-Where do you come from?"

The Man remained immovable.

The governor took a vase off an end table and heaved it across the room, shattering it on the wall. "Why do you still refuse to speak to me?" His face flushed red. It seemed his voice might shake the foundations of the palace. "Don't you grasp who I am? Don't you understand who rules this city? Don't you see the future set before you if you don't open your mouth?"

Stillness.

The governor approached The Man and quieted his voice, giving The Man one last chance. "Don't you realize I have the power to either release you or crucify you?"

The Man lifted his bloody head and stared at the governor. His passionate gaze penetrated the governor's confidence and authority.

At once, the governor regretted coming close to The Man, as his stare covered the governor with a wet blanket of apprehension and discomfort. He felt like somehow The Man could see the hidden fear buried deep within his heart.

The Man's labored smile looked excessively unnatural on his disfigured face. "You would have no power over me at all unless The Father gave it to you. The people who handed me to you have committed the greater sin."

* * *

The irony couldn't have been more tangible.

There stood the governor, well-groomed and rich, wearing Roman rings on his fingers. There was no one in the entire region who wasn't forced to obey his every command. His word was always absolute and final.

And there slouched The Man, beaten and poor, wearing a crown of thorns. Only a handful of people submitted to him. His word was often mocked and discounted.

And yet, it was The Man who claimed the situation they were in wasn't, at first glance, all it appeared to be.

It was The Man who claimed to be in complete power even though he was in chains. It was he who declared *real authority* in the situation even though he stood face to face with an emperor-appointed governor. And it was The Man who claimed to be in total control of his grim circumstance.

Yes, as The Man slid into a steeper and steeper descent into the jaws of death, he still stood unshaken, holding unmitigated control in his left hand and absolute sovereignty in his right.

* * *

Although the governor scoffed at the idea that The Man was fully Divine, he grew absolutely sure of one thing; he wanted nothing more to do with the Jew standing in his house. The governor was set on doing everything he could to free The Man without ruining his own political reputation.

The Man and the governor sauntered to the porch. For the next ten minutes, the governor disputed with the Jews the charges against The Man and tried to show them why his initial punishment was enough. They would have none of it. No matter what the governor said, the Jews responded with unified shouts to crucify The Man. Like metal being shaped in a furnace, the Jews continued to dial up the heat as they molded the governor to their wishes.

"But I'm the governor of this city, and I'll do what I see best! I'll let this man go!"

"If you let this man go," the high priest said through gnashed, yellow teeth, "you're no friend of the emperor. Anyone who claims to be a king opposes the emperor."

The governor understood this to be true, but the way the high priest said it made the governor consider the statement in a personal manner. As much as he desired to release The Man, he desired even more to have the favor of the emperor. Knowing the high priest would surely take this to Rome if The Man wasn't crucified, the governor saw no way out of this mess without relinquishing.

The governor pushed The Man to the front of the porch then stepped backward. "Here is your king!" he said sarcastically.

The crowd roared their disapproval as they tasted the mocking tone in the governor's words.

"Take him away!"

"We don't want him!"

"Crucify!"

"He's not one of us!"

"Crucify him!"

"R-Really?" the governor said in a cracked voice. "Is this what you really want? To crucify your king?"

"We have no king but the emperor!" the high priest said.

The crowd thundered in agreement and cheered joyfully.

The Father's heart hurt as he listened to his own priests pledge their full allegiance to a mere human they'd never even met.

The governor didn't see a path forward. He ordered his soldiers to bring a large basin of water to the front of the porch along with a towel. "Jews, watch me!"

The gathering hushed.

The governor washed his hands in the basin of water. He rinsed his palms, wrists, forearms, and elbows. As he did, he peered across the crowd and made eye contact with its leaders to confirm they saw what he was doing. He dried himself with a towel. After ordering a servant to take away the water and towel, he lifted his dirt-free hands toward the people for their consideration. "As I wash my hands in the basin, so I also wash myself of this situation. No matter what happens, I am innocent of this Jew's blood! It's your responsibility!"

"He deserves to die!" the high priest reminded him as the mass cheered. "Let his blood be on us and on our children!"

"And it will"—the governor lifted his hands once more—"because my hands are clean."

The people cheered.

Somewhere toward the back of the crowd, The Accuser nodded with pride as he laughed quietly.

* * *

The appearance of clean hands was one of The Accuser's oldest tricks in his book. For ages, he had deceived humanity with the impression they really could cleanse themselves from their offenses toward the Divine. Many times, the scheme seemed almost too easy for him.

"*Just do something good later.*"

"*Don't worry. You have an upright character.*"

"*Double your sacrifices.*"

"*Make more of an effort in the future.*"

"*Create more laws so you don't break The Father's.*"

Of course, The Accuser understood perfectly doing these things never made people right with The Father, and it definitely didn't cleanse them of their sin.

Oh, The Accuser thought, *how foolish they all are to believe removing their sin is this easy.*

And that's why The Accuser laughed as he watched the governor wash his hands. He didn't have to whisper any useless suggestions into the governor's ears to help remove the holy guilt within him. The governor himself had devised his own pathetic way to cope with his guilt. He, like the rest of humanity, believed he could rid himself of sin by performing some inept gesture that steered his feelings about himself in a more positive direction and allowed his shame to fade gradually.

Nothing made The Accuser happier than watching The Father's children try to pull themselves from their own sludge and muck, thinking they've succeeded, while failing to notice they're only deeper in it.

* * *

"His blood is on your hands," the governor said quietly in defeat. "He's your king, after all." He stepped beside The Man but refused to look him in the eye.

The crowd quieted in anticipation.

"I hereby sentence this man to death. He'll be crucified immediately."

At his announcement, the Jews screamed and cheered. They raised their hands in celebration as they praised The Father. Many priests thanked and hugged the other Jews for coming and supporting their movement.

Many in the courtyard strained to listen to the governor as spoke. For one of them, though, she heard no sounds at all—his mother. For her, in that moment, everything stood still. Her throat tightened. She grew chillingly numb as she gasped for air. She tried to loosen the clothing from her chest and neck but couldn't as her hands shook.

The disciple next to her moved in and tried to console her. The three other women wailed as they surrounded the mother. The five of them fell to the ground as despair and hopelessness set in.

The Man stood on the porch, watching them, as tears flowed down his face.

At once, the governor ordered for crucifixion documents to be sent to him for his approval and seal. He also regrettably directed soldiers to bring out the thug.

After a few minutes, the soldiers arrived at the porch with the thug in chains.

"In honor of my tradition, here's your prisoner," the governor said as he dropped his chin to his chest and shook his head slightly.

Much to the thug's delight, the soldiers loosened and unlocked the chains. He let out a sly snarl, revealing his rotting teeth hiding behind his lips. Once freed, the thug walked leisurely down the left staircase and into the crowd. He strutted to the high priest to chat, his eyebrows bouncing as he did. "Thank you for—"

A priest swooped in-between the two and struck the thug across the face, sending him backward. "*Don't address the high priest, you swine!*"

The thug barely winced. He slurped up the blood falling from his now-opened lip into his mouth and swallowed deliberately, as if he enjoyed it. He said nothing more as he exited the courtyard and into the city. As he went, people kept their distance from him.

Although the thug was given a legal second chance, society gave him a cold shoulder. For the rest of his life, people treated the thug like the evil, vile, and foul person he was.

* * *

Yes, the thug was despicable in every way. He was a murderer and a liar and a rebel. He was unclean and unwelcomed. He refused to respect authority and refused to change his ways. He was the worst of sinners.

And yet, the crowd chose the thug.

The governor had given them the choice of who they wanted to live next to and who they wanted to see die. They had chosen to live next to the worst of sinners while voting to crucify the Treasure of Heaven.

But it wasn't only the crowd who made that choice that day.

The Father did too.

Yes, it was The Father's good and pleasing will to see the thug freed and The Man crucified. Of course, the price of the thug's freedom was astronomical. But the cost wasn't insurmountable—not for the mighty love of The Father. The Father's choice was no different than the crowd's, but his heart was.

The crowd simply desired to see The Man crucified no matter the cost. The Father wanted to live next to the sinner no matter the cost. The crowd wanted to prove that buried deep within The Man was true evil. The Father wanted to unearth the true beauty buried deep within the sinner. The crowd sought to strip The Man of his dignity as he hung on a cruel cross. The Father anticipated the moment where he'd clothe the sinner in his own robes of righteousness.

The Father, with the help of The Man, was executing his plan set long ago to forever demonstrate to the world that his heart was for the sinner.

* * *

The crowd buzzed as the governor reviewed the crucifixion documents and, with a trembling hand, stamped and sealed them. He handed them to a soldier who would supply them to the centurion in charge of the execution.

The governor turned and regarded The Man one last time. He strained to say something but couldn't find the words. He eventually nodded, turned and went inside.

Chapter 8

The Half-Mile Road

"It's time to get dressed." The soldier met The Man and ripped off his scarlet robe, leaving him standing in front of the crowd in just his bloodied undergarments.

The Man moaned and arched his back as the robe's fibers tore open the cuts on his body.

Additional soldiers brought over his original tunic and forced him into it. His wounds caused dark brown streaks to appear gradually across the tan garment.

The Man teetered as he watched his mother weep for what seemed like an eternity.

Just a few minutes later, another soldier appeared through the double wooden doors with a plaque of scrap wood with a thin rope attached to it. The soldier tied the rope around The Man's neck. Scribbled on the plaque of wood in three different languages was his crime.

The soldiers chained The Man's hands and neck and led him from the courtyard under an archway and to the scourging hall. After the short walk, they released him to the centurion and gave him the crucifixion documents.

"The governor now wants this?" the centurion asked with a raised brow. "We don't normally flog *and* crucify the same criminal."

The soldiers escorting The Man simply nodded. They unshackled him and headed toward the governor's palace.

The centurion ordered his four soldiers to prepare for crucifixion.

One grabbed a basket loaded with a small sledgehammer, some rope, and multiple iron spikes. The three others grabbed thin leather whips.

"Carry your swords as well. From what I understand, the people may grow agitated. We need to be prepared."

They forced him outside the room and down a poorly lit cobblestone hallway to another room.

As The Man peered in, his stomach churned.

Olive wood crossbeams lined the walls. Two soldiers entered and chose one for The Man. Together, they carried the beam outside as the others followed. Once outside, they met a cobblestone road and stopped. Bewilderment swept over them as they gawked at what they saw.

"This is why we have our weapons," one soldier said in a hushed tone to another.

Hordes of people crowded the road like never before.

* * *

The cobblestones lay uneven in the road, tripping anyone forgetting to occasionally glance down. The road wound around buildings, market stands, and housing units, eventually leading its travelers out of the city. Even though the execution site sat only a half-mile away, The Man felt as if the road was endless.

In front of The Man and the centurion's unit stood a sea of people who crammed together on the sides of the road. Although the road was just over ten feet wide, the men never saw more than five feet of its width due to the mass pressing inward. Men, women, and children all packed in. Jews and Gentiles alike bumped shoulders with each other. The rich, the poor, and the slave all gathered close. Some shouted insults, and some wept. Some praised The Father, and some didn't make a sound. People swarmed the half-mile road, covering it from end to end. Nobody wanted to miss the demise of the famous Jew.

The two soldiers tossed the sixty-pound crossbeam to the ground. As loud as the crowd was, the beam's weight thundered as it hit the stone.

"Pick it up," the soldiers said.

The Man obeyed his orders. He bent and put his hands underneath one side of the beam. He noticed how different the rough wood felt compared to the smooth material he was used to working with in his carpentry shop back home. His teeth clenched and his neck muscles strained as he fought to hoist it up. With one end in the air and one still on the ground, The Man bent again and put his shoulder in the beam's center. He struggled to find his balance. Once he did, he inhaled sharply and strained to lift the beam into the air.

His success lasted mere seconds before he lost his balance, and the beam fell behind him. A punishing slap of leather met him across his back.

"You fool, pick it up, I said!"

Exasperated, The Man made another attempt as the soldiers watched. This time, he hugged both arms around the center of the beam and tried to stand with the beam pressed to his face, but it fell again.

"Help him," the centurion said to the soldiers. "We don't have all day."

Two soldiers lifted the beam high into the air and centered the wood on The Man's right shoulder.

His legs shook slightly, but he didn't fall. The Man glanced up and considered the crowd. Even in his hellish situation, he loved each one of them. As he took his first steps through the swarm of people, his heart had no second thoughts. Not once did he entertain the thought of throwing down his beam and revealing through might and power his true identity. He *was* determined to reveal his true identity but chose to do it through weakness and humility.

He toddled by countless faces. In his Divinity, he knew them all personally, even though in his humanity, he recognized none of them. Amid it all, one face caught his attention.

A young boy, no more than ten years old, stood on an elevated ledge. The Man and the boy made eye contact. The boy's parents didn't appear to be nearby, although The Man knew he had a Jewish father who provided well for his family.

He was sure of this because the boy was holding a young lamb in his arms.

That weekend, the boy would be reminded of the gravity of his sin as he watched his father, with the help of local priests, cut the lamb he held in his arms until it bled to death.

The significance of watching The Man traverse the half-mile road that day eluded the young boy. His innocent eyes failed to notice there were actually *two* sacrificial lambs on the street that day—one he held in his arms and one he made eye contact with. Both lambs faced the same fate: death for the removal of sins. One's blood brought limited and temporary relief, like the wrapping of a bandage, while the other brought a deep and sweeping healing once and for all.

* * *

The first half of the half-mile road tortured The Man. Most of the road twisted as it climbed upward through the city. The sun's intensity increased, driving The Man to a nagging thirst.

As he inched up the street, the crowd's demeanor escalated. Many people tried to approach The Man to hurl abuses at him, but they were met with the leather whips from the soldiers. The Man heard wailing from multiple directions as some of his followers were scattered throughout the route. Numerous onlookers extended their arms toward The Man. Some reached aggressively while others did so longingly. The range of emotion felt suffocating.

With each step, The Man's suffering compounded. The scourging hall was horrific, no doubt, but his flogging lasted mere minutes. The Man now faced an anguish that specialized not in intensity but in longevity. His pain was slow, consistent, and unending. There'd be no more pauses to catch his breath. There'd be no more breaks.

He did his best to obey his orders, but in his humanity and physical weakness, he struggled mightily to keep his feet underneath him. Four times in the first quarter mile The Man fell to the ground. Each time, the soldiers met him with leather whips that slapped against his tunic as the crowd yelled.

"Get up you dog!"

"We didn't give you permission to stumble!"

"There'll be no more rest for you!"

"Let's get going, King!"

"Stop putting on a show for the people!"

The centurion grew concerned after watching him fall for the fourth time.

The soldiers placed the beam on the crest of The Man's back to help him balance, but after a few hundred feet, the beam's weight took its toll. Hunched over, The Man frantically tried to find his footing with each step on the stone but eventually tripped and crashed to the ground. He was simply emptied of his energy and had nothing left to give.

The crowd screamed as The Man failed to pick it back up.

The centurion recognized he needed to try something else, so he summoned two soldiers. "He can't continue on his own. Find someone to help him."

The soldiers scanned the crowd for an able-bodied man.

"You there!" one said as he pointed to a tall, well-built, middle-aged Jewish peasant.

The peasant stepped backward, turned and looked behind himself.

"Come here now," the soldier said.

After realizing the soldier was talking to him, the peasant stepped through the crowd and into the open. He licked his lips repeatedly as his eyes darted back and forth.

"Carry this crossbeam," the soldier said.

"S-Sir, I don't know th-this man. I-I haven't seen him before. I haven't done anything wrong . . . Please don't make—"

"I didn't mention any wrongdoing. And I don't care if you're acquainted with him or not. I just told you to carry the beam."

"But p-please! I have two children. I can't be involved in this. I haven't done anything—"

"You haven't done anything wrong *yet,* but, if you refuse to carry this beam, I can assure you that you won't like the consequences."

The peasant said nothing. He lifted his muscular arms behind his head and interlocked his fingers as he took a deep breath. Shifting his weight, he bit his lip as he closed his eyes and quickly shook his head, like a dog trying to rid himself of a flea.

"We'll let you go once we get to the execution site," the centurion said. "You have our word."

The peasant opened his eyes and took another deep breath. Rather than continue to press his luck in refuting the soldier's request, he stepped forward and set the beam squarely on the center of his own back. He assured the soldiers his footing was secure even though his knees wobbled anxiously.

The Man hobbled to the peasant and placed his shoulders underneath the beam and threw his arms over it.

The peasant eyed The Man up close for the first time then read the wooden sign dangling by rope from The Man's neck. His eyes widened as he read The Man's crimes.

The Man peered into the peasant's heart and sensed the dread.

The peasant tried to look away from The Man's distorted figure. "Oh, I d-don't want any part of this," the peasant mumbled as he looked away from The Man. "Why's this happening? I just want to go home . . . I don't want to be here."

The Man's heart went out to the peasant as he saw angst swell in his eyes. "Look at me," The Man murmured to the peasant.

Glancing at The Man and beholding his gruesome figure, the peasant hyperventilated. His eyes darted in every direction as anxiety rose in his throat. He tried to swallow but couldn't.

Then, amid the noise from the crowd, the pressure from the soldiers and the fear growing inside, The Man did something to help the peasant focus; he said the peasant's name.

How The Man knew the peasant's name was a mystery to the soldiers who had stopped to listen. But it was clear he did, for he repeated the name over and over in a nurturing way as the peasant struggled for air.

"It's okay," The Man said to the peasant in a soft, gentle tone. "You're okay. It's okay."

The peasant fixated on The Man's calming gaze. After just a few seconds, his breathing normalized.

"It's okay," The Man said again. "It'll all be over soon."

The peasant nodded. He looked up the road, refocused and composed. His nerves still shook his legs, but he became filled with an unfamiliar kind of peace.

In unison, they trudged up the half-mile road.

* * *

They didn't have much farther to go. Both men had traveled this road several times and knew the city walls loomed. The Man fought to suppress the images that crept to the front of his mind of several hills outside the city where sizable wooden beams were permanently embedded into the earth. Sometimes the beams were empty, and other times they held dying criminals lifted high for all to view.

But even though they were over halfway there and had less than a thousand feet to go, The Man was struggling. Although he no longer shouldered most of the beam's weight, he stumbled along the path. The Man watched the peasant straining under the beam's weight. *Thank you, Father, for providing help.*

In the chaos of his suffering, The Man believed it critical to remain steadfast in his thankfulness.

* * *

The Man suddenly became dizzy. His tongue felt dry and stuck to the roof of his mouth. "I don't . . . feel well," The Man said quietly to the peasant.

The peasant looked over just in time to see the consciousness fall from The Man's trance as he fainted. His arms became limp around the beam, causing the peasant to lose balance. Both men toppled to the ground.

As the soldiers whipped both men, the crowd saw their opportunity to push close. The space the soldiers had created for the men to walk through now dissipated as the screaming mob packed in, shoulder to shoulder. Realizing their mistake, the soldiers turned their whips on the crowd. People several streets away heard shrieking and crying as the centurion barked commands and tried to regain control.

Nobody noticed what wandered to The Man underneath all the pandemonium.

The Man opened his eyes. A warm, tingling sensation flooded his frame as he crawled from his unconsciousness. When his mind composed itself, The Man sat upright and looked around. Confusion overtook him as he was at first unsure of where he was. But the thorny crown and the buzz of the crowd reminded him all too quickly that he was in the middle of his death march.

And then he made eye contact with it.

Beneath the commotion of the soldiers and the crowd stood a lamb. It had accidentally wandered toward The Man during his unconsciousness. It wasn't just any lamb—it was the lamb The Man had seen the young boy holding at the beginning of the road.

The moment didn't last long, but, for a few seconds, The Man and the lamb stared at each other.

The boy who owned the lamb frantically pushed through, searching for his lost animal. He swooped in and attempted to grab his animal when the soldier kicked him over.

"Get out of here, you Jew!"

The boy sat on the street with tears streaking his face. His lamb ran away again, but the boy didn't move.

The soldier grabbed the boy's shirt and lifted him. "Didn't you hear what I just said?"

"I'm sorry," the boy said through tears, "b-but I have—"

"The only thing you have to do is leave!"

The boy sobbed as the soldier threw him to the ground.

"I said, get—"

"*Enough*," said an unfamiliar voice. It was The Man.

The soldier looked behind him and saw The Man standing and staring at him.

The soldier started toward The Man. "How dare you tell—"

"I said *enough*," The Man said as he lifted his palm toward the soldier.

The soldier stopped dead in his tracks. He wouldn't stand to have a Jew order him around, let alone a criminal. But he sensed something different, perhaps strangely authoritative, in The Man's demeanor that didn't permit the soldier to finish his thought or even step closer.

Other than a few crying women, silence filled the street.

"Leave the boy alone. Punish me if you want . . . but be done with the child."

The soldier stood dumbfounded and at a loss for words. He tried to speak, but his mouth could only open and shut.

The Man turned and regarded the sobbing women in the crowd. "Daughters of the capital, don't cry for me! Cry for yourselves and for your children."

The soldiers started to move in on The Man to force him along, but the centurion motioned for them to pause. The centurion squinted and glued his gaze to The Man, as if the centurion believed the Jew might have something important for everyone to hear.

"Listen to me!" The Man said to the women.

Some of them hushed and stifled their gasping to hear his words.

"Listen," The Man said painfully but in a more conversational tone. He found himself out of breath the longer he talked. "The days are . . . coming when they'll say, 'Those who've . . . never had children are happy. Those whose bodies have never given birth are . . . happy. Those who've never fed babies are happy.'" The Man clearly wanted to say more, but his exhaustion made conversation difficult. He paused to catch his breath. "They'll begin to say to the mountains, 'Fall on us.' They'll say . . . to the hills, 'Cover us.' If they do these things to a . . . green tree, what will they do when it's dry?"

An eerie silence lay steadily on the street as the people pondered what The Man meant.

After a few moments of silence, a soldier finally stepped in. "That was a lovely speech," the soldier said sarcastically as he approached The Man. "Now it's time to get back to work, don't you think?"

The peasant bent and forced the beam into the air as The Man took his place under it.

The soldiers pushed the people backward to create space for the men to walk. As they went, the shouting and the wailing resumed.

Right as they reached the top of a hill, The Man peered backward and caught one final glimpse of the boy. He kissed his lamb as he held the creature in his arms.

* * *

Time crawled by as midday turned to afternoon. With each step, The Man inched his way to his final destination.

The Man didn't appear to be the same after he had fainted. Trudging up the remainder of the road, the peasant saw The Man couldn't shake the ominous daze plastered to his face. As he walked, the peasant kept a close eye on The Man so he could help him if he fell.

For the first time since shouldering the crossbeam with The Man, the peasant allowed his eyes to fully comprehend The Man's wounds. The Man's right eye couldn't open. Bruises and lacerations covered his body. Blood and sweat soaked through his tunic and stuck to his skin. The peasant finally noticed the thorny vine digging into The Man's skull; the peasant had missed it earlier because blood caked The Man's forehead.

Suddenly, the peasant felt a spark of panic resurge as his stomach felt uneasy. *What did this man do to deserve this?* His mind started down the rabbit trail. Maybe he had been caught trying to overthrow the government. Perhaps he had been caught assisting other criminals. It was possible The Man was some type of slave who had continually showed contempt toward his Roman master. Or maybe he was a murderer.

The thought that the peasant was possibly walking with a murderer so wicked that Rome felt it necessary to completely obliterate him unnerved the peasant.

Then the peasant's Jewish mind returned to the Divine and how egregious The Man's sins must have been in The Father's eyes. The peasant shuttered at the thought of how intense The Father's wrath would burn against The Man.

* * *

Of course, The Father's wrath wouldn't burn against The Man. How could it? The Man was the definition of good and perfect.

But the peasant, like the rest of humanity, assumed The Father's natural disposition concerning people bent toward wrath due to their sinful nature. Humanity always supposed it was their job, through their religious efforts, to change The Father's mind about themselves. For some, this notion eventually evolved into the idea that it was the *messiah's* job to change The Father's mind about people. But neither could be further from the truth. The Father's heart, soul, and mind had always been *for* his children. Nothing would change that.

Yes, The Man was The Father's promised messiah. But it wasn't his job to change The Father's mind about people. That wasn't why he came.

He hadn't come to change The Father's mind about people but rather he had come to change people's minds about The Father. He had come to show them The Father's mind was unchangeable regarding his children, and *that was a good thing*. He hoped they wouldn't view The Father any longer as a distant deity who demanded to be pleased through religious ceremony and activity. The Man longed to reveal that The Father was much kinder than humanity originally presumed, and he wasn't demanding people to please him but inviting them to come closer. The Man yearned to convince people that the Divine really was a good father who'd settle for nothing less than bringing his wayward children home so he could celebrate who they really are.

* * *

They saw the city walls and the gate that would lead them outside the capital. Even though the end of the road was near, the crowd grew. More people pushed closer despite the soldiers' best efforts to ward them off. Most shouted a variety of things toward The Man and the soldiers.

"Show us a miracle and free yourself so we might believe!"

"You've disgraced our nation!

"A cross suits you perfectly!"

"Teacher, what should we do?"

"Where are your disciples now?"

"Please don't take him! Please!"

"If you execute him, we'll riot!"

"Whip him some more!"

"Injustice!"

The Man's presence completely divided the people. It saddened him to watch many of the people he loved spew vile words. The Father had given them all working tongues to uplift each other as they praised him, but none of them chose to do so that day.

And the violence.

If their speech saddened The Man, their violence repulsed him.

Violence caused a particularly agonizing ache in The Father's heart. Violence was mankind's uncanny ability to tear down the physical form of their own kind because they couldn't stand to admit that, deep down, their enemy bore the resemblance of The Father to the same degree they did. Violence was such an aggressive form of pride that it never cared to hide its ugly face. Violence was hatred in action.

In the past twelve hours, violence had surrounded The Man like never before. He had witnessed violence in the orchard and in the home of the high priest. He had suffered from it at the hands of the regional king and the governor's minions. He had writhed underneath its weight in the scourging hall and had watched it enacted on an innocent boy trying to collect his lamb.

Violence sickened The Man. It needed to be taken care of and dealt with. It needed to be conquered.

The Man knew a violent hate could only be conquered by a nonviolent love.

Although the violence saddened him, he sensed love brooding deep from within his being ready to burst forth and overcome.

Yes, as The Man walked with the beam on his back, he walked full of sorrow *and* love.

* * *

The stones in the road disappeared as The Man felt firm dirt underneath his feet. The path stretched no more than fifty feet before it curved around a large hill on the right. Many people left the path and started up the hill. As they quieted, The Man heard two faint, bone-chilling sounds—hammering; erratic, thundering hammering—and after every thud of the hammer: prolonged blood-curdling screams.

The path curved around the hill and led The Man toward the top.

Over a hundred individuals gathered at the top of the hill in a semi-circled cluster. More people trickled up and joined them. Once at the top, their faces reflected the brutality their eyes absorbed.

In front of the semi-circle, three large wooden beams rose from the ground, standing about thirteen feet high with vertical slots cut into their tops. The left beam was already completed; a crossbeam was already dropped into the vertical slot. Bleeding on the cross hung a criminal crucified about ten minutes before The Man arrived. The criminal hung unconscious from the pain. Above his head was a sign fastened to his cross that explained his crime—theft.

A second criminal was sprawled on the ground in front of the crowd. His beam lay underneath his back with his arms already nailed to the wood. Heavy breathing escaped through his gnashed teeth as he tried to remain still. After discussing their strategy, a handful of Roman soldiers hoisted him into the air, fastened the beams together and finished his crucifixion. The crowd found the criminal's screams awful to hear as soldiers hammered the criminal's feet to the vertical beam.

The Man shambled through the semi-circle as the soldiers commanded the people to back away. He and the peasant let the beam fall to the ground. He watched as the soldiers sorted through the nails in their basket.

"Oh, Father," The Man said as he looked skyward, "please strengthen me." He eyed the peasant as he tried to stifle his tears. Pinching his face inward, The Man's quivering lip vibrated as he choked for air. The Man looked helpless, like a young boy overcome with sadness, needing to simply be held by his mother.

The centurion approached them both. "Let's get this over with."

Chapter 9

The Man was Lifted Up

THIS WAS IT.

The Man had been born for this moment. The Bread of Life was about to die. Prepared to lay his life down so others may take theirs up, he was set to reunite people back to The Father, launching a new age in motion.

All Creation leaned in as it watched in agonizing anticipation.

* * *

"Please, Father," The Man said, "be with me."

The soldiers grabbed The Man's arms and led him to the right side of his beam laying on the ground.

"Please . . . *be with me.*"

"Give it to him," the centurion said to a soldier.

The soldier retrieved a small brown pouch of liquid from the basket. He opened it on his way back and poured the contents in a cup and held it out to The Man. "Drink."

The Man looked in the cup and smelled the sharp aroma of alcohol—wine mixed with myrrh. The Roman soldiers sometimes offered this concoction to their crucified criminals. The practice was more practical than merciful. If the crucifixion victims drank, they'd be slightly numbed and more relaxed, making the jobs of the crucifiers easier.

The Man considered the drink. A part of him desired to consume it, but another part of him knew he ought not to. It wasn't to prove his toughness. It wasn't to defy Rome in some way before he died. He believed to do what he was determined to do, he must fully deny the Romans' cup so he might fully accept The Father's. The Romans' cup offered an escape from the suffering and sorrow set before him. The Father's cup embraced the worst of suffering to unleash the best of love.

The Man shook his head at the soldier.

"You don't want the drink?" the soldier asked.

He shook his head again.

"Please drink it," the centurion said. "It'll make this easier."

The Man remained still.

The centurion considered whether he'd force The Man to drink the alcohol.

The crowd failed to notice this interaction, as they were fixated on the two crucified criminals.

"I'd really prefer—"

"Haven't you heard why I've come?" The Man asked in a high-pitched voice full of desperation, and his chin trembled. "I haven't come to live a lavish life like the one you live. I haven't come to be treated like royalty."

"Obviously," one soldier said with a snicker.

The Man considered the soldier and loved him. "I haven't come to be served but to serve." The Man's voice shook. "And it's on this hill where I'll give my life in exchange for many."

The centurion weighed The Man's words.

"Thank you, but I can't accept your drink."

The peasant overheard him and grew troubled. Even though they had barely talked, he felt like he had come to know The Man as they had walked along the half-mile road. No one observed The Man's sorrow and suffering in a more personal way than he did. He couldn't believe The Man wanted more. "Take their offering," the peasant said as he came close. "You've had enough today."

"Go away!" a soldier said as he shoved the peasant.

"Just accept it!" the peasant said to The Man as he struggled with the soldier. "Don't embrace . . . more pain than you have to."

The Man once again called the peasant's name.

The soldier released the peasant, allowing him to approach The Man one last time.

"You don't have to—"

"I do."

The peasant's jaw hung low. He attempted to find words to say but failed.

Moved at the sight of the growing compassion swelling inside the peasant, The Man cried. "I must do this," he said through tears. "There's . . . There's . . . no other way. I must . . . *I must* drink this cup of suffering." Then

The Man explained to the peasant he wasn't just doing this for The Father but also for the peasant's wife and his two sons.

The peasant wept as The Man miraculously spoke each of their names.

"It's only by my wounds that they'll be healed of theirs."

At once, the unconscious criminal hanging on his cross awoke to his horrifying reality. His relentless screams broke the bittersweet moment between The Man and the peasant and gave the soldiers their excuse to interrupt the exchange.

Two soldiers slipped behind The Man, loosened his tunic and removed it from his back.

He moaned as the fibers of the cloth aggravated his open lesions.

They tossed the garment aside, along with the piece of wood the governor had tied around his neck, leaving him standing in just a loincloth and wearing his crown of thorns.

A soldier gave him a command that would echo throughout eternity. "Lie down."

* * *

I'm the Good Shepherd, The Man thought. The Man had anticipated this moment. He had predicted he'd eventually lay down his life, like a true shepherd would for his sheep. He had taught for years about the significant difference between a good shepherd and someone who was only hired to care for sheep. He had witnessed the distinction himself. A hired hand was someone who was brought in to watch the sheep even though they didn't know the sheep. Because they didn't know the sheep, they never went above and beyond. They would do the bare minimum to ensure they got paid at the end of the day. They cared about the sheep's wellbeing only because they cared about their own wellbeing.

But a true shepherd was different, The Man had always explained. The real shepherd of a flock wasn't in the business for his own rewards. He was in it because he loved the sheep. He knew all their names and spent time with them. He slept next to them. He only wanted the best pastures for them. He ushered them into the sheep pen and *laid down* across the gate opening so any predator who tried to harm the sheep must deal with him first. The real shepherd was *good*, because he always put the sheep's wellbeing over his own wellbeing.

"I am the Good Shepherd," The Man said, as he had to countless people over the past few years. "And the Good Shepherd lays down his life for the sheep."

* * *

The crowd turned and watched The Man tremble as he bent onto his hands and knees. As the two crucified criminals screamed, The Man's shaky voice muttered the same thing over and over through tears. "I am . . . the Good . . . Shepherd." The Man turned and lay on the ground with his back propped against the beam. He now wailed and extended his arms across the beam as soldiers took rope and secured both wrists to the wood. The Man felt a dreadful darkness creep over him, like an evil shadow he couldn't escape. His shoulders felt heavy and burdened, as if Evil Itself was entering him. "*Father*! *Oh, Father*!"

Many in the crowd covered their eyes and ears.

As the peasant watched, he joined The Man in crying.

Three soldiers proceeded to lay across The Man, using their own weight to restrain him. One lay across his legs, one across his chest, and one across his left arm. The last soldier approached with a nail and a sledge.

"I am . . . the . . . Good . . . Sh-Shepherd," The Man said as he sobbed bitterly.

The crowd, boisterously loud ten minutes earlier, fell strangely silent.

The soldier took his sledge in his right hand and wound it through the air a few times to loosen his shoulder. He knelt and pressed the point of the nail in the middle of The Man's left hand between the bones of his palm. He glanced up at the centurion and waited for his approval.

The centurion nodded.

All Creation held its breath in holy horror.

The soldier lifted his sledge high and drove it onto the nail head with all the force he could muster.

The nail went clean through The Man's hand and cut into the wood beneath. The Man tried to scream but was silenced as the pain choked him into submission.

The soldier swung again and drove the nail deeper. The body of the nail widened the deeper it went. Blood spurted from The Man's hand onto the soldier's garment.

The Man thrashed. His head banged against the top part of the beam. As a stabbing, hot sensation darted up his arm into his shoulder, the soldier swung on the nail seven more times, bringing the nail head even with the skin on the palm. The Man knew unconsciousness would come soon.

The soldier hit the nail two more times, driving the head of the nail lower than the skin itself.

The Man's teeth clamped so hard he thought he might break them. Agony paralyzed him. He remained mute as his blue and purple fingers twitched erratically. His vision blurred.

The soldier laying on his left arm stood and lay on his right.

The soldier with the sledge grabbed another nail, moved down the beam and dropped to both knees.

The centurion strolled to The Man's left hand and inspected it. After a few seconds, he stood back and nodded in approval toward the soldier.

The soldier aimed the nail in the middle of The Man's right palm and swung down, shooting the nail through The Man's hand.

The crowd clenched their fists as their muscles tightened in agitation.

The initial swing on the right side jolted The Man from his temporary paralysis. The Man released a choppy scream as the sledge swung again. "*Father*!" He cried as he stared into the blue sky. "Father!"

The nail opened The Man's hand wider with each swing. The crowd groaned in unison.

"They . . . d-d-don't know," The Man said as he sobbed. "They . . . don't . . . know."

The hammering persisted.

"Forgive them, Father. Forgive them . . . because . . . they don't know what . . . they're doing."

The crowd grew uneasy as they listened to The Man's heartfelt pleas on behalf of his crucifiers.

The peasant dropped to his knees and put his hands over his head.

An overwhelming and terrible darkness engulfed The Man. He found this dark, new spiritual sensation more revolting than his physical pain. He looked up at the soldier who hammered the nail head deep into his palm. "Forgive him," The Man said softly through gritted teeth. "He doesn't know, Father. He just doesn't know."

* * *

The Man lay bleeding on the ground for a couple minutes as the soldiers strategized their next step. No one checked on him or attended to him. He dared not move. If he did, scorching pain would fill his arms and shoulders. As he waited, he prayed for The Father to strengthen him to finish his work.

"Time to get up," one of the soldiers said.

Two soldiers approached him, squatted and wedged their hands underneath the beam. "We're going to lift this up. You need to use your stomach to help you sit up when we do," they said. "Does that make sense?"

The Man said nothing.

They hoisted the beam as level as possible, three feet into the air, forcing The Man to sit upright.

The Man's face contorted as his palms strained against the nails.

Two more soldiers wrapped their arms around The Man's torso.

"Altogether, now," the centurion said.

At once, the soldiers raised The Man to his feet. Although the soldiers were assisting him, the weight of the beam across his shoulders felt like it might break his upper back—a sensation that nauseated The Man. The soldiers put their shoulders underneath the beam to ensure The Man remained upright. If he fell, the force from the drop could cause the nails to rip through the top part of his palms and ruin their work. They walked in unison toward the barren middle beam.

"Steady," the centurion said.

As The Man looked up, he saw two crucified criminals. Wooden signs hung above their heads explaining their crimes. The Man's vertical beam rose from the ground between the two criminals. His beam was by no means his own personal beam. Many victims had hung on the beam before The Man and more would hang on it after him. Crucifixion had proved so effective at sending messages that the Romans crucified countless people. Therefore, they reused the beams.

Two wooden ladders rested on both sides of the beam. The basket of nails and the sledge sat underneath the left ladder. Once at the foot of the beam, the soldiers forced The Man to turn his back toward it.

The centurion faced The Man. "We're going to lift the beam across your back above the vertical beam and let it fall into the slot. We'll support your weight as we do. It's crucial you don't fight us in doing this. If you do, we might drop you. You don't want that, do you? That'd cause much unnecessary pain. Do you understand?"

The Man nodded.

The centurion stepped backward.

One soldier knelt and clutched The Man's knees. "I've got him."

"Proceed," the centurion said.

The two soldiers holding the horizontal beam on top of their shoulders climbed the ladders leaning against the vertical beam. Careful not to fall, they took sluggish steps in unison with each other as the ladders groaned under their weight. As they climbed, they hoisted the horizontal beam above The Man's head. The soldier around The Man's knees also elevated The Man into the air.

With each movement and jerk, The Man winced in pain. Even though the soldier around his knees did his best to support The Man's bulk, the weight held in The Man's palms grew heavier the higher he went.

The soldiers stepped to the top of the ladder.

"At my word," one said to another. "*Now!*"

The soldiers extended their arms and lifted The Man as high as possible as his horizontal beam hovered above the slot at the top of the vertical beam. They quickly lowered the horizontal beam into the groove. It eventually dropped into the slot with a jolting thud, forcing a scream from The Man as an unfamiliar kind of pain in his upper back overcame him. The soldiers scurried down the ladders. Time wasn't their friend; if they didn't finish the crucifixion soon, The Man's weight held entirely in his hands might cause the nails to rip through.

Once on the ground, the two soldiers adjusted their ladders and leaned them against the horizontal beam. They climbed halfway and grabbed The Man around the waist. With a heave, they lifted and pinned him against the vertical beam.

The crowd stirred as they watched the scene unfold.

"Hustle!" the centurion said.

The two other soldiers swooped in and grabbed the sledge and two nails. They took The Man's left foot and raised it a dozen inches from where it dangled and placed his heel flush against the front of the beam. A soldier pressed his weight into The Man's ankle to ensure it wouldn't move. The other took a nail and placed the point against the top of The Man's foot. With one powerful strike, he drove the nail through The Man's foot.

Due to the pooling in his feet, blood surged from The Man's new wound, streaming down the wood. As the soldier drove the nail into the beam, The Man descended deeper into spiritual blackness. Twelve strikes later, the head of the nail was planted firmly into the flesh of The Man's foot. His teeth gnashed.

"Quickly," the centurion urged them. "Hustle now!"

The soldiers secured The Man's right foot and held the heel flush against the beam next to his left foot. They let go momentarily and dried off their hands on their clothing to ensure a firm grip and grabbed him again. They collected the sledge and nail and took aim.

With each blow, the nail wedged itself tighter between the bones of The Man's right foot. He wailed as his head swung back and forth, knocking against the wood.

Finally, the nail was planted deep in the wood.

"Done," the soldier said, facing the centurion.

The centurion swept in to examine their work. Pleased, he addressed the soldiers on the ladder. "Slowly release."

They released their grip on The Man.

The cross creaked under The Man's weight as he dropped into his final position. Pain unnervingly knifed through his body. Struggling to breathe as his upper back flexed and pushed against his lungs, he took short half-hearted breaths. His attempts to find a new position only induced more agony. He felt sure the nails would rip through his hands—*sure of it.* His eyes, blinking hard and often to swat away the blood dripping down his forehead, darted back and forth to his palms, waiting for it to happen.

The soldiers stepped backward to admire their work.

Both criminals ceased their cries.

No one in the crowd spoke.

A haunting silence coated the hill as an inappropriately pleasant breeze swept through the people.

The Man's mouth moved as his eyes closed. In the silence, only the soldiers at the foot of the cross heard him murmur, "Forgive them, Father." His quiet words struggled to pierce through the wind. "They . . . don't know w-what they've . . . done."

As he whispered, the vertical beam turned dark red. The blood ran down the cross and puddled on the ground.

* * *

The soldiers didn't realize it, but they were witnessing the beginning of the greatest act of intercession the world would ever see. As The Man hung, he implored The Father to grant them forgiveness.

This was nothing new. The Man had pleaded to The Father many times to forgive his enemies. He'd even claimed to personally forgive numerous people himself throughout his life. But this time was different, for it wasn't just his words that spoke to The Father.

His blood was speaking too.

Yes, as his blood trickled down the cross, it spoke a convincing word to The Father. The Man's blood immediately interceded on behalf of all people—past, present, and future. His blood whispered in The Father's ear a new language that no priest ever could. As The Father listened, it boldly proclaimed a new covenant for The Father's children to live from. No longer would they be defined by sin; now they'd be defined by sacrifice—a Divine sacrifice of suffering love.

Although the hilltop was quiet, The Man's blood lifted an echo of reconciliation toward Heaven.

* * *

"Sir," a soldier said as he approached the centurion, "we forgot something." The soldier presented the wooden plaque that had hung around The Man's neck from a rope as he had walked the half-mile road. On it was written The Man's crime in three different languages.

The centurion cursed. "It has to be done right." He snapped his head toward the crosses and pointed. "Why didn't you attach it when you climbed the ladder?"

"We must've forgotten about it in the—"

"I don't want your excuses. I want it hung!"

The soldiers eyed each other.

"*Now!*"

Startled at the sternness in the centurion's voice, the soldier dropped the sign. He reached for the rope as the other soldiers snatched the ladder and placed it against the side of The Man's cross. Plaque in hand, the soldier grabbed the sledge and a nail from the basket and climbed the ladder.

Four steps up, his eyes met The Man's.

The Man's head fell to the left as he made eye contact with the soldier. The Man's entire face clenched as he tried to be still. Short, shallow breaths forced their way from his throat.

The soldier's eyes became trapped by The Man's. He paused.

The Man knew the soldier's heart; he knew the soldier's heart was filling with an odd sensation, like he was naked. No—*exposed.* A sense of wrongness overwhelmed the soldier and brought him to a halt. The soldier longed to look away but couldn't.

"Hustle!" the centurion said.

The soldier shook his head as he forced his gaze away and climbed two more steps. He nailed the sign to the highest part of the vertical beam, about a foot above The Man's head. He descended the ladder and jumped off with three steps to go. He took the ladder and strode from the cross. He threw it down at the back of the crowd and returned to his fellow soldiers. What he saw next upset him. He watched the three men crucified justly for their crimes against Rome, but the middle one was strangely different from the two on either side of him. The soldier stared for minutes, attempting to figure out why.

Sure, The Man was in worse condition than the other two. He was bleeding more. He was also responding to his crucifixion more . . . *submissively.* But those things weren't what separated The Man from the other two.

And then he saw it.

The soldier's eyes finally connected the dots that his subconscious had already done but hadn't yet communicated to the rest of his mind.

The Man was wearing a crown. And not just any crown—*a crown of thorns.*

The soldier would never in his life explain why that crown bothered him so much. The thorny vine hadn't bothered him hours earlier when he had helped weave it together and had fixed it to The Man's skull. He and his unit had mocked plenty of their crucified subjects. That was, in a way, part of their job, after all. Words wouldn't come together to make sense of why the crown now seemed so . . . *disturbing.* Intensely focused, the soldier couldn't keep his eyes from darting back and forth from the thorny crown to the sign above The Man's head.

For it was above The Man's head, in three different languages, that the soldier had nailed a plaque of wood declaring who was really on the cross.

The sign read: Jesus, King of the Jews.

* * *

The only things that would ever matter from that point forward could be traced to the name inscribed on the plaque of wood nailed to The Man's cross.

It was his name.

It was his name that would forever strike fear in The Accuser's heart. It was his name that would always be associated with victory. It was his name that would make the demons flee.

The Alpha and Omega. The Lion of Judah. The Mighty One.

It was his name that would bring comfort to the brokenhearted. It was his name that would give hope to the hopeless. It was his name that would unite all languages and cultures across the globe.

The Prince of Peace. The Wonderful Counselor. Immanuel.

It was his name that would inspire faith in fickle hearts. It was his name that people would look to when they scraped rock bottom. It was his name that would shine a bright light in the darkest of places.

The Author of Salvation. Redeemer. The Champion of Heaven.

It was his name that would bring healing to the nations. It was his name that would forever be found worthy of breaking the seal and opening the scroll. And it was only his name that would hold the power to make mankind right with The Father.

The Way. The Truth. The Life.

Messiah. Savior.

The King of Kings. The Lord of Lords.

It was his name that stood above all other names.

And his name was Jesus.

* * *

More people lumbered up the hill.

"Please," the criminal on the left said as he struggled for air. "Please let . . . me . . . down. Please."

The Man gasped as he labored to breathe. He tried to put himself in a different position in the hopes it'd bring him relief, but with each movement, the pain just shifted. All three crucified men cramped and grew nauseated.

Even though most on the hill believed they were looking at society's scum, the mood was still somber. After a few minutes of silence, the soldiers noticed something of interest.

A group of about twenty Jewish men wearing elaborate robes sauntered to the top of the hill to inspect what was transpiring. They pushed through the crowd toward the front. The soldiers knew what group these men belonged to, as the centurion recognized their leader—the high priest. He brought a few of his men to confirm The Man's death.

One soldier approached the group with a smirk. "Ah, our Jewish friends! Have you come to pay homage to your king?"

The high priest ignored the soldier.

The crowd turned from the crosses to watch the interaction.

"Well, aren't you going to bow before your king?"

The high priest didn't even acknowledge the soldier. His eyes remained glued to The Man.

"Don't you see his crown?" The soldier pointed and laughed. "The sign *clearly* says he's your king. You're all Jews, correct? Then why won't you bow? He's the King of the Jews!"

The other soldiers laughed and moved closer. Anxiety bubbled as the tension tightened.

"Bow to your king!" the soldier said as he met one of the priests eye to eye.

The priests continued to ignore.

"Do you think you're too good to bow before the king? Or have you forgotten how? How about I show you?" Laughing, the soldier grabbed the priest in front of him and forced him to his knees. He attempted to take the priest's hands and extend them in an act of worship.

"Enough!" the centurion interrupted.

"I'm just trying to help these filthy Jews learn how to honor their king." The soldier returned to the crosses and faced the crowd. "Why won't you all bow before your king? Why won't you show him the proper respect he deserves?"

The three other soldiers howled.

The rest of the Jews on the top of the hill avoided eye contact with any of the Romans.

"I'll tell you why! You don't understand how to bow before a king, because you don't have a king, because *you're a pathetic people*!" The soldier's smirk left his face, leaving behind a nasty snarl and flaring nostrils. "Your king isn't Jewish. He's Roman and always will be! You people don't know how to survive in the real world, because you live in your religious fantasies. What god will save you now?" He pointed to the middle cross as his tone lowered ominously. "What god will save you when it's your turn to hang on a cross?"

Silence.

"Let's show them how it's done," the soldier said to his comrades as he turned. He bowed before the cross with extended hands and mocked The Man. "Oh, mighty king!" he said as the others giggled. "You sit high above us on your wooden throne! Your crown is covered with splendor, and all your subjects adore you!"

The soldiers roared with laughter.

The centurion stood with a blank expression as he let them have their fun.

One of the criminals smirked.

The soldiers then took The Man's clothes and divided the garments between themselves, boasting their delight to walk away with a souvenir to remember the special day. They made a game out of who got what as they cast lots for the best pieces.

All the while, The Man's blood flowed down his cross.

* * *

They mocked him for his kingship and made fun of his crown.

And it was true; The Man wasn't just a king.

He was the King of Kings. His crown and his title weren't ironic at all. They were fitting for what The Man, fully Divine, was doing.

As his blood ran down, he revealed to the world he truly was the King of Sorrow and Suffering. By doing this, he made a way for The Father to have complete access to the hearts of those *defined* by sorrow and suffering. The King of Sorrow and Suffering was paving a road that allowed The Father entrance to a world marked by sorrow and suffering.

The road was paved by The Man's blood and was marked by his wounds.

* * *

An hour passed.

The three crucified men fell deeper into their anguish.

The soldiers packed up their items and sat to the side of the crosses to ensure no one tried to rescue the men.

The priests ordered for servants to fetch them water and food, as they planned to watch in comfort.

People came and went. Their responses to The Man on the cross differed wildly. Some just stared. Some wept loudly, others quietly. Some hurled insults at him. Some flung clogs of dirt. Some spat on him, and some worshiped him.

But nobody's heart broke quite like the woman who eventually climbed the hill—his mother.

The disciple and the three other women joined her.

Paralyzed by the news her son was to be crucified, she had found herself unable to follow him along the half-mile road. After more than an hour of weeping outside the governor's mansion, she had composed herself and had gone to find her son. Nothing could've prepared her for what she saw. The sight of the nail heads embedded in her son's hands and feet churned her stomach. Her heart broke as she watched her son struggle to breathe, spewing blood through his clenched teeth. She sobbed as she ran through the crowd toward her son.

At the foot of his cross, she wiped the blood off his feet. She quietly repeated her son's name as she tried to console him. "What have they done to you?" she asked through tears.

The disciple held her as she wailed.

The three women came close.

Realizing the woman was his mother, the crowd quieted.

Bitter tears fell from her eyes for over five minutes.

One soldier grew irritated that the woman was ruining the mood. Instead of heaping shame on the criminals, she was turning this crucifixion into an emotionally charged goodbye. He couldn't allow sympathy to sprout in the heart of the crowd. He got up from the ground and met the mother. "Listen, Jew! Back away from—"

"This is *her son*!" the disciple said as he whipped around. "Don't you dare take this away from her!"

The women got between the mother and the soldier and cursed him.

"I couldn't care less!" the soldier said as spit flew from his mouth. "Step away from the criminals!"

"Please, sir," the disciple said. "Please don't—"

But the struggle began. The three women placed their hands on the soldier and shoved him backward. The onlookers moved in along with the other soldiers. People roared like thunder. Three soldiers drew swords and forced the crowd backward. The three women backed down as the disciple turned his back toward the mother to protect her.

"I said that's enough!" The soldier pushed aside the disciple and grabbed the mother. He started driving her away from the cross.

"*No*!" she said as she thrashed. The mother tripped over a rock and fell.

The crowd grew more disorderly.

The centurion saw things were getting out of hand.

Out of nowhere, the peasant ran toward the mother and threw his arms around her. He'd never seen her in his entire life but felt like, in a bizarre way, he owed it to her. "Make them stop!" he said to the centurion. "Enough is enough!"

The crowd roared and stirred up dust.

The soldier yelled at the mother.

The peasant, visibly growing upset, shouted back.

The passion covering the hilltop became denser as each second passed.

"Stop!" the centurion said. "Enough!"

Some onlookers hushed while others continued.

"*I said enough*!"

The soldier backed away.

The mother lay on the ground as the peasant held her, both sobbing as they rocked back and forth.

For a few moments, no one spoke. The crowd watched the mother and the peasant—strangers before but now brought together through The Man's final hours—cry together.

Eventually, the peasant and the centurion locked eyes in a raw gaze. Both longed to leave but knew they couldn't. As the peasant sobbed, the centurion quickly found himself at a loss for words. His breathing increased as his eyes swelled. He clenched his jaw to control his feelings.

The Man saw the centurion's emotions swirling inside. Normally, the centurion was steady and unmoved. He had to be for this job. But something about that morning had set him off and troubled his heart. He couldn't sense if it was good or bad, but he knew he'd never felt this stirring before.

The peasant broke the gaze and fixed his eyes upward at The Man.

The centurion followed suit.

As they gazed upon the King of the Jews, their hearts burned.

The Man was gradually transforming them as he hung on his cross.

Chapter 10

The Horror and the Wonder

A COUPLE HOURS PASSED. The sun climbed to the highest point in the sky, signifying the end of morning and the arrival of afternoon.

The Man lost track of time. How long had he been hanging on his cross? Was nightfall approaching, or was there plenty of daylight left? In his humanity, he was unsure. The longer he hung on his cross, the more he couldn't think straight.

His heart struggled to move blood throughout his frame. The nauseating feeling of the lack of blood in his body repulsed him. With each beat, blood leaked through his many open wounds. An ominously dark black and blue color streaked from each nail across his hands and feet.

The Man felt dizzy. He'd vomited once already and feared he might do so again. His stomach also churned painfully. The Man grasped for his dwindling dignity but forfeited it as he lost control of his bowels. Worst of all, the spiritual darkness that engulfed him drowned his ability to feel The Father's presence.

The Man was near the end.

* * *

The crowd remained atop the hill. If anything, more people had arrived. Some stood their distance and watched. Others mourned. Others made fun of the criminals. Many brought their lunch and camped on the hill to see what would happen.

The Man's mother, the disciple, and the three women were propped against a boulder. The mother stared silently skyward as tears rolled down her cheeks.

The group of about twenty councilmen also had found a spot to camp. Servants brought them food and drink as they relaxed. Most of them sat on the ground, but the high priest had ordered a small table with four chairs on which he and his inner circle could recline.

The centurion and his unit relaxed underneath the crosses just off to the left. They too had slaves bring water and towels so they could wash. They spoke casually as they enjoyed the pleasant breeze.

"The allegiance of his followers is unlike anything I've ever seen," the centurion said to the soldiers.

They all watched a family of six approach The Man's cross. The father prayed as the mother bent over to worship. The two older children cried as the two younger ones simply watched.

"It's pathetic," one soldier said.

"Pathetic?" the centurion asked. "Not even the emperor's followers act like this."

"Yes, pathetic—the Jew's a scam . . . a hoax."

The centurion didn't respond as he watched the family.

"Yeah," another soldier chimed in. "If he truly was a king, his followers would retaliate and stand up for him. But he's a Northerner from a no-name town. He's a laborer hiding his peasant ways through gifted speeches. He's no king. And, if he's no king, then he's scamming all these people."

The centurion remained silent.

"You know he's a hoax, right?" the first soldier inquired.

The centurion looked at the two soldiers then up at the three crosses. "I've overseen hundreds and hundreds of crucifixions. Sure, their families come and mourn. Sometimes even a slight crowd shows up. But nothing like this. This is just . . . *different*."

The soldier's shoulders drooped as his head slumped backward. He let out a dramatic sigh. "Don't tell me you're falling for his tricks!"

"I'm not falling for anything, I just—"

"Look at these people!" the soldier said in frustration. "All these people who've given their allegiance to this man . . . they're fools! In their stupidity, they worship and adore a man who easily could've avoided this. All he had to do was say he wasn't a king, but he couldn't do it!" The soldier pointed up at the middle cross. "The Man brought this upon himself. He's a fool worshiped by fools."

"I understand—"

"Do you? Because it appears you need help seeing things for the way they are."

The other soldiers chuckled.

The soldier relaxed and bit his lip. "I'm sorry for speaking sharply to you, sir," the soldier said with sincerity. "Forgive me if I've spoken out of line."

The centurion shrugged.

"But let me ask you a question." The soldier stood and pointed again to the middle cross. "If he's a king worthy of worship, why's he up there?"

The centurion looked up and considered the question.

"Don't fall for their stupidity. Don't give consideration to their foolishness."

* * *

Foolishness. The soldier couldn't see what The Man was doing. All the soldier saw was a weak lowlife who claimed to be a king dying a slave's death.

What a fool, the soldier thought. *A truly powerful king would never be subject to such a pitiful fate.* The soldier's spiritual blindness was nothing new.

For the rest of history, mankind everywhere would fall into the trap of looking upon The Man's cross, just like the soldier, and failing to see what was really happening.

The Man claimed to be doing The Father's will by suffering and dying on a cross.

To the soldier, this seemed utterly foolish. But in the eyes of The Father, The Man's cross radiated with Divine wisdom. As The Man died, he took the wisdom of men and turned it on its head.

For on that day on top of that hill, The Man redefined power.

The King of Sorrow and Suffering wouldn't, *couldn't,* be worshiped and embraced by people who were chasing the powers of the world—fame, riches, authority—for their own narcissistic gain. The Man would forever bid his followers to relinquish their selfish pursuits of worldly power and take up a life of sacrificial love. For it was in sacrificial love—his followers would soon find out—that authentic power and strength are found. For some, this idea was difficult to swallow. For others, it resonated. For those looking to manipulate power to their own advantage, The Man's cross *and its ways* were foolish. For those who looked to it for salvation, it made sense.

* * *

The peasant didn't leave. How could he? He felt inexplicably connected to what was happening. Earlier that morning, he never could've predicted what would take place that day, how he would have to carry a Roman cross, witness a crucifixion, and console the victim's weeping mother. He wanted to leave and return to his family but felt like his feet were stuck on the hill. He was now part of this story; he couldn't leave. Something deep within him urged him to stay and watch. The longer he gazed upon The Man's cross, the more his heart filled to the brim with . . . *something*. He didn't have the slightest idea what it was or even if it was good or bad. He just felt—*he knew*—something deep within him was changing. For hours, he stood at the top of the hill toward the back of the crowd and watched everything unfold.

As he watched, a fresh batch of wealthy Jewish men and women pushed through the crowd to taunt The Man.

"Look at him!" one woman said as she pointed up. "Look at him squirm!" Her laugh sent a shiver down the peasant's spine.

The Man grimaced with his eyes closed as he shifted his weight.

The woman snapped her fingers at him to get his attention. "Look at me! Look at me! Didn't we tell you this would happen if you didn't shut your blasphemous mouth?"

"Looks like that mouth isn't doing much talking anymore," another woman said.

The whole group chuckled, along with a couple soldiers who overheard. Some in the crowd wanted in on the fun and stepped forward to insult him.

"You're no better than swine!"

"Where are your powers now?"

"Your crown looks good on you!"

"Give us another sermon!"

"What part of the scriptures describe this part of the messiah's journey?"

"Your carpenter-father would be so proud of your wooden throne you now sit on!"

Fresh tears slid down his mother's face.

Listening to the taunts caused the peasant's eyes to grow wet and dull as his chest felt heavy.

A Jewish teenage boy stepped forward. Because he was being groomed for the Jewish priesthood and learned from them daily, the boy knew all about The Man's wild claims. "Didn't you say you'd destroy the temple and rebuild it in three days? Seems like a difficult task. If you can do that, why not just come down from that cross?"

"Because he can't!" the first woman said. "He isn't who he claims to be!"

The Man opened his eyes.

She made eye contact with him. "You're a disgrace," she said softly. "You're nothing more than a breeze that blows and then is forgotten. You say you love this nation and have come to help us, but you haven't done anything for us. You claim The Father is proud of you, but we all know that can't be true." She touched the vertical beam, turned around and announced to the crowd what they were already thinking. "This man is cursed by our Father. He's hanging on a tree. And you know what our ancient laws say about anyone who hangs on a tree—they're cursed! The Father isn't proud of this man. The Father's disgusted by him."

The crowd erupted in agreement.

"If you're the King of the Jews, then do something!" she said. "Do anything! Save yourself!"

The Man looked down at her as fresh tears slid down his face.

The crowd cheered as they watched him cry.

As they did, The Father watched and wept.

* * *

They couldn't see it, but The Man was in a battle. It was The Man, fully Divine, against The Accuser. This hidden war had been going on for ages, and now the struggle had finally come to a climax. On the top of the hill, both The Man and The Accuser positioned themselves to deliver what they both believed to be the final blow that'd push them over the edge. They battled for unquestioned sovereignty and dominion. Neither would allow the other a portion of the kingship they both sought.

The Accuser had The Man right where he wanted him. Using The Man's cross to force The Father's hand to curse his own messiah, The Accuser supposed it was a foolproof strategy. The Father's plan to rescue his children from The Accuser's reign would fail, because The Man would forever lay in a grave, defeated by The Accuser.

But what The Accuser didn't see coming was The Man would use The Accuser's own weapon against him. The Father desired for The Accuser and the power he held over The Father's children to be defeated completely. To do that, he'd allow his own messiah to be crushed by Death.

Yes, The Father foresaw the only way to cripple The Accuser's power was to turn Death against him. The Father would show the world it was sacrificial love, not Death, that held ultimate power.

No one could see it, but The Man was dying so he could once and for all crush The Accuser and disarm him of the powers he'd been holding over The Father's children since the beginning of time.

* * *

The high priest sat at his table relaxing. He said nothing but smiled as he watched his archenemy get publicly degraded.

One of the high-ranking priests sitting with him stood and approached The Man to have fun with him. This priest removed some of his elaborate garb due to the increasing temperature. "You're our king, right?" he sarcastically asked The Man.

The Man didn't move or make a sound.

The priest turned toward the crowd. "He's the king of this nation! He's apparently Divine too! He oozes with power." The priest clasped his hands together in a beggar's posture. "I say we beg him to come down from this cross. If he does, I'll give him my allegiance!"

Many in the crowd verbally agreed and laughed.

The priest faced The Man. "Come down from that cross, so we may all believe in you!"

The Man kept his eyes closed as he focused on keeping his position on the cross.

"You trust in The Father! Let The Father rescue you now!" The priest waited for a Divine hand from Heaven to pluck The Man off the cross, but none appeared. "I've heard of your wondrous deeds!" The priest's hands raised dramatically. "The people rave about your power. You've apparently fed thousands of people with the scraps of a simple lunch. You make concoctions from mud that help the blind see. You can touch the leper without getting sick. You keep parties going when the barrels run dry. Lame people walk when you tell them to. Rains and winds bow before you in obedience. Some people have even claimed you tear open graves and demand the dead to rise . . . *and they do*!"

Some in the crowd chuckled in disbelief.

"And yet, you're going to let *this* be your end?" The priest frowned as he rubbed his chin. "Seems like a man as powerful as you could bend back these nails and heal yourself."

The Man remained silent.

The priest stepped closer and, baring his teeth, whispered so only The Man could hear, "You Samaritan-loving fool. You deserve every minute of this." The priest faced the crowd once more and snickered. "He saved others, but he can't save himself!"

Many in the crowd erupted in laughter.

* * *

The priest didn't know it, but what he had said was absolutely correct; The Man couldn't save others *and* save himself. He never could. The Man's blood held the power to give life to all. But he couldn't give the world his life-giving blood if it stayed in his own body. To save the world, he couldn't save himself.

And even though the priest mocked him for the decision, The Man's followers would forever worship him because of it.

* * *

Another hour passed.

The criminal on the right wept quietly after a group of children threw dirt clogs at him. Once the children left, he turned his head toward The Man. "Can . . . y-you help . . . us?"

The Man locked eyes with the criminal. Mercy and compassion overflowed from The Man's heart as he recalled in his deteriorating mind just how much he loved the criminal. The Man miraculously called out the criminal's name and told him how much The Father loved him.

The criminal wept louder as he shook his head in disbelief.

"Stop it," came a quiet, agitated voice in the other direction. The other criminal had heard the entire conversation and grew aggravated with The Man. "Is that really . . . all you can do?" the criminal on the left asked with difficulty to The Man. "That's it? You have . . . all these powers inside you, and all you can . . . do at this point is tell him some mindless deity—" The criminal shifted his weight and took a painful, shallow breath. "Some deity has feelings of affection for a cursed thief . . . hanging on a tree?"

The Man's focus remained on the weeping criminal.

"Aren't you the messiah?" the criminal on the left continued. "Save us! If you can actually help . . . people, then show us now! Do something!"

"D-Don't you fear The Father?" the weeping criminal asked through tears and broke his gaze with The Man. "We're under the same s-sentence. We're p-p-punished justly. But this . . . man has done nothing wrong."

The criminal on the left grimaced as he chuckled. "Nothing wrong? Everything about him is wrong. He is—" The criminal on the left winced as a fresh line of pain crawled up his back and stole his breath. He took a few seconds to compose himself then continued in a softer voice. "He's a liar and . . . a fraud. He's done nothing for us. Instead of rescuing us from these crosses, he chose to climb his own and hang . . . here with us!"

A few in the crowd who heard the conversation snickered.

"Sir," the criminal on the right said softly as he locked eyes with The Man once again. "Remember me when you come into your kingdom."

The Man's heart embraced the criminal. A smile forced its way onto The Man's face as he considered how The Father was using him, even as he hung on a cursed cross, to redirect people's hearts toward Heaven. "I tell you the truth. Today, you'll be . . . with me . . . in paradise."

Upon hearing this claim, the crowd exploded once again as they hurled insults toward The Man. They called down curses upon The Man and the criminal on the right. They shook their fists at them and gnashed their teeth.

"Love your enemies," The Man said to the criminal on the right. "Love them as The Father loves you."

The criminal on the right flinched as dirt clogs hit his face.

* * *

The Man panicked; this nightmare proved terribly real. He felt the nails. He heard the crowd. He tasted blood. He tried to open his eyes more to break the fog his mind was trapped in. His mother's cry sent him back to reality.

The Man understood he was in no nightmare; he'd fallen unconscious for a period of time and was waking from it. He was unsure how long ago he had conversed with the criminal on his right.

"He's alive!" the disciple said as he shook The Man's mother and encouraged her to look up.

The mother fell to her knees and repeatedly cried her son's name. For a few minutes, she had assumed he was dead. Her smothering despair lifted temporarily.

The Man was tempted to use his Divine power to return to his unconscious state and ease his pain. But he resisted.

"*Don't do that to me*!" his mother scolded her son. "Don't do—" She couldn't finish her thought as she buried her face in her hands.

The Man looked at her through the eyes of The Father. Of course, he saw his own mother, the woman he had adored his whole life. She was his comforter and his hero.

But through her aging face, he also saw the heart of a fourteen-year-old virgin who'd miraculously conceived The Father's messiah. She passionately cared for each of her children but believed The Man was The Father's chosen one who'd set all things right. She protected him with an extra measure. When her son was hurt or fell sick, her heart dropped to the pit of her stomach. *What if something happens to him?* she would worry. In a way, she felt as if the fate of the world rested in her ability to mother him. If she couldn't protect him, how could he do The Father's will?

The Man saw his mother's pain multiplying. Sure, her heart broke to see her son dying on a cross—this would be true of any parent—but it wasn't just her son dying on the cross; in a way, her motherhood was being crucified as well. And if her motherhood was crucified, so was her role in The Father's Divine plan.

"I'm . . . sorry," The Man said as he held back tears.

"Why are you doing this to me?" the mother asked.

The Man said nothing.

"We all know who you are!" She eyed the disciple and the three other women. "We all have seen your power! We believe you can come down from that cross! Do it! Why are you waiting so long to relieve me of this pain?"

The Man shook his head slightly. "You don't understand," The Man said quietly. "You don't . . . remember . . . my words."

"Please, just do it," the disciple said with frustration mounting in his voice. "Do it for your mother!"

"Do it for me!" she said.

The Man shook his head again.

The mother sobbed. "But you have to!"

The Man didn't move.

"You must go on with your ministry!"

The Man's face tightened as he attempted to suppress his tears. Seeing his mother this way burdened his heart. Finally, he locked eyes with her as he whispered, "This *is* my ministry."

The mother paused in confusion. "Then you must go on with your healing!"

"This is . . . my healing," he struggled to say.

"You need to keep teaching the people The Father's ways!"

"This *is* The Father's way."

"Your life must be preserved!"

At that, The Man looked away as he shook his head again. His face was full of sorrow.

Defeated, the mother fell to the ground and into the arms of one of the women with her.

The crowd didn't know how to respond, so they stayed mostly silent.

The Man waited as he, in his humanity, came to internally accept what he was about to say. He asked both his mother and the disciple to stand and step closer.

The disciple stood, but the mother refused.

"Dear woman," The Man said as he started to cry, "here is . . . your son." He nodded toward the disciple. "And you, here—" He choked up as his crying intensified. Fresh lines of tears left vertical paths on his cheeks as they fell across dried blood. "Here is your mother!" He nodded toward his mother, indicating from that moment on he wanted the disciple to take care of his mother and treat her as his own.

A few in the crowd who had held dirt clogs now felt their eyes water as they listened to the heart-aching conversation.

The disciple lifted the weeping mother to her feet. He regarded The Man and attempted to respond but found he couldn't. He simply nodded in agreement.

The Man had set his affairs in order. Now all he had to do was wait for Death to swallow him.

He glanced up and noticed buzzards circling high above him.

* * *

His mother collected herself. She didn't know what to think. Her son was her Master, after all. She obeyed him because she believed he was the messiah. And yet, her Master was her son. As her child, he was to obey her. This confusion gnawed at her heart as she wrestled with how to respond to the fact her will lay out of line with her son's.

All she could think to do was pray for rescue. "Please, Father,"—she touched and kissed her son's bloody feet—"please. Listen to my spirit and save my son." She repeatedly prayed this in desperation. A half-hour passed. Seeing no immediate results, she grew more animated in her prayers and clenched her fists. "Father! Show your face to me! Listen to me! For the sake of your name, save your messiah!"

Nothing.

She dropped to her knees and pounded the dirt. "Do something!" She buried her face in her hands. The silence of The Father flattened her. *Where are you? Why won't you fight for your messiah? Will you really turn your back to us now?* She looked around and saw no evidence of The Father's presence. She lifted her trembling hands to her face and pressed her palms firmly against her temples. Closing her eyes, she reached deep within herself and mustered all the spiritual might she had left in a last-ditch effort to move the heart of The Father. "Show me you're still with me," she said faintly.

The temperature dropped dramatically. Her tears now felt cool on her face as a sharp breeze sent a shiver down her spine.

The crowd on the top of the hill gasped collectively. Some people screamed. A distinct hum of insects buzzed.

She opened her eyes, looked up and grabbed the arm of the disciple standing nearby. Her skin grew clammy, and her pulse raced as she watched the sun recede in the sky. She couldn't tell what covered it, but, after thirty seconds, the sun simply . . . *disappeared.* Twinkling, faded stars appeared in the now-dark afternoon sky.

The crowd on the hill panicked. Nobody's eyes had time to properly adjust. Many pushed down the hill and blindly ran home. Some stood speechless and in awe. Others accused The Man of sorcery and demanded him to stop. The priests yelled for their servants to run into the city and grab lanterns. They returned a few minutes later and lit them, providing a faint illumination.

After waiting for her eyes to adjust, a young woman who was one of The Man's followers darted to the centurion. "Do you see what you're doing? The Father's judging you! He's judging all of you for this great tragedy! Let this man down before something worse happens!"

Rigid and tense, the centurion's mouth opened and shut repeatedly, like a fish out of water. His eyelids refused to blink, opening wide enough to show, even in the dark, the clear whites of his eyes. This was unlike anything he'd ever experienced.

"Do it now!" she said.

The centurion turned to command his soldiers. "Q-Quick, grab your—"

"*You will do no such thing*!"

The centurion spun around to the familiar voice of the high priest.

"Don't you *dare* bring that man down."

"But I . . . I think—"

"Let me tell you exactly what is going on!" The high priest's nostrils flared. "This woman is correct: this darkness is the work of the Divine. But it's not because the Divine is judging your actions. The Divine is judging The Man. He's filled with a nasty evil; the Divine is now enveloping him in the dark judgement he deserves."

The centurion considered both sides. As he did, the crowd's eyes adjusted finally, and their alarm dimmed. "But what if—"

"If you know what's good for you, you'll do the job the governor ordered you to do." The high priest's eyes communicated an intensity the centurion hadn't yet seen. The high priest backed away gradually, but before he turned to return to his table, he looked up and pointed at The Man. "This is all on you," he said loud enough for the entire hill to hear then returned to his seat and relaxed.

The afternoon sky contained a few wispy streaks of pink on the horizon, as if the day had just a few minutes of light left.

The Man whimpered as his head darted back and forth and up and down, as if he was searching for something that was previously there but now was not. An awful dread plastered across his face as his breathing quickened. He murmured something over and over, but the centurion couldn't make it out.

"What's happening?" the centurion asked himself.

* * *

"*Come and look*."

The peasant's eyes widened, and his pupils dilated. The hair on his neck stood up. The familiar burn in his heart returned with intensity. It wasn't a painful burn but rather a passionate one. The sound of the voice that had spoken to him didn't enter into his ears but rather into his heart.

A half-hour had passed since darkness had covered the land. Around half the people on the top of the hill had fled the area once the darkness had overtaken them.

But not the peasant. His feet seemed to be stuck to the ground. In a way, he felt as if he and the crucified Jew were forever linked together because of their journey on the half-mile road. Even though the peasant wanted to leave and return to his family, for some strange reason, he believed he couldn't abandon The Man. And although he couldn't stomach watching the dying, crucified Jew hanging between two criminals, he also couldn't keep his distance. So, at the top of the dimly lit hill, he sat by himself, trying to ignore the three men's disturbing cries.

"Come and look."

The peasant disregarded the voice he heard in his heart. A few more moments passed.

"Come and look."

"No." The peasant surprised himself; had he just verbally communicated with himself? Were the events he had experienced in the last few hours causing irrevocable mental damage, so much so that now he was hearing voices? And why was he suddenly feeling so passionate *and* nervous inside, like he was about to discover something that might change him forever? Shouldn't he be overwhelmed with sorrow and revulsion?

"Come and look."

The peasant didn't understand what was happening. Who was talking, and how could he hear it? He knew no one else could hear it, for it came from deep within his own being. The voice was persistent and authoritative, yet gentle and inviting. The voice was, in a good way, *daring*. And the peasant couldn't say what it was exactly, but the voice was breaking down something foundational at his very core.

It was the voice of The Father. *"Come and look."*

"I've had enough," the peasant whispered as he noticed The Man's dried blood plastered across his own tunic. Suddenly, something burst within his heart, and his emotions flooded. He grabbed his bloody tunic as his body tensed. As he rocked back and forth on the ground, he tried to stifle his tears but eventually lost control. He wept by himself as he understood who he was talking to. "I've had enough," he said again through tears. "I just . . . I want to go home. I want to see my family. I want it all to go back to normal."

"I want to give you a new normal."

The peasant stopped and considered what this meant. He wasn't sure if it was good or bad. Fear mounted inside him.

"I want to open your eyes. Come and look."

The peasant wiped his cheeks and glanced up. He wasn't sure what to expect or what he was supposed to see. He scanned the hilltop for something significant, but nothing had changed. But then his heart raced wildly as his eyes panned The Man's cross. He shot his gaze down and away. "No. I don't want to look. It's too much."

But, in the peasant's heart, he sensed The Father wasn't budging. He felt The Father's eyes staring into his soul—not in a judgmental or intimidating way but in a patient way, like when a parent waits for their child to do something difficult but ultimately good.

The peasant gathered his strength and stood. Shaking, he meandered in the dark through the crowd and finally knelt at the foot of The Man's cross. He looked up. After a moment of staring at the bloody wooden beams and the tortured Jew whose flesh was nailed to them, the peasant heard one last whisper.

"This is my love for you."

* * *

From that day on, people all over the world would be met with jarring, emotional responses when beckoned by The Father to come and look at The Man upon the cross. To be sure, the idea that The Man, fully Divine, was left to die alone on a cross was nothing short of disturbing. For centuries, worshipers would grimace at the mental image of the nails being hammered through his skin while his thorn-wrapped skull banged against the beams in agony. Tears would flood their eyes as they imagined the sound of his screams. Terrible irritation would overtake listeners as they heard the stories of his death. His Divinity made this irritation even worse.

To simply gaze upon The Man's cross would soon become equivalent to inviting a kind of holy horror into one's heart. And yet, horror wasn't the only jolting response people would experience when they looked upon his cross.

They'd also be filled with wonder.

For The Father's whispers wouldn't be limited to the ears of the peasant. For ages to come, the curious worshipers who'd open their hearts to the holy horror of The Man's cross would also give their hearts the ability to hear the same whisper that the peasant heard that afternoon.

"*This is my love for you.*"

Worshipers around the world would always be filled with wild wonder when they focused the eyes of their hearts upon The Man's cross. The longer they did, the more their hearts would burn as they realized The Man's cross was everlasting proof of how The Father felt toward his people.

Horror *and* wonder—walking hand in hand—would forever be the appropriate responses that would bubble up in the hearts of the people who chose to kneel before The Man's cross and look up.

* * *

The walls in his heart crumbled. On top of the hill, the peasant raised his hands, barely illuminated by the few lanterns, and wept silently. He allowed the sight of The Father's love to wash away the grime of his soul. He felt brilliantly free, a sensation he'd never experienced before.

He bowed low to the ground in worship. "Thank you."

He was the first worshiper—although certainly not the last—to gaze upon The Man's cross in complete awe of the horror *and* the wonder of The Father's love.

* * *

A couple more hours passed. Late afternoon inched toward early evening. A chilly breeze whipped the landscape as travelers bundled up. The miraculous darkness still blanketed the land, causing the hilltop to remain dim.

The Man fell in and out of consciousness. When he awoke and saw the sun had still refused to shine, he fell deeper into his despair. The darkness covering the hill caused a physical reaction for the people who observed it. But, for The Man, it was a terrible spiritual fright.

He felt utterly alone.

In his Divinity, The Man had *never* been alone. Even before the creation of the world, he existed alongside The Father. Their closeness was never broken. But now, The Man felt this closeness evade him. For the first time in his life, he looked for the comfort of the Divine but only saw darkness. In his humanity, The Man wasn't sure if The Father was present or not. He just knew he *felt* utterly alone.

Please come closer, The Man begged in his heart.

But he was met only with silence. And darkness.

Ever since the darkness had covered the land, The Man searched blindly for The Father. His heart reached for anything to grasp onto in the malevolent spiritual fog he was trapped in. But he failed to latch onto anything.

Doing this for hours as he fell in and out of consciousness took its toll. The Man was broken. Hopeless, he began to cry.

His mother ran to him and attempted to comfort him, but he paid her no attention. Even though several dozen people remained at the top of the hill, the hill might as well have been completely empty. His loneliness crushed him.

The Man looked upward into the darkness. "Father! I don't want to be alone."

Silence.

The Man wept loudly. "Father! Father! Why have you forsaken me?"

At this, his mother and the disciple standing close to her joined The Man in his crying.

"Why have you forsaken me?" The Man asked repeatedly through tears.

* * *

Forsakenness.

Forsakenness was one of The Accuser's greatest weapons. In mankind's times of trial and suffering where The Father seemed to be distant, The Accuser had always been quick to flaunt the idea in people's faces.

The Father has forgotten you.

Your sinfulness has pushed him away.

If The Father was going to help, he would've done so by now.

So, when The Accuser heard The Man's words, joy filled his heart like never before. The Accuser's plan to crush The Man was going well . . . *but now this*? This seemed too good to be true.

The Divine Man feels the Divine Father has forsaken him, The Accuser thought. *How wonderful! I won't have to persuade men that their Father abandons them; the proof is on the cross!*

And yes, while it was true The Man *felt* The Father had forsaken him, The Accuser could've never imagined how the Divine would use that truth for mankind's benefit. Sure, it didn't happen overnight. It took years for mankind to uncover the hidden glory in The Man's feelings of forsakenness.

The wisdom and the glory of The Man's feelings of forsakenness were this: because of The Accuser, every person who ever lived would experience *feelings* of Divine forsakenness at some point or another. This was inevitable. But now, because The Man, fully Divine, had *also* experienced the feeling of the Divine forsaking him, he was allowed a new level of access into the human experience. Because of his feelings, The Man became instantly relatable to everyone who ever lived. No human being would ever feel abandoned, rejected, or forsaken by The Father without hearing The Man reply, "Me too." Because The Man felt The Father had forsaken him, he was the undisputable and rightful Deity to those who'd also felt The Father had forsaken them.

* * *

"Why have you forsaken me?" The Man softy asked to himself. Devoid of energy, his head hung low. He was losing body heat. His will to continue waned.

A flash of lightning illuminated the faint horizon. The city was supposed to be bustling, but its terrified visitors chose to take shelter in the daytime darkness. A storm loomed, and it wouldn't be long till it arrived.

The birds circling high above the crosses lowered themselves to just a couple hundred feet. Their instincts told them the three struggling creatures below them were just minutes from death.

Chapter 11

Giving Up

"He's awake again!"

The Man stirred. He tried to stretch his body across the vertical beam to take weight off his shoulders but no longer possessed the strength. Light red lines fell from his eyes where tears mixed with blood. He was lethargic and slow. And silent.

"My son!" his mother said as she approached.

The criminals on his left and right also grew silent. They realized speaking required energy, a luxury they simply didn't have.

The Man regarded his mother with a blank, empty gaze. His mouth moved, but no words came forth.

"What did he say?" the disciple asked as he came close to the mother's side.

"I couldn't hear," she answered as lightning illuminated the dark hillside. "Tell us, my son, what you need. We'll get it!"

The Man looked back and forth at his mother and the disciple.

"Tell us!" the disciple said.

"I'm . . . thirsty," The Man said in a faint whisper.

His mother searched frantically for anything to help her son. She ran to multiple people in the crowd and begged for whatever water they had. After finding none, she advanced on the centurion. "Please show mercy! My son needs a drink. He won't last much longer without one. Give us your favor. Please show us mercy. *Please*." She bowed her head low and kept her gaze on the ground.

The centurion blinked rapidly, his eyes barely illuminated by flickering torches. He jumped at the sound of a crow's caw as the bird flew close over his head. Clearly uneased by the miracle of darkness surrounding him, he shook his head as he shot his glance downward. He turned and snapped his fingers at a soldier. "Get him a drink."

The soldier stood and grabbed a spear nearby. He approached the boulder where their supplies were laid, grabbed a jar filled with wine vinegar and opened it. Taking a sponge set aside for cleaning, he dipped it in the liquid. He pierced the sponge with the spear as he reached The Man's cross. Lifting the sponge high in the air, he offered it as a drink.

The Man bit the sponge. Wine vinegar ran down the front of his chin and neck. The Man released and grimaced as the liquid washed through his wounds.

"Dip it again," the mother said. When no one responded, she repeated herself. "Again!"

The soldier walked to the jar, took the sponge off the spear and dipped it. He reset it on the tip of the spear and offered the drink once more.

The Man opened his mouth wide and sucked on the sponge. The drink tasted awful, but he hardly noticed due to the temporary relief his mouth felt.

Eventually, the soldier lowered his spear, taking away the sponge.

The wind whipped the hillside. After a moment, rain fell—drizzling at first but then increasing into a soaking shower.

His mother asked the centurion if she and the disciple could place ladders against the cross and use their clothing to shelter The Man from the rain, but the centurion declined.

"Leave him alone," one of the soldiers said. "Let's see if anyone comes to save him."

The disciple stood next to the mother and the three women. He took off his outer garment and put it over the mother's head as he shielded her from the rain.

* * *

Twenty minutes passed as the rain plastered the hill. The afternoon darkness intensified with the storm clouds moving in. Lightning illuminated the three crosses and their victims. The few people left on the hill watched in silence.

The Man seemed to be losing the power to control his thoughts. His mind raced aimlessly through memories from his distant past. He bounced back and forth, recalling his favorite foods, childhood friends, time spent in his father's carpentry shop, and of playing with his younger siblings. His mind wandered to pleasantries he had exchanged with people in his hometown fishing village to funny interactions with rabbis he knew. Every time he thought of something, his mind shifted to another memory; he couldn't control it even though he could sense it happening.

A strange sensation overtook him in a pleasant yet frightening way. The Man's extreme thirst left him, as if his body no longer cared about his physical needs; he wondered what might happen next.

A few moments passed when he developed a bizarre tickling deep in his throat. Powerless to stop it, a strange rattling noise increased in his throat as he exhaled.

He knew his time was over.

The Man opened his eyes and peered at the fifty or so people huddled together on the hill. He could barely discern their faces, but he didn't care. He had one last declaration for them to hear. He mustered all the strength he could and extended his chest off and away from his cross. The words he would boldly bellow as his throat rattled in the rain would echo throughout history as the rallying cry in the battle against The Accuser.

"It is . . . *finished*," The Man said with all his might.

His mother and the disciple rushed close and stood underneath him. Pelting their eyes as they looked up, the rain became a downpour, blowing sideways across the hill. They both rose on their tiptoes to listen to The Man's final words.

"Father," The Man said as thunder cracked, "into your hands . . . I . . . commit my . . . spirit." He tried to cry, but nothing came out—only the deep rattling sound from the back of his throat. He opened his eyes again and looked down at his mother. Unable to speak, he opened his mouth to tell her he loved her, but his tongue couldn't move.

As he stared at her, his peripheral vision began to blur. The blur moved gradually from the outer bands of his vision toward the center. Quickly, his entire vision darkened. With each blink, his sight grew dimmer. And then his vision was completely gone.

The Man hung on the cross and listened to the thunder. He blinked rapidly and opened his eyes wide to help his vision return, but it did not.

Over the next two minutes, his hearing faded. He could tell his mother was speaking at one point but couldn't decipher what she said. When all the noise disappeared, his eardrums hummed slightly, but that too ultimately faded to nothingness.

Even though his pain was gone, he knew he was still on his cross. Mute, deaf, and blind, all he could do was feel the vibration of the rain pelting his skin. He didn't know how long he hung there, because the concept of time had slipped through his fingers as his mind waned.

And then he sensed absolutely nothing.

Then he exhaled his last.

The crowd watched calmly as The Man's head fell sharply against his chest. Eyes wide, all of Heaven leaned forward in silent anticipation.

The Man was dead.

And then, seeing what had transpired, all of Creation wailed.

* * *

"*No*!" His mother collapsed to the ground. She dug her fingers deep into the wet earth.

The disciple bent down to comfort her as the three women rushed to her side.

Slowly, the surging storm drowned out her cries. Lightning relentlessly struck the capital city. It struck trees and buildings. It struck the temple and the marketplace and homes. The peals of thunder blended, making a terrifying and unending roar of explosions. In their wake, fires blazed throughout the city and countryside.

Although it seemed impossible, the weather intensified as the wind thrashed the hillside, extinguishing all the remaining torches. All three crosses shook. The onlookers panicked and scattered from the hillside. The criminals screamed for help, but the thunder overpowered their pleas. The rains blew sideways across the hill as it bombarded those looking for shelter.

"Hold steady!" the centurion said to his soldiers at the top of his lungs. "Be brave! We must perform our duty to the end!"

But the soldiers who had taunted The Man just hours earlier now looked terrified. Bewilderment overtook their faces. Blind and disoriented from the rainy assault, they moved together across the hilltop, peering through the torrent for a large boulder to provide something of a shelter.

"Over here!" the centurion said.

The soldiers followed the overmatched sound of his voice as the peals of thunder reverberated. They found the centurion on his knees, bracing himself against a sturdy boulder. The soldiers surrounded him and pressed against the rock for security. In unison, they peered across the hillside. Through the flashes of lightning, they saw the three women, the disciple, and the mother huddled on the ground. Looking up, they noticed the three crosses swaying in the wind. They couldn't tell if the men on the crosses were dead or alive.

The earth moaned. The soldiers glanced at each other. Choked by fear, they grimaced as they listened to rocks smashing against each other.

Maybe it's a landslide, the centurion thought. But then he felt it. And then he *witnessed* it. The ground trembled. The boulder their backs were pressed against vibrated ominously.

"We can't stay here!" one soldier said and darted across the hillside away from the soldiers and crosses. Right before he departed down the trail leading to the city, the air hummed. Lightning cut through the atmosphere and exploded on top of the hillside, striking a tree in front of the fleeing soldier, sending him to the ground.

The earth shifted. The city walls cracked and gave way as rocks collapsed against each other and city structures toppled inward. The ancient temple's foundation quaked as its holy curtain tore in half. Confused livestock scampered in every direction.

The soldier brought to the ground by the sheer force of the lightning strike stood and continued down the path illuminated now by new wildfires born from the strike. The centurion watched him as he came to the bottom of the hill. To the left, the path forked to the city; to the right, the countryside. The soldier chose the latter. As he hurried, he sprinted by many graves carved into the hillside. As each lightning bolt brightened the landscape, the centurion noticed many tombstones were cracked into pieces and broken.

What he witnessed next was something that would frighten him and haunt his dreams well into his old age.

People were appearing through the mouths of the open tombs. And not just any people—*dead people*. People who'd just recently died but now were no longer dead; no, they were very much alive. Their skin wasn't rotting or decaying; it appeared completely healthy. They didn't have wrapped bandages or any clothes. These dead people, who were now very much alive, were entirely naked and walking out of their own tombs.

And as they staggered into the storm, they too appeared petrified.

The three soldiers and the centurion standing on top of the hill during the tempest were all struck mute and immobile as they stared at the countless naked *dead people* running hysterically across the hillside and fading into the darkness. Another lightning bolt to the hilltop shocked them from their frozen, numb state and back into a terrifying awareness. They turned simultaneously.

The centurion couldn't help but have his gaze drawn up to the dead man upon the cross. In the rain, he cautiously approached the three crosses as he wandered from the shelter of the boulder.

"Come back!" one of the soldiers said through the wind.

But the centurion didn't listen. He staggered toward the crosses and stood directly behind the wailing mother and the four others who comforted her in the mud. His gaze never left the middle cross. Lightning illuminated everything the centurion saw. And as he gazed up at The Man, his heart finally broke. "We've sinned," he said to himself.

Just then another lightning bolt struck a nearby hillside, sending rocks and boulders tumbling to the bottom.

The centurion cried as he stood by himself in the rain. The tightness in his chest wouldn't loosen. A horrible, heavy guilt sat in the pit of his stomach. He pinched his eyes shut in an attempt to block the tears, but it was no use. "I've sinned," he said loudly, as if he wanted someone to hear. He turned toward his soldiers.

A hopeless terror stretched across their faces.

He pointed to the dead man. "We've sinned! This man was who he claimed to be! The wrath of the Earth has turned against us! Surely this man was Divine!" The centurion fell to the ground, and his knees dug deep into the mud. He lowered his body, allowing his face to touch the earth in submission to the dead man upon the cross, and wept. "What've I done?"

* * *

During his life, The Man had radiated with power—not the kind of power kings inflicted upon their subjects. No, it was a humble and holy power, a kind that forced the eyes of those it met toward Heaven.

The Man had opened the eyes of the blind. He had spoken to the religious leaders with surprising authority. Nature had submitted to his will. Demonic forces had trembled before him and begged for mercy. And the people had been held captive at his every word.

But his influence didn't stop there. *Even in his death*, The Man radiated with power.

In his death, he brought faith to the faithless and belief to the skeptic. And through his death, he raised rotting corpses to life.

Even though The Man had died, he was still changing the world.

* * *

The centurion didn't know how long he buried his face in the earth. He didn't care. He didn't care if he was struck by the lightning exploding around him. He didn't care his men saw him weeping. He was broken to his core as he lay in the mud.

After what seemed like ages, the rain tapered off. The earth stopped shaking, and the lightning subsided. Once the rain slowed to a light drizzle, the centurion raised his head and looked around. His eyes locked with the mother's eyes just a few feet in front of him. In his emotional turmoil, he had completely forgotten that she, the disciple, and the three other women remained on top of the hill. He squinted to see her better in the darkness. He searched for words, but nothing of significance came to mind. "I'm . . . I'm sorry."

The mother stared at him blankly. She didn't look mad or upset. She didn't even look sad. She looked empty, like nothing was inside her anymore.

"I didn't know." The centurion refocused on the ground. "I just didn't know."

A few more minutes passed. The centurion dared not look back at the five people kneeling in front of him. An incredible shame overtook him. As the drizzle hit the top of his neck, he decided to just close his eyes as he listened to one of the criminals calling for help in the darkness.

The rain finally stopped, and the clouds rolled back in the sky. People across the city strayed from their shelters and lifted their eyes skyward. Slowly but surely, the sun revealed itself again, throwing soft wisps of pinks and yellows across the city. Eventually, the sun reclaimed its place high in the sky and shone brightly. It warmed the land once again as the flooded streets dried out. It leisurely inched across the sky as if nothing had ever happened.

The three soldiers joined the centurion and helped him stand. Lifting their heads, they eyed the crosses. The criminal on the left hung unconscious while the one on the right took short and shallow breaths as his head tilted back and rested against his vertical beam.

The Man's lifeless body hung limp. The entire top of his thorny crown was exposed as the crest of his head sagged down. His cross no longer moved. Although the intense rain almost washed The Man clean, small amounts of blood still found ways to escape his wounds. A slight breeze rustled his wet, curly hair.

The sun revealed what Creation couldn't bring itself to believe: The Man was really dead.

* * *

Three hours passed, and the city returned to its typical ebb and flow. The bleating of sheep could be heard everywhere as people prepped for their holy celebrations. The storm didn't return, and the sun didn't stop shining. Few people returned to the hilltop to see what had become of the three crucified men. The mother, the disciple, and the three women never left. As evening approached, the land cooled as the sun crept to the horizon.

The Jews wanted no bad omens during their holy weekend. They believed anyone who hung on a tree was cursed by The Father, so a group of the Jewish Council met the governor and asked for the bodies of the three crucified men be taken down before sunset.

The governor obliged and sent soldiers to communicate the orders to the centurion.

The soldiers meandered up the half-mile road and exited the city gate. After trudging up the muddy hill, they found the centurion.

"Sir," one of them said, "we have direct orders from the governor."

The centurion regarded them with a void stare. He remained shaken to his core, unable to focus.

"In order to appease the Jews, the governor wants you to take all three bodies off their crosses and have them buried before nightfall."

The centurion's eyes seemed glossed over, complementing his white-washed face. He seemed as if he wasn't really paying attention.

"Sir," the soldier said, "are you all right? You look like you've seen a ghost."

"We'll do what the governor wants," the centurion said matter-of-factly. "Now leave."

The governor's two soldiers returned to the palace.

The centurion told his three remaining soldiers to take the three bodies off the crosses.

"But sir," they said, "at least two of them are still alive."

"Figure it out," the centurion said dismissively.

One soldier walked to where their crucifixion supplies lay, grabbed the hammer and returned to the other two.

The centurion drifted toward the back of the hill, staring apprehensively at the open graves.

"I guess this'll do?" The soldier raised the hammer for their inspection.

The other two nodded in confirmation.

The soldier approached the criminal on the left.

The criminal didn't speak even though his grief-stricken face communicated a terrible sadness.

The soldier bashed in the criminal's tibia bones until both his shins had a noticeable dent.

The criminal howled in pain as he thrashed.

The soldier made his way up both legs. He didn't stop till he heard loud cracks in the bone.

The criminal's palms now supported all his weight. He had no strength left in his shoulders to shift his weight. The stretched muscles in his back couldn't do anything to help his lungs expand to take in air.

The soldier stepped backward and watched the criminal attempt to gasp for air. He moved to the criminal on the right and did the exact same thing. After a few minutes of both criminals gasping, an eerie silence covered the hill. The soldier turned his back and walked away from the crosses.

"You forgot one," the centurion said.

"He's already dead," the soldier said.

"Confirm it."

The soldier grabbed a spear and approached the middle cross. He knew The Man was dead; he hadn't moved in hours. The soldier thrust the spear through The Man's lower abdomen. Once inside, he shoved it up even farther, piercing his ribcage.

The Man didn't react.

When the soldier removed his spear, blood and water sprayed from the open wound. He backed away just in time to avoid being splattered with it. "He's dead," the soldier said as he returned to the soldiers and the centurion. "They're all dead."

As the sun set, the soldiers grabbed their ladders and hammers and bent the twelve nails back on the three crosses. The bodies of the three men fell to the earth with a thud.

For the soldiers, their job was almost over.

* * *

The mother stood at a distance as she observed her dead son dropping to the ground. She didn't cry. How could she? Her emotions had already spilled from her in an agonizing way. There was nothing left to feel. She was empty and void. She wasn't sad, nor was she angry. Just completely numb.

Tears trickled down the disciple's cheeks. Two of the women clung to the mother's garments as they cried quietly. The other woman crouched low to the ground with her hands above her head in disbelief. She kept her gaze on the dirt as she breathed heavily.

Two soldiers grabbed one of the dead criminal's hands and feet and trekked down the hill and out of sight. They carried the body to a community grave outside the city. When they returned fifteen minutes later empty handed and winded, they did the same thing with the other criminal.

Before they could return, two unlikely guests—councilmen—climbed the hill and kept their gazes down somberly as they approached the centurion. The councilmen talked with the centurion for less than five minutes. They kept their voices quiet as their eyes darted between the centurion, the mother, and The Man's dead body lying on the ground.

The centurion's expression looked weary and dejected; it communicated an inexplicable hopelessness.

Finally, the men approached the mother and her companions. "Excuse us," one councilman said gently, "but we were hoping we could talk with you."

The mother didn't acknowledge them; her gazes never left her son's dead body. At first, no one responded; the councilmen were only met with soft crying.

But then one of the three women lashed out, "This is all *your fault*! What do you want with us now? Do you want to crucify us as well? Would that be—" Her tears interrupted her thought.

The sun snuck down below the horizon. Twilight faintly illuminated the people on the hill. Darkness would take over again within minutes.

"We're sorry this has happened," the other councilman said.

The mother broke her gaze and considered him. The tenderness in his tone revealed he truly meant what he had said.

"Unlike the rest of the Jewish Council, we hoped your son was the one who'd restore this nation to our rightful glory. We believed his message. We were ready to declare him King."

The mother watched her son's lifeless body. Just like these two councilmen, she also believed he was the promised messiah. She believed he was The Father's Chosen One who'd make all things right. But now that dream was in the past. She couldn't protect her son. She had completely failed The Father's mission given to her over thirty years ago. It was over.

"Do you have a tomb to lay him in?" the first councilman asked.

The mother didn't reply.

The disciple simply shook his head.

"We want to honor his ministry in the best way we can. I own a tomb close to this hill . . . I'd like to offer it to you. I want him to rest there. We've brought wrappings and spices for his body."

The mother remained silent.

"May we . . . May we bury your son?"

The mother's eyes dilated as her focus intensified. Her heart raced as her palms grew clammy. The back of her throat tightened as a wave of dismay brought her closer to reality.

Bury your son.

Something in those words stomped on the mother's heart in a fresh way. Emotion rushed throughout her body as she considered the dreadful thought of saying goodbye to her firstborn child . . . *forever.* She closed her eyes and bit her quivering lip as she mustered all her strength to suppress her tears. She merely nodded her head.

"Thank you for giving us this honor."

The two councilmen stood for a moment, trying to decide whether to embrace the woman and her companions or say something else. Eventually, they descended the hill and grabbed their supplies. Returning with clean linen cloth and over seventy-five pounds of myrrh and aloes, they knelt by The Man's feet and packed the spices against his legs.

Multiple servants illuminated their work with lanterns.

The Man's head lay clumsily on the ground as they went. It rocked back and forth in the dirt as the men worked the spices into the cloth.

As the mother watched, streams of tears fell from her eyes. "P-Please be . . . *be gentle*," she whispered. She covered her face with her hands and watched between the slits of her fingers. Her shoulders bobbed as her crying increased, and her stomach contracted. She gasped for air between sobs.

"Do you want me to hold him?" the disciple asked her.

"No, I'll—" the mother said as her tears choked her. "I will."

She shuffled to the two men wrapping the body.

Working rapidly in a race against nightfall, they quickly moved past The Man's knees.

The Man's lifeless body rocked back and forth in the dirt.

The mother kneeled by her son's torso and held his limp head and neck against her stomach. She used her garments to clean the grime off his face. Memories raced to the forefront of her mind of nightly rituals of washing her son's face before supper just a few decades earlier. For the first time in days, she studied her son's face. It was basically unrecognizable from the child she used to nurse and kiss. No joy or light could be found on his face—only a stiff barrenness. Her body tensed as she felt the flood of sorrow approach. She hunched her upper back low and grabbed his head and brought it to her chest. His thorny crown cut into her forearms, but she didn't care as she wailed.

The three women rushed to her side.

The disciple fell to his knees as he buried his face in the mud. He covered his ears as the sounds of the mother's cry was too much to bear.

"I'm so sorry," the mother said between gasps for air as she looked at her son's face. "I wasn't—I wasn't strong enough to save you. *I'm . . . so . . . sorry.*"

The women around her held the mother's arms.

The mother didn't realize it, but her maternal instincts kicked in as she started to rock back and forth on the ground while she coddled her son's body.

The two councilmen worked up The Man's torso. They wrapped his arms closely to his chest as they packed him with spices. Only his head and neck remained unwrapped.

"It's time," the disciple said softly to the mother. He outstretched an arm, inviting her to stand and let the councilmen finish.

She moaned as she kissed her son's cheek for the last time. His blood covered her mouth while her tears fell on his face. She wailed again as the disciple helped lift her to her feet. As her son's limp head fell from her hands and was received by the councilmen, she bellowed. She watched them take the linens up his neck and wrap them around his mouth, nose, and eyes. Eventually, they wrapped his forehead and covered the thorny crown still buried in the skin. Her heart shattered in an irreparable way as she knew she'd never see her son's face again.

And with that, the twilight gave way to darkness.

* * *

The councilmen ordered for servants to light more lanterns to brighten their path to the tomb. The councilmen thanked the centurion and his soldiers for allowing them to give a proper burial to the body.

The centurion and his soldiers didn't say anything. They eventually left the hill and returned to their homes equally disturbed and distraught. They left the stretcher for the councilmen to use to carry the body.

Servants holding lanterns led the small group down the hill and into the countryside. The councilmen followed them as they carried the body on the stretcher. The five others walked closely behind. They all wept as they went, except the mother; she wailed.

They soon found themselves passing tombs cut into hillsides. The councilman's tomb wasn't far from The Man's execution site. Many tombs sat peacefully as the flicker of the lantern revealed them. A few tombstones were split open, giving the people in the group an unnerving feeling. One opened tomb had a family inside looking for the missing bodies of their loved ones.

Finally, they arrived at the councilmen's tomb. The opening was small, no more than four feet tall. A narrow, square-shaped stone sat elevated to the right of the opening ready to seal forever the tomb's inhabitants. They couldn't see inside the pitch-black tomb.

The mother dropped to her knees as the disciple and the three other women embraced her.

"Take courage," the disciple said reassuringly into the mother's ear.

A servant entered the tomb and disappeared. After a few minutes, he returned. "It's ready."

The two servants bent down and lifted The Man's body that lay wrapped in linen on the ground. They ducked carefully under the low entryway and carried him into the dark tomb while the tomb's owner followed them with a single lantern. They didn't stay inside long. After a minute or so, all three men stooped through the tomb opening and returned to their group.

Through her tears, the mother stared into the mouth of the grave. She felt the cold draft exiting through the doorway. In just a few days, the dark tomb would become drenched in the smell of rotting flesh. She choked back her sobs again as she pictured her son lying in the dark alone. Forever.

The two servants stepped to where the tombstone lay against the right side of the grave. They pressed their shoulders against the rock and shoved.

Slowly, the right side of the stone lifted off the ground. The tombstone scraped harshly against the hillside as it rumbled toward the opening. Finally, it dropped with a deep thud into its place as it covered the entrance to the tomb.

The mother rose and covered her head with her shawl. She couldn't look at the tomb any longer. She turned and walked up the path to return home.

The disciple and the three women followed immediately.

On her way, she imagined how she would tell her other children that Roman hands and Jewish hearts had crucified their oldest brother. The thought alone made her sick.

* * *

For some reason they couldn't explain, the two Jewish Councilmen along with their servants stood at the grave for a long time, contemplating the gravity of the situation. They wanted to leave, but every time they tried, they couldn't, as if the tomb had a gravitational pull, refusing to let their hearts wander off. They struggled to fathom what they both truly believed; Heaven's Treasure would begin to decompose in a pitch-black grave that night, that their people once again had ruined the Divine's plan to bring real salvation to the nation.

"Father, forgive us," the tomb's owner said.

Silence followed the councilman's plea for a moment before the other councilman asked himself a question that even he himself, at the time, couldn't comprehend how horrifying the answer was. "What've we done?"

They didn't know how long they stood alongside their servants, but it was long enough for guilt and shame to overwhelm them. Their messiah was dead, and so was their hope for the future.

Chapter 12

All is Lost

ALTHOUGH NIGHT HAD FALLEN, the city was wide awake.

As she wove through the streets, the mother avoided eye contact with everyone. She kept her head down, only looking up to ensure she didn't run into anything as her four friends followed closely behind.

The group passed closed market stands and houses packed with people. Laughter bounced throughout the corridors as foreigners enjoyed each other's company. The scent from countless animals filled the cobblestone roads. The moon shone brightly, and the breeze dissipated.

The mother scurried through the capital. She too was a foreigner from the north, and the place she and her children were staying was beyond the gates on the other side of the city. As she moved, fear set in and consumed her. She sensed the courage and fortitude it would require to be a rock for her children. She hesitated to peer into her soul to see what she had left to give.

She assumed there was nothing.

* * *

A half-hour passed once she exited the city and took the dirt road to the home where she was staying. After a brief walk down a steep hillside lit only by scattered moonlight, the mother descended on a poor village and approached a small house cut into the hillside. She put her hand against the rough walls made of small gray stone and mortar as she rested. Although there were no windows, she knew someone was home by the flicker of light escaping through the slits of the wooden door.

The mother stood motionless, staring at the flicker of light. She wanted to go inside, lock the door and never come out. And yet, she couldn't go inside. Going inside meant telling her family what had happened, making her current nightmare grow all the more real.

The disciple and the three women caught up and stood behind her. One woman embraced her from the side. None of them said anything. They didn't need to; nothing they could say would help.

Weeping, the mother lingered in the dark. After a few minutes, she opened the door and entered.

Large flat stones with compressed dirt between them created a smooth but uneven floor. The home was one open room. In the corner, multiple straw-filled sacs lay lined up to sleep on, while a sturdy wooden table sat opposite. Bread and wine sat on the table with ten chairs surrounding it. All of them were empty. Except two.

At the far end of the table sat the home's host. Wrinkles crawled from her elderly eyes. She emanated a quiet, gentle spirit. She took a special interest in the mother's children who were staying with her, for she was a distant relative.

The mother's youngest daughter, beautiful and innocent, sat next to the host. Together, they prepared herbs to cook with. As the door creaked open, both turned their heads to see the mother.

"I didn't know where you were during that storm," the daughter said. "Where have you been all day? You made me nervous." She stood and started across the room. Once she noticed her mother's wet and heavy eyes, she slowed and tilted her head down. "Mother . . . what's wrong?"

"They—" The mother lifted her fist to her forehead and pushed her closed palm against her brow. As she took a deep breath and exhaled, her tears returned.

"Mother! What's wrong?"

"They took him!" She moaned loudly and gulped another breath of air. "They took him. They took your brother."

The daughter's eyes widened.

The mother knew the daughter understood which brother she meant—the oldest brother, the one who had claimed to be the messiah, the one who had performed the miraculous signs and wonders. And although, at first, he was her older brother, the daughter too had come to place her faith in him.

"Where . . . is he?"

The three women who had followed the mother walked through the door, appearing distraught.

The disciple followed, but his face was devoid of a smile.

"Where is he? Where is my—"

"*They put him on a cross*!" the mother wailed.

The blood drained from the daughter's face. Her jaw dropped in horror as if she'd seen a spirit.

"They put him on a cross and mocked him! They laughed at him."

Silent tears fell from the daughter's eyes. "Where is he?" she asked softly. "Is he all right? Did he use his powers to overcome his enemies?" The daughter needed no response; her mother's sobs clearly answered her question. Her shoulders slumped as she came to understand her brother had been hanging on a cross all day just a few miles from where she had spent her quiet afternoon doing household chores.

The daughter lost control of her emotions. She embraced her mother as they both fell to their knees and wept.

* * *

The host fetched them water then joined the disciple and the three other women as they went to search for the other siblings to tell them what had happened.

The mother and the daughter stayed inside and experienced various emotional highs and lows over the next few hours. Sometimes they prayed. Other times they sat silently. They shared fond memories of The Man. Often they cried as their faith in him and the future of their nation was shattered.

Unsure of where the rest of their family was or if they were safe, they meandered to the bed on the floor. They laid down on the straw sacs and held each other as they wept. The mother knew she couldn't sleep with her other children out and unaccounted for.

She surprised herself as her weary eyes grew harder to keep open. Eventually, her body gave in as she fell asleep.

* * *

The mother found herself on a small, crowded fishing vessel in the middle of a lake. Taking a deep breath, she smelled the familiar scent of home: lake water and fish. She knew none of the people who packed the boat. A handful of men cast nets while the rest watched. Tall green hillsides surrounded the shores of the picturesque lake as a light breeze skimmed the top of the water.

Two men called for assistance as they pulled in a heavy catch of fish. People pressed shoulder to shoulder as they stepped backward to allow the net onto the boat. A couple fish fell from the net and flopped against the wood deck.

The mother bent and grabbed one. She took the fish to the edge of the boat, leaned over and put her hands below the surface of the cool water to release it. She smiled as she watched the ripple it created as it fled. After shaking the water from her hands, she looked up.

Night had fallen. From nowhere, rain pummeled the landscape. Lightning illuminated the sky as the waves rose.

The mother looked around.

No one seemed to be worried, let alone notice. They continued fishing.

The mother felt a claustrophobic panic sweep through her. She wanted to get back to shore but had no way of doing so. The waves crashed over the boat. She screamed into the spray of the storm, but still no one seemed to care. After peering across the water to see how far the shoreline was, she saw him.

Illuminated by bursts of lightning, The Man stood on the surface of the water. He wore his normal cloak but had it pulled over his head to shield himself from the rain as he approached her. His form flashed before her eyes as it took turns hiding in the darkness and revealing itself in the lightning.

She turned and attempted to get the other's attention but failed. She called out to The Man, unsure if he could hear her. The constant spray in her face obscured her vision.

Then her stomach dropped.

Lightning illuminated The Man once more, but this time he looked different. He no longer stood erect but hunched over, naked. Blood covered his body. His skin looked shredded. He couldn't open one of his eyes. Something twisted tightly around his skull. "Mother!" he cried from afar.

She called back, desperate this time. She grabbed her neighbors' cloaks and forced their gazes across the lake, but they still didn't seem to care. She scanned the surface for him in the crashing waves. She found him with the help of a lingering bolt of lightning, but he no longer stood on the water.

He slowly sunk through the spray, like quicksand. He thrashed to escape but was overpowered, as if something sinister beneath the waves had a hold of him and was pulling him down. "Help me!" he said as he choked on the water. His chest was now underwater. Signaling for rescue, his arms flailed.

The mother jumped in and attempted to swim to him, but her cloak dragged her down. She struggled to stay on top of the water as she screamed his name. Wave after wave pummeled her. She turned to retreat to the boat, but it was nowhere in sight. Her feet felt restricted and tangled—possibly in her own garments. She couldn't kick. Finally, the last wave engulfed her and towed her underwater, cutting off contact with the sights and sounds of the world above.

She opened her eyes. All was black. Even when lightning illuminated the sky, the water was murky at best. She waited for the lake to fill her lungs.

But it didn't. Miraculously, she didn't die. She floated weightlessly in the middle of the inky darkness not quite sure which way was up or down. She felt warm and oddly at peace. Then she bumped into something behind her. When she turned around, her eyes widened at her son's lifeless, rotting corpse.

She gasped and felt a horrible panic as water rushed into her lungs. She sunk deeper into the lake. Her lungs felt heavy as water sloshed inside them. She tried to scream but couldn't force out anything as the water filled her. She pushed and pushed and pushed—

The mother screamed loudly as she sat upright in bed. She panted as sweat drenched her face. Squinting as she tried to peer through the darkness, confusion overtook her. She couldn't remember where she was or whose bed she was in. All she knew was it wasn't her own.

"Mother," her daughter said as she sat upright. "Mother, it's—"

"Nobody helped me!" the mother said in a daze. "I tried! He kept calling for me! He—" She looked around and realized where she was. Bits and pieces of her dream gradually came together as she recalled the scene that had played out inside her mind. Temporary relief set in as she understood the dream wasn't real.

Then she remembered her son.

She embraced her daughter. Tears silently stained her cheeks.

From the dark corners of the room, four others came and embraced her—the host, the disciple, and two of her other sons. They had snuck in quietly at some point in the night and had chosen not to disturb the mother. Even though a few of her children were still unaccounted for, she embraced the ones in front of her, thankful they were safe.

It took almost an hour for everyone to fall back asleep. No one said another word.

* * *

Early the next morning, one of the governor's guards knocked on his bedroom door to wake him. "Governor, the Jewish Council wishes to see you."

The governor sat upright, irritated. He squinted and stretched his back as his wife pulled up the sheets to cover herself. "Is this a joke?" the governor asked gruffly, rubbing his eyes.

"They want—"

"Think they'll knock on my door tomorrow morning?" The governor paused even though he knew the guard wouldn't answer. "What about the next morning? What about the morning after that?"

The guard bit his lip and looked down.

"They claim what they wish to discuss with you is of utmost importance."

"Of course." Although early in the morning, the governor's sarcasm was sharp as ever.

"It's about The Man you crucified yesterday. It's about his tomb."

The governor grew in his agitation. *Don't they understand I need sleep too? What could possibly be wrong now?* "Do they want me to open his tomb and . . . I don't know, crucify him again?" the governor said with a sarcastic yawn.

The guard stood silent, knowing this question was rhetorical. He shut the door and allowed the governor to get dressed.

After a few minutes, the governor came downstairs.

Seven Jewish Councilmen, including the high priest, waited in his dining hall. "We are sorry to wake you again," the high priest said. "But we would not do so if we did not believe our concerns to be crucial for you to hear."

The governor sighed and lifted his palms toward the ceiling and raised his hands above his shoulders. He lowered them and pursed his lips as he tried to not verbally lash out at them.

"Sir," a councilman said, "something came to our minds this morning that we feel you should know."

The governor gave them a cool, blank stare.

"We remembered that when The Man was still alive, he said, 'After three days, I will rise again.'"

"Alright." The governor blinked slowly. "And?"

The councilmen glanced at each other, as if trying to telepathically communicate what their next move should be.

"We believe you should give the order for the tomb to be guarded until the third day," the high priest said. "Otherwise, his followers may steal the body and tell the people he's been raised from the dead."

The governor's stare was no longer blank; it narrowed as he shot his gaze back and forth between the high priest and the other councilmen. Considering the ramifications of the hypothetical scenario the priest was painting, the governor carefully weighed the situation.

"He first lied to us and told us he was the messiah. If he rose from the grave, he'd claim equality with the Divine. We can't let his followers stage this one final trick. The hoax of a faked resurrection might ignite the people even more than his false claims to kingship."

The governor knew this was true. It'd be easy for his followers to steal his body and claim something . . . *wild*. Too much excitement surrounded this Jew and his death. The governor refused to allow more drama to unfold as The Man decomposed. The governor motioned for two guards standing by the entryway.

They approached the table.

"Take a guard," he said to the councilmen. "Do you know where this tomb is?"

"We do," the high priest said as a smile snaked across his face.

The governor faced his soldiers. "Go make the tomb as secure as you know how."

"Yes, sir."

The governor pointed at the councilmen. "And as for the rest of you and your friends, stop knocking on my door and giving me problems."

They nodded and left with one of the soldiers. Journeying beyond the city walls, the soldier and the councilmen found the grave where The Man lay. Taking small stones, they jammed them into the crevices of the tomb's doorway.

Armed with a sword on his right hip and a dagger on his left, the soldier stood in front of the tomb and defended the entrance. Anyone who wished to steal from the tomb would have go through an armed Roman soldier first.

* * *

Warming the earth as it crept along its route, the sun perched high in the sky. A cool breeze swept through the tall grass, covering the hillsides.

Mating calls bounced across tree limbs as birds attempted to lure each other into creating new life. Peace shrouded the land—and rightfully so, for it was the Sabbath.

Except for the host's house.

In the afternoon quiet, the small house grew congested and filled with distress and anxiety. And fear.

To the mother's relief, all six of her children huddled inside the home—four sons and two daughters. The four reclined at an old, worn table. The youngest daughter went with the host to collect water at a nearby well. The oldest daughter anointed her mother's feet with oil to help relax her.

The disciple and the three other women also sat at the table, picking at bread. A handful of The Man's followers who had been scattered in the olive grove two nights before returned. The fisherman stood behind the three women while the tax collector sat on the floor against a wall with another one of the disciples; this follower had been a political zealot.

Conversation was awkward. Because no one knew what to say, they often chose not to talk. In the silence, tears rolled down the mother's cheeks as her oldest daughter massaged her heels and calves.

Abruptly, the fisherman spoke up. "Where are the others?"

No response.

The fisherman glanced down at the tax collector and the zealot. "Hey!" The fisherman snapped his fingers. "You ran into the woods with them. Where did they go?"

"I told you." The zealot rolled his eyes. "I don't know where they went."

The fisherman bit his lip. "Well, do they plan on seeing us again? Do they plan on anointing the body? Do they even know *he's dead*?" The fisherman saw the mother grimace, making him grimace as well. "Well . . . do they?"

"I told you what I know," the zealot said with clenched teeth. "This morning, I checked where we ate two nights ago. I hiked up to the olive grove. I haven't seen anyone."

"Did you check the temple grounds?"

"No."

"Well, they could be there if—"

"Then you go check."

The fisherman paused and shot the zealot a look. "You *know* I can't go there. After going to the high priest's home, everybody recognizes me. It's not safe—"

"And you think it's safe for me to go?"

"Safer than me."

"I won't risk my life searching for them. They might crucify me too!"

"Stop arguing," one of the women said. "It isn't safe for anyone to go to the temple. The others will eventually find us."

For a moment, conversation paused.

"How do you know?" the disciple asked gingerly.

"I just do."

A knock on the door interrupted the conversation.

The four brothers stood in unison, shooting alarming glances at each other.

The fisherman broke for the door, ready to defend his friends.

Their hearts raced. There was no back door to escape through. If the governor had sent a legion of soldiers to crucify the rest of The Man's followers, they were doomed.

"It's us," the youngest daughter said on the other side of the door.

The fisherman breathed a sigh of relief and dropped his shoulders. He opened the door and let them in.

The oldest daughter sprang up to fetch a cup and dipped it in the bucket. She brought it to her mother and let her drink. A heavy silence filled the room for a moment as they resumed their places.

Eventually, the disciple spoke up. "So . . . what now?"

The fisherman's face carried a hint of irritation. "What do you mean?"

"I mean, what are we supposed to do now? What would he want us to do?"

"We'll go to the tomb tomorrow and anoint his body," one of the three women said. "We have the supplies prepared."

"No, I mean . . . you know, after that. What should *we do*?" The disciple pointed at everyone.

When no one responded, the fisherman decided to say what everyone else was thinking. "Go home, I guess."

"Right, but once we get there, how will we continue doing what—"

"Continue?" The fisherman's brow furrowed. "Continue? There's no continuing. It's over."

"But quitting isn't what he would've wanted. He would've wanted us to continue the mission he gave us."

"But the mission he gave us requires him!" one of the brothers said hopelessly. "Without him, there's no mission. Without him, we're nothing."

"I understand it'll be hard," the disciple said, "but we have to press on."

"No," the brother said. "The mission won't be hard; it'll be nonexistent. *It is nonexistent.* What don't you understand? How does this not make sense to you?"

"I disagree. We must spread the good news about The Father and his coming kingdom!"

"There's no kingdom without a king," the mother said in a whisper.

Even though all attention was now pinned on her, her gaze didn't leave the floor. She wasn't sad about what she had said. She had said it as a matter of fact.

The disciple grew frustrated. "But we dishonor his legacy if we act like nothing happened. Do you forget what he did? He made the blind see and the deaf hear. The weather did his bidding. No one has ever taught like him. Ever! *He even raised the dead to life.* Why would we act as if none of this even happened?"

"Because we want to live," the fisherman said. "They'll kill you if you pick up where he left off."

The conversation paused. Everyone knew the fisherman was right.

"But . . . I think—" The disciple was at a loss for words. He saw no path forward existed if he wanted to continue to follow The Man and his mission. The disciple's eyes brimmed with tears.

One of the three women stood and embraced him.

"We followed him for . . . for three years!" The disciple buried his face in the woman's shoulder. "Does all of that just go to waste now?"

"It wasn't wasted," the zealot said. "I wouldn't trade it for anything. We saw and experienced things that'll never be seen again. So no, it wasn't wasted . . . *but it's over.*"

As the disciple sobbed, he attempted to speak to the group with his mouth pressed against the woman's garment. His speech was muffled and choppy. No one quite understood exactly what he said, but it was something about how he really did believe The Man was the promised messiah.

Everyone at the table stood and embraced the disciple. And, as they did, they joined in his mourning.

* * *

A strange feeling hovered over the house for the rest of the day, a feeling they'd all felt before in trivial doses but never of this magnitude. It shrouded their souls and choked out every ounce of optimism until nothing remained but darkness. Like a vulture waiting eagerly for an animal to die, this feeling lingered close to their hearts as it waited for Hope to take its last breath.

The feeling was Defeat.

As The Man's family, friends, and followers all huddled fearfully inside the house, this insidious reality enveloped them. Not only had they failed as his followers, but they started to grasp *he had failed as their messiah*. The Man had failed. They all had failed. And now their ill-begotten movement was over. They were nothing without him. They'd lost.

In the past, The Man had been the one who swooped in at the last second to ensure evil wouldn't be victorious. He had bailed out his followers on countless occasions. He had fed thousands of people after his disciples had run out of food. He had even chased away demons when his followers had declared nothing could be done.

But not this time. The Man couldn't help them anymore, because he was rotting inside a hole in the earth. Nothing more could be done. The mission was over. Evil had won.

And as they felt Hope take its last breath deep within themselves, they could sense Defeat beginning to feast.

Hope was dead. All was lost.

And their faith in him was permanently destroyed.

* * *

The rest of the day was a mix of emotions.

The huddled group went back and forth. Sometimes they talked casually, and sometimes they chose to sit silently. Many found themselves throughout the late afternoon crying. A few shared fond memories of The Man. Some chose to remember the times The Man's power and abilities had left them in awe. And during the variety of emotions and memories bouncing around the group, one response kept reappearing above all the rest.

Fear.

No one spoke the word, but they all felt terrified. Every time they heard someone outside, their hearts raced. Images of their own crucifixion became engrained in their minds. The men often stuck their heads out the door and scanned the street, checking for trouble and halfway expecting it. Their stomachs churned at the thought they might find the other missing followers hanging on their own crosses. They spent time in fervent prayer as these thoughts invaded their minds, unsure if The Father was even listening anymore.

As evening set in, the host set out bread and vegetables for supper. Everyone crammed around the table and attempted to eat. Except the mother. For her, she couldn't put anything in her stomach.

As the group picked at their food, the sun started to set.

* * *

Two slaves from the governor's mansion exited the city and descended the winding slope. One carried a small pillow and a jug of water. The other carried a lit torch in one hand and a basket filled with bread and fruit in the other. After a short walk, they found The Man's tomb.

The Roman soldier sat with his back against the squared stone sealing the tomb shut. His sword lay across his lap for sharpening as he scraped it with a rock and eyed the basket. "What's this?"

"Refreshments," one slave said. "The governor wants you to guard the tomb throughout the night. You'll be relieved tomorrow at noon. We'll bring you supplies."

The soldier sighed as he rolled his eyes.

The slaves set out the food and stuck the torch in the ground. They left him oil to keep it lit throughout the night.

"Thanks, but I won't be needing it."

"Don't you want to be able to see if anyone comes to steal the body?"

"If this torch is lit, it'll ward off his followers."

"Is that not what we want?"

"No, I want them to come."

"But why?"

The soldier continued to sharpen his sword. A handful of scrapes later, he set down the rock and lifted the sword into the fading amber sunlight, admiring his work and running his fingers gently across the blade. "Because I want to stick this in their stomach."

Not sure how to respond, the slaves told the soldier they'd return at dawn to bring him food. Then they left.

As the sun set and darkness covered the graves throughout the hillside, the soldier stood and extinguished the torch. He gathered his supplies, carried them to the left side of the tomb and up a small, steep hill and set them behind a tree. He sat behind a bush, out of sight from any passersby. With an elevated view, he could see graverobbers coming from a long way away.

* * *

The host blew out all the candles except the one sitting by the door.

The zealot and the disciple locked the door and pushed the table against it, hoping they could prevent any Roman soldiers from kicking it open. They decided they'd take shifts watching the entrance of the home; the possibility of soldiers taking them away in the middle of the night was all too real.

The huddled group found their places on the ground and attempted to shut their eyes and doze off. Every sound ignited their anxiety, making sleep difficult. Their fear was tangible.

At some point in the night, they all fell asleep.

* * *

And then the next morning, as soon as dawn arrived, something strange and terrifying happened.

Once again, the ground shook.

Chapter 13

A New Age

All was silent at The Man's tomb. Slumped against a tree, the soldier slept soundly in the grass toward the top of the hillside and out of sight. The sun's early morning rays clambered over the still knolls as hundreds of thousands of people throughout the capital rested peacefully. No breeze blew. The roads were empty. The temple area was barren. Everyone was asleep.

Except The Father.

The Father looked down upon the stone that sealed what would become the most renowned grave in all of history. Inside lay the rotting corpse of The Man, The Father's promised messiah.

The Father considered the stone. He remembered the day he had fashioned the rock and placed it in the earth, fully knowing one day it would be used to seal, in a way, a part of himself in a cold, dark grave. All his handiwork, including the stone, was good. It was *very good*. But there was nothing he hadn't made that sin hadn't touched and marred. The Father had created the stone for his glory, but it was being used as a symbol of death.

Although the thought sickened The Father, he wouldn't let The Accuser prevail. The Father's mission was to redeem and restore everything he formed to its original condition and purpose, including the stone sealing the grave of his messiah. The Father was about to use the stone for his glory once again in a way that would permanently change the world.

Peering through the stone, The Father saw the corpse. The soft, white linens that once wrapped tightly around the body now felt rigid. Dried blood stained them scarlet. Through the tainted linens, The Father saw the body, bruised and cut. The Man's thorny crown remained pressed firmly into the now-stiff skin. His face was tortured and devoid of life.

The Father's heart sank. Filled with sorrow, he allowed the gravity of the situation to engulf himself. He remembered how much he cherished The Man. In an instant, he recalled every moment of The Man's life. He remembered how precious and vulnerable The Man had been as an infant. In his mind's eye, The Father again watched him grow into adulthood. Looking back at his baptism, leadership, teachings, and compassion stirred feelings of extreme pride within The Father.

But now his messiah lay lifeless in a menacing grave.

The Father took a deep breath and paused. He closed his eyes and looked into his own being. "Thank you. With you, I am *still* well pleased." As he paused, victorious joy filled his heart. "For the sake of my glory, be eternally exalted." And with that last syllable, his Spirit fell on the corpse. It slipped through the slits in the linen and penetrated the rigid, cold skin.

All at once, the flesh on the corpse moved, and the countless open wounds closed. As the skin on the head rippled, the crown of thorns relaxed its grip on the corpse's brow and lifted from the skull. The puncture wounds and cuts on the face healed instantly. The dried blood became wet again and miraculously pooled off and away from the linens and the skin, as if it knew it was no longer welcomed. Fresh skin replaced the raw and exposed flesh that circled the wounds in the palms and feet, leaving clean holes the size of a crucifixion nail. The blood vessels under the swollen eye healed, restoring the eye to its normal state. Bruises faded. The linens softened and loosened.

The atmosphere changed instantly. A cool rush of air swept into the tomb seemingly out of nowhere. Power reverberated off the walls as a low hum rattled from within the corpse's chest. After a moment, the hum came to an abrupt halt. All was still.

Silence.

Darkness.

Nothing.

Then, breaking the stillness, the once-dead body took a deep, long breath.

And, at that moment, the stone that sealed the grave scraped the outside walls of the tomb as it rolled away, allowing marvelous light to flood in.

* * *

Adrenaline rushed through the soldier as he heard the harsh sound of a boulder scraping against another. He sat upright in a fog and touched the earth with both hands. It was moving. The vibrations escalated as more rocks around the hillside quaked. His legs wobbled as he staggered to his feet, grabbing a tree for balance. He noticed thousands of birds leaving the trees and taking flight into the pink and orange sunrise. Nearby livestock bellowed. Even though the earthquake lasted no more than thirty seconds, it violently shook his nerves.

Eventually, the tremors ceased, and the hush of the countryside returned. The soldier bent down and gathered his things. When he stood and looked down the embankment, he saw a strange glow proceeding from the front of the tomb. Since he was stationed above the tomb on a steep ridge and off to the left, he couldn't quite see the source of the light.

They've come for the body, the soldier thought as he reminded himself of his duty.

He drew his sword and raced down the hill. At the bottom, he jumped in front of the tomb and raised his sword to strike.

He saw no one. He paused, wondering if his eyes had deceived him. Then he noticed the tomb. The stone that sealed the tomb no longer sat in its place. The soldier approached the opening, stooped down and took a cautious step across the threshold. He glanced over his shoulder to confirm he was alone then looked inside.

Although it was open, the tomb seemed unusually dark to his unadjusted eyes. He hesitated then squinted. The slight hint of myrrh and burial spices filled his nostrils. The man's corpse lay to the left wrapped in linen on a low slab of rock. The soldier took a few more steps into the tomb. He wasn't sure why, but he felt nervous and full of apprehension. An abnormal chill filled the tomb. With eyes now fully adjusted, he turned to his right and saw something etched into the wall. He walked over, straining to decipher it. They seemed to be—

The soldier heard a faint noise behind him. He stopped and turned, eyeing the body. Growing perplexed, he stepped toward it. He stared at the wrapped corpse for a moment, not quite sure why. Something seemed . . . *off*.

And then it hit him; the linens were clean. And not just clean, but . . . *perfect*. Not a single stain on them. *How's this possible? Wasn't he crucified just a few days ago?* He reached over the chest of the body and felt the linen, bewildered at how smooth and soft—

His eyes widened. A dreadful panic seized him as he felt his hand rising and falling as the corpse took a deep, quiet breath. The soldier gasped as he scurried backward and crashed into the wall behind him. His heart raced like never before as he watched the body he presumed to be dead wiggle and stretch. Keeping his attention on the body, he shuffled toward the mouth of the tomb and hit his head on the low-lying opening as he escaped.

Breathing heavily, his gaze didn't leave the grave. His throat tightened as his lungs strained to open fully. After a few short breaths, he noticed light coming from behind him. He turned around, not sure what to expect.

All at once, confusion and terror crashed down on him.

Someone—or *something*—stood behind the soldier just twenty feet from the now-opened tomb. It had to be over ten feet tall. The being's back was turned to him. It remained motionless.

The soldier's knees shook as the hair on his neck raised. His sword fell from his now-clammy hand and hit the ground with a clang.

The being's head tilted as it listened. It turned gradually. Once it squared off with the soldier, its body jolted to a stop.

The soldier's jaw dropped as he struggled to breathe. Instinctively, he slowly lifted his left hand to partially cover his face.

The being had the form of a human, but it was *nothing* like a human. It had two legs and two arms like a human, but it didn't have skin. At least, it didn't *look like* skin. The soldier didn't have any idea what covered the being's body, but it wasn't skin, and it wasn't garments. Whatever it was, it was bright and jarring, like permanent lightning. Its body flickered and shimmered as if on fire. Something behind the being produced physical heat that the soldier could feel. Whatever it was, it distorted everything behind the being, bringing on a wave of disorientation to the soldier's senses.

The soldier tried to speak. Trepidation consumed him when he felt his tongue powerless to move.

He considered the being's head. It had similar facial features to a human but had no hair. Whatever covered its face also shimmered and rippled. But the most terrifying feature of all was its eyes. They were sizeable and without pupils. They didn't blink. And they were a color the soldier had never seen.

The being reached across its waist and grabbed something the soldier failed to notice. As its arm moved away from its body, it revealed an imposing sword. The sound it made as it exited the sheath cracked like thunder, causing the soldier to cower. The blade glowed emerald-green. The being took one step toward the soldier.

To the soldier, the step alone was overwhelming and devastating. His head felt light, and his knees buckled as his body collapsed. He was unconscious before he hit the ground.

* * *

They woke in a panic as they felt the ground shake. The host rushed to light a few lanterns, because the early morning sun couldn't penetrate the home yet. When the quaking ceased, they questioned each other as to what it might mean.

After a few chores, one woman approached the mother. "Would you like to visit his tomb? We have spices to anoint the body."

The thought of looking at her son's dead body once again reopened the wounds of the mother's heart. She took a few moments to contemplate it. "Yes. I need to."

The woman gently helped the mother to her feet. As they were about to walk out the door, another woman joined their group.

"Please be careful," the disciple said.

The three women nodded. They grabbed oil and their spices and shut the door.

* * *

"Who's going to roll the stone from the tomb's entrance?" the mother asked.

They were the first words uttered since they left the home a half-hour ago. The women came around the corner on the dirt road that led to The Man's tomb. If they couldn't move the massive stone themselves, their entire morning would be wasted.

"I don't know," one woman said. "I didn't think about that. Do you suppose if we all pushed together, we can move it?"

"I'm not sure," the other woman said. "Maybe if we—"

She was struck mute at the sight of The Man's tomb. The stone was already moved away, resting to the left against the hillside. A Roman sword lay abandoned in front of the opening. The mother's eyes flooded with tears as she lifted her hands above her head. "W-What's happened?" she asked with a quivering voice. "Has someone desecrated his resting place?"

One woman dashed into the tomb. "He's not here! Someone's stolen his body! We need—" The woman screamed.

The other two rushed into the tomb behind her and gasped.

A young man sat on the ground against the right-hand wall of the tomb. He didn't look to be more than sixteen years old. Freckles covered his white, pasty skin. He wore a white robe as he rested his elbows on the top of his knees; he wore no shoes, and his feet didn't have a spot of dirt on them. As if his presence wasn't odd enough, his short hair was completely white. "Don't be alarmed," the young man said with a lingering smile.

"But—" the mother said. "But . . . I need . . . Who are—"

"Don't be alarmed." The young man stood. His arms stayed at his side as his chest came forward. He continued to smile.

The three women didn't say it, but they all felt it; something was different about this young man. They knew he wasn't a local; nobody from there looked like he did. But where would he have come from?

He didn't break his gaze with the three women, and he didn't blink. Not once.

"Who are you?" the mother asked.

"Don't be alarmed. You have no reason to fear."

"Where have you taken the body?" the mother said sharply.

"You are looking for The Man who was crucified. Is that correct?"

"Yes, where is he?"

The young man smiled. "He is not here."

The mother huffed. "Where is he?" she said sternly.

The young man paused and calmly regarded the mother. A quizzical look crossed his face. His body language communicated that he knew something he assumed the women ought to already know as well. "He's risen."

Puzzlement swept over their faces.

One of the women started to speak but stopped. "What do . . . What do you mean?" she finally asked.

"He is risen from the dead. He is not here! He is risen!"

The hair on the mother's arms and neck raised. Anger and hope and excitement and fear all battled for her heart. She wasn't sure how to respond.

"Look." The young man pointed across the tomb. "Look at the place where they laid him."

The three women turned to see pristine white linens folded neatly where the body had once laid.

The mother's heart raced with passion as she wondered if this could be true. "So," the mother asked cautiously, "where . . . is he?"

The young man stared at the mother. As his smile grew, he turned his head to the left and looked out the tomb toward the beautiful slopes that surrounded the city. He nodded.

The women didn't know what to think. The young man seemed confident, and yet something about him seemed so foreign. They weren't sure if they could trust him, let alone stay with him another moment.

"Go," the young man said, "and tell the disciple and the fisherman this: 'The Man is going ahead of you into the northern province. There you will see him, just as he said.'"

"How do you know our friends?" the mother asked quickly. "*Who are you?*"

The young man turned his head back to the three women and smiled again. He still hadn't blinked.

The mother's hands trembled. Without warning, she turned and ran from the tomb and the young man. The other two followed. The mother didn't stop running until the tomb was out of sight. Bent over and panting, she waited for the other two to catch up. "I want the others to look for him. I don't feel comfortable out here alone. I thought I would, but I don't. I want the others to be here."

"Agreed," one woman said. "But what if your son is out here right now?"

"Do you really think he's alive?"

"I don't know. Maybe. Either way, the body isn't in the tomb."

"I know."

"That's why we need to get the others."

"Yes. Let's go."

The three women started on a brisk walk down the road.

"Wait," the other woman said to the mother. "Do you think the young man knows where your son is? If he's actually alive?"

"I don't know. Perhaps he knows where the body is if someone has taken it."

The woman thought for a moment. "You continue. I'll go talk to the young man. I'll find out the exact location of your son or where his body is. You both hurry home and bring the others back. I'll wait for you in front of the tomb."

The mother nodded. She took the hand of the other woman and strode away, leaving the one eager to talk to the young man alone.

The woman turned and darted up the road. She approached the tomb and ducked inside, but the young man was no longer there. She went outside and scanned the hillside but saw no sign of him. Cupping her hands to her mouth, she called out for him but heard no response. He seemed to have vanished into thin air.

There was no use trying to catch up to the other two. She sat against the tombstone and waited, bewildered as to how the young man had evaded her.

Her breathing increased as her muscles tightened. She lifted her cloak to cover her head. With her face in her hands, she bent down to pray. "Our Father in Heaven, help us find him."

* * *

Almost an hour later, the woman heard heavy breathing along the road. She stood and brushed off her cloak. Climbing a boulder off to her right for a better vantage point, relief swept over her once she saw it was the disciple.

He sprinted toward the tomb. He lifted his eyes and saw the woman standing at a distance. "Have you found the body?" he asked through cupped hands. "Is he here?"

The woman shook her head.

The disciple ran up the embankment and embraced her in front of the tomb. He tried to talk more, but he doubled over and panted. He glanced into the tomb and saw the slab of rock where he had witnessed The Man's body placed a few days ago.

The woman noticed the fisherman struggling up the road.

As he ran, he clutched his chest, straining for air.

The woman went out to meet him and opened her arms to embrace him, but the fisherman ignored her.

He glanced at the disciple and ducked into the dark tomb to investigate the claims himself. Completely winded, the fisherman grabbed the folded linens in both hands and lifted them. Perplexed, he viewed them as if they were some mysterious object he hadn't seen before. He let the soft fabric slide between his calloused fingers.

Not long after, the disciple joined the fisherman inside the tomb and did the same thing.

"What do you . . . think," the fisherman asked through short breaths, "this means?"

The disciple beheld the fabric in awe, not sure what to say. He noticed the slab of rock didn't have a drop of blood on it. Something behind the head of the slab caught his eye. He couldn't tell what it was. Without speaking, he curled around the fisherman and bent to pick it up. Once the sun's rays landed on his hands and revealed the object, the disciple's jaw dropped as he realized he was holding a strand of thorny vines tightly woven together. He looked at the fisherman whose eyes were just as wide as his. "They wrapped this around his head. I saw it. No doubt . . . this was it."

The fisherman usually had plenty to say. This time, words eluded him.

"He's out there," the disciple said. "*He's alive.*" He dropped the thorns and ran from the tomb.

The fisherman followed. They both ran past the woman and down to the road, going back the direction they had come.

"Wait!" the woman said. "Where are you going?"

"We have to tell the others!" the disciple said over his shoulder as he sprinted, tripping over stones along the way.

"Tell them what? Should I go with you or wait for the others?"

But it was too late. The two men were already down the road and out of sight.

The woman grew furious and agitated at the same time. *Why would they leave me?* She tried to catch up with them. Weaving up and down the twisting road, she called their names as she panicked. "Please wait for me!"

No response.

She took her hands and placed them over her head, opening her lungs to allow in more air. She stood on the road once again by herself, not knowing where the fisherman and the disciple went and wondering when the mother and the other woman would return. She decided it'd be best for her to wait by the tomb rather than wander through the city by herself. She turned and walked back, crying.

* * *

A half-hour passed.

The woman paced in front of the tomb unable to control her emotions. She hadn't stopped crying since she turned back on the road. Frustration and confusion mounted inside her. But mostly, she felt alone and without direction. It was times like this when she found comfort in placing her faith in The Man.

If only he were here, he could tell me what to do. As her mind ruminated on his absence, she felt the pain of missing him even more. And the more she missed him, the harder she wept.

She stopped pacing and looked toward the road. She thought she heard someone. She waited and watched for a minute or two, hoping for one of her friends to appear, fearing it was one of her enemies. But no one emerged.

Am I hearing things now? Why is it taking—

She felt something warm on the nape of her neck. A low buzz, some kind of reverberation, hummed from behind her. Her heart skipped a beat, and her stomach churned. She whirled around and saw a light inside the tomb. It produced some kind of heat. She knew no one was inside, because she'd been standing in front of the tomb since she had returned to it. Somewhat curious and absolutely afraid, she bent over and crossed the threshold to see what was inside.

When she saw what it was, she fell to the ground, screaming as she covered her head. She didn't get a good look at them, but it was enough to fill her with a type of dread she'd never experienced before.

Two beings sat on the slab of rock where The Man once lay. They weren't human; they weren't even of this world. From what she initially saw, they took the form of a human but were much, much larger. They were extremely bright. Their sizable eyes were altogether disturbing.

She couldn't see what produced the heat, but she felt it on the back of her hands. "Please don't hurt me. Please!"

"Don't be afraid." The voice spoke her native language, but it was unnerving and bizarre and exceptionally deep—deeper than any human vocal cord could make. The voice produced an echo after *and* before it spoke.

Assuming she would die in the presence of these horrible beings, the woman screamed and wept bitterly.

"Don't be afraid," she heard the same voice repeat.

But she couldn't help it. Terror was the only true response in their presence. She wanted to flee but felt paralyzed.

"Woman," the other being said with a voice that seemed to rattle inside the woman's chest, "why are you crying?"

"Don't be afraid," the initial one repeated.

"W-Who . . . *Who are you*?" the woman asked through tears as she trembled. "Where are you from? W-Why are . . . you here? Who sent you?"

"The Father sent us."

The woman considered what the being had said and the implications of it. Although her breathing calmed, she hid her face as she dared not look up. The initial sight of them had upset her too much. *Am I really speaking with two of The Father's servants?* "Are you the ones who've taken his body?" the woman asked carefully.

"No."

"Do you know who has?" She waited, but the beings didn't respond. "Because someone has! Someone's stolen his body. They've taken my Lord away, and I don't know where they've put him. Our group, especially his mother, has suffered from the injustice we've experienced. We can't bear any more. It's too much. So, if you know where—"

Something changed. It felt as if all the air was sucked from the room. The low hum halted. The coolness of the tomb returned. She no longer felt the heat on the backside of her hands. Confused and unsure, she waited a moment before she uncovered her face and opened her eyes. The beings were gone without a trace. As she lifted herself to her hands and knees, she heard something outside.

She buried her head to the ground again, assuming it was the beings. She listened. Something moved. She peeked through the slits of her fingers and saw someone just outside the entrance of the tomb.

He had his back toward the woman. He grabbed something in front of him and rocked back on his knees. He strained as he pulled and eventually removed a large weed from the ground then placed it in a basket full of pulled weeds next to him.

She tried to be quiet, unsure if he knew she was there. She took her cloak and wiped the fresh tears from her eyes.

"Woman," he said casually without looking, "why are you crying?"

The woman felt exposed. *How did he know I was crying? Has he been here the whole time?* "I'm . . . It's because . . . I'm t-trying to find—" The tears returned.

"Who is it you're looking for?" He didn't turn to face her, as a stubborn weed wedged underneath a boulder preoccupied him. He took a rag from his basket and wiped the sweat from his face and arms. He set it down, regripped the weed and yanked, pulling it out along with the root. Without hesitation, he moved to the next one protruding from the crevice.

He must be the gardener. Maybe he knows who opened the tomb. "I'm looking for the body of a crucified man who was buried in this tomb three days ago. I think someone stole his body. Have you been working here all morning? Did you see who opened this tomb?"

Still with his back toward her, he stopped and considered what the woman had asked. He rocked off his knees and sat on the ground. As he placed his hands on the ground behind him and leaned back to recline, he let out a light chuckle.

"Please, sir, if you've carried him away, tell me where you've put him, and I'll go get him." She stood and stepped forward to confront him. When she looked down at him, she froze as her pupils dilated. She tried to swallow but couldn't.

Each of his hands contained a clean hole the size of a small coin. With a familiar gentleness and warmth in his voice, he called her name.

All at once, a powerful hope from deep within her came to life as she knew, without a doubt, she was speaking to her now-risen crucified messiah. In an instant, her faith in him returned as she believed, without hesitation, he really was the Lord of the Universe.

The Man stood and faced her. He smiled.

Overwhelmed with emotion, the woman fell at his feet and kissed them as she wept tears of elation. "*My teacher*!" The woman recoiled into a ball as her hands trembled, hovering above The Man's feet. "*My Lord*!"

The Man bent down and comforted her.

The sight of his resurrected body amazed her. It was completely healed and restored. She couldn't explain how, but she knew his body would never again see decay. For although it was his original body, it looked *transformed* by a mysterious power that could only be attributed to resurrection.

The Man kept saying the woman's name. When she stayed low to the ground, continuing to kiss his feet, he laughed, but she couldn't help it. She was overcome with love for her messiah. In that moment, it was the best way she knew to express it.

She paused and leaned back. As her tears blurred her vision, she stared at the small holes in his feet while The Man continued to laugh. Her mind had a difficult time processing what she was seeing. It was truly unbelievable, and yet, she believed. How could she not? He was standing right in front of her, laughing and smiling.

She took his hand and stood with her jaw hanging open, unable to speak. Faith exploded in her eyes as The Man took his cloak and wiped away her tears. He beamed with pride. Her heart raced as she stood in a state of wild and uncontrolled wonder. She raised both hands and covered her mouth, trying to control the mixture of crying and laughter that bubbled out. *It really is you.*

"Yes, it really is," The Man said aloud before bursting into a new round of laughter.

She was speechless and filled with awe. It really was her messiah. The Man was alive. And in that moment, the woman's eyes opened as to how his resurrection changed everything.

* * *

It was true. From that point on, The Man's resurrection changed everything.

Because of his resurrection, the Divine finally beat Death at Death's own game. No longer would human beings be forced to fear the finality of death or even make daily decisions based on it. Even though they'd never be fully sure what lies on the other side of their death, they knew someone who did. They knew a man who was called the Resurrection and the Life, and he told them they had nothing to fear. Although their bodies were destined to decay one day in a grave, they understood a day was coming when The Father would also breathe on them new life and call their name, waking them up to a glorious new age.

Because of his resurrection, the eternal significance of his crucifixion was confirmed. On the cruel cross that wondrous day, The Man redeemed all who'd believe in him and commit their lives to his lordship. Through his blood, the strongholds and powers that held sinners in chains were forever destroyed. But without his resurrection, none of it would matter. For his resurrection was the only thing that actually verified he was fully Divine. And his Divinity validated his blood, proving it to be the only thing valuable enough to save people from their sins.

Because of his resurrection, The Accuser was left humiliated and overcome. Three days earlier, The Accuser had celebrated, thinking he'd won. But when the stone rolled away and The Man walked from his grave, The Accuser was completely undone. The Father's messiah wouldn't stay dead, and the Divine refused to be defeated. The Accuser's time was limited, and his influence would one day come to an end.

Because of his resurrection, The Man officially ushered in his kingdom. From that point forward, the world would run differently, and new rules would be set. His followers would give their lives, proclaiming his reign to every corner of the Earth. As they did, they'd help men and women of every nation experience the freedom of living under his rule and reign. His people would be known as a resurrection people, calling sinners everywhere from their own spiritual graves into a wonderful new reality. Their mission was to renew and restore everything on Earth, bringing it under The Man's lordship.

Nothing would ever be the same again.

* * *

The woman embraced him and held him tight. Unabashed joy filled them both. She sensed a mighty, righteous hope swelling from the pit of her being.

The Man let go and stepped backward. "Don't hold on to me too tightly," he said with a smile, "because I still have to return to The Father. Go instead to my brothers and tell them I'm returning to my Father and to your Father."

The woman's hands shook. A warm smile crossed her face even though she remained somewhat confused. "Aren't you coming with me? Don't you want to see everyone?"

"I'll see them in time. For now, there's much to do."

Her brow wrinkled. "You just want me to tell them . . . you're returning to The Father?"

The Man smiled. "Tell them Death couldn't hold their messiah. Tell them I'm alive."

She beamed ear to ear as she hugged him one last time.

"Go," he whispered.

She let go and stepped backward.

He pointed at the road.

She turned and took off down the road toward the city, exploding with fits of laughter as she went. Unable to contain herself, she felt like she might burst. She had to tell the others The Man was alive.

And then they would tell the rest of the world.

Epilogue

A FEW WEEKS LATER, The Man met with his disciples one last time on a mountainside.

The past forty days had been nothing short of unbelievable for the disciples. The Man would appear to them, but he wouldn't prolong his stay. They knew his body was physical, for they shared meals with him and watched him eat. And yet, his body was so *different* from theirs. It didn't seem to grow tired. Other than the holes in his hands and feet, it was flawless in every way. The disciples often felt The Man appeared from nowhere, confusing their physical senses. They came to accept The Man's body was filled with a kind of mysterious wonder that could only be attributed to resurrection power.

"Is it time for you to free our nation and restore our kingdom?" one disciple asked.

The Man stood on a sloping field, observing the horizon, and smiled. He knew they still didn't understand fully. He didn't blame them. How could men understand the plans of the Divine? He'd soon need to send The Father's Spirit to inhabit their hearts to help them remember all the things he had taught them. For them to push his kingdom into every corner of the world, they'd need Divine help.

The Man turned, looked at his disciples and loved them. "Only The Father has the authority to set those dates and times, and they aren't for you to know." The Man pointed skyward. "But you'll receive power when the Spirit dwells in you."

The disciples eyed each other, perplexed. Even after all they'd endured, they still struggled to process what their messiah had said.

"What will we need power for?" the fisherman asked. "What kind of power is it?"

"You'll be my witnesses, telling people everywhere about me." The Man pointed in the direction of their nation's capital. "In the city, throughout Judea, and in Samaria." As The Man spoke, the areas he pointed at grew larger. Then he lifted both hands wide. "And even to the ends of the Earth." Then, without warning, The Man slowly rose into the air.

Many of the disciples gasped. All were speechless. As The Man ascended higher, the disciples noticed a rippling cloud forming in the sky. The higher The Man went, the more the cloud moved. The disciples strained their necks as they could barely see him. Eventually, the cloud engulfed him. After a few minutes, it dissipated. Shielding the sun from their eyes, the disciples searched the sky for The Man.

"Men of Galilee!" a voice boomed, startling them all. Lost in awe at The Man's ascension, the disciples had failed to recognize the two visitors standing behind them. Two men—if they could even be called men—with pasty-white skin and snowlike hair stood on a boulder. They wore dazzling white robes that made the sun look dim.

The disciples knew they ought to be afraid but, for some reason, weren't.

"Why are you standing here, staring heavenward? The Man has been taken from you into Heaven, but someday, he'll return from Heaven in the same way you saw him go!"

While the disciples pondered these words, the two men disappeared, leaving the disciples huddled together on the mountain's scenic slope. Some looked for the two men. Others strained their necks skyward.

Eventually, the tax collector broke the silence. "What now?"

After a moment of silence, the fisherman said, "Our messiah has gone into Heaven but is someday returning, correct?"

"That's what they said," the zealot replied.

"Then we ought to prepare ourselves for his arrival."

The tax collector opened his mouth to speak but then retracted.

"Afterall," the fisherman said with a joyful smile, "he'll return in the same way he departed. He'll return soon."

Smiles crept across each of the men's faces as they imagined the day when their messiah would return. As they did, hope stirred their hearts.

The fisherman nodded as he whispered to himself, "He's coming back."

Yes, he's coming back.

The Man is coming back.

Amen and amen.

CPSIA information can be obtained
at www.ICGtesting.com
Printed in the USA
LVHW081438100821
694968LV00027B/967

9 781666 706857